PRAISE FOR
Indians on Vacation

"The beauty of King's writing is that, like all good authors, it seems effortless. Like those words always have and always should be in that specific order on the page, and that was the way the great literary gods planned it. . . . I like reading Tom King because he does, succinctly and cleverly, what all good writers should do—he educates, illuminates, and entertains with every paragraph."
—Drew Hayden Taylor, author of *Motorcycles & Sweetgrass*

"Funny and deeply sensitive. . . . *Indians on Vacation* presses sharply against the world with humour and heart—personalized demons and all."—*Quill & Quire* (starred review)

"*Indians on Vacation* is a witty, funny striking story that ponders the importance of history from the smallest personal connections to big-picture politics." —*Vancouver Sun*

"As more and more Indigenous writers create new and exciting works, trailblazers like King have endured. Canada, in turn, is better for it. . . . I could spend my time dissecting the skill in King's writing, how he layers complex ideas and themes underneath his trademark humour (which is pretty much unmatched). . . . Readers find essential truths King has laced within the narrative thread."
—David A. Robertson, author of *Black Water*

"[Bird and Mimi] are winning, funny protagonists: bickering, falling ill, eating bad food and confronting old truths. A sly and wise book." —*Chatelaine*

"King, . . . winner of the RBC Taylor Prize for *The Inconvenient Indian*, offers armchair travel and wry observational truths about contemporary life in equal measure." —*Zoomer* magazine

Indians on Vacation

OTHER WORKS BY THOMAS KING

Fiction

Medicine River

Green Grass, Running Water

One Good Story, That One

Truth and Bright Water

A Short History of Indians in Canada

The Back of the Turtle

Sufferance

DreadfulWater Mysteries

DreadfulWater

The Red Power Murders

Cold Skies

A Matter of Malice

Obsidian

Non-fiction

The Truth About Stories: A Native Narrative

The Inconvenient Indian: A Curious Account of Native People in North America

Children's Illustrated Books

A Coyote Columbus Story, illustrated by William Kent Monkman

Coyote Sings to the Moon, illustrated by Johnny Wales

Coyote's New Suit, illustrated by Johnny Wales

A Coyote Solstice Tale, illustrated by Gary Clement

Coyote Tales, illustrated by Byron Eggenschwiler

Poetry

77 Fragments of a Familiar Ruin

INDIANS
On Vacation

A NOVEL

THOMAS
KING

HarperCollins*PublishersLtd*

Indians on Vacation

Published by HarperCollins Publishers Ltd

First published by HarperCollins Publishers Ltd in a hardcover edition: 2020
This trade paperback edition: 2021

HarperCollins Publishers Ltd
Bay Adelaide Centre, East Tower
22 Adelaide Street West, 41st Floor
Toronto, Ontario, Canada
M5H 4E3

www.harpercollins.ca

Library and Archives Canada Cataloguing in Publication

Title: Indians on vacation / Thomas King.
Names: King, Thomas, 1943- author.
Description: Previously published: Toronto, Ontario, Canada: HarperCollins Publishers Ltd, 2020.
Identifiers: Canadiana 20210172932 | ISBN 9781443465465 (softcover)
Classification: LCC PS8571.I5298 I53 2021 | DDC C813/.54—dc23

Printed and bound in the United States of America
LSC/H 9 8 7 6 5 4 3 2 1

For Helen, one last time

I

In Prague, we stay at the Hotel Certovka in the shadow of the historic Charles Bridge. Second floor. Some of the rooms overlook the Vltava River.

Ours doesn't.

However, we can see the tourists on the bridge, can hear them talking, as they stroll from the Lesser Quarter to Old Town and back again, and if we were so inclined, we could lean out our window and engage them in conversation.

We don't.

But we could.

We arrive at our hotel after a twelve-hour flight from Toronto. The room is hot. There is no air conditioner, no ceiling fan to push the heat around. We're exhausted. We fall onto the bed, thinking we'll sleep until dinner, when a band somewhere below us begins playing a fortissimo, quick-step arrangement of "Hello, Dolly!"

I'm sweaty and sticky. My ears are still popping from the descent into Vaclav Havel. My sinuses ache. My stomach is upset. My mouth is a sewer. I roll over and bury my face in a pillow. Mimi snuggles down beside me with no regard for my distress.

"My god," she whispers, "can it get any better?"

About six years ago, Mimi decided that we should travel.

"We can follow the postcards," she told me. "Maybe we'll find out what happened to Uncle Leroy. We might even find the Crow bundle. Wouldn't that be great?"

"Why don't we look for the Lost Lemon Mine while we're at it?"

"And the travel will give me a chance to paint other places in the world."

"You paint water. You don't need to travel to paint water."

"You could take your typewriter and your camera. Just like the old days, Bird. You were one of the best."

"I haven't used a typewriter in years."

"Maybe it will inspire you to finish your book."

"And there is no book."

"But there could be."

It's a losing battle, but I try anyway. "Why would we want to travel, when we can stay home?"

"Travel is broadening," said Mimi, though that old adage has never been proven. "And it will help take your mind off your health."

So we're in Prague.

It's too hot to stay in the room. We go outside and follow the music to a small park that is awash in food vendors and craft stands.

And musicians.

The "Hello, Dolly!" band is not alone. They have come to Prague with friends, an assortment of musical troupes from around the world—Germany and Spain, Austria and Slovakia, France and Portugal—all armed with a frightening array of North American show tunes.

The "Hello, Dolly!" folks are from Brussels. They finish off the Jerry Herman hit with a flurry and give way to an assault by an Israeli ensemble and the overture from *Oklahoma!* A band from Italy waits

its turn in the shade of the bridge. The Italians have fashioned their instruments to mimic kitchen appliances and bathroom fixtures.

One guy has a French horn that looks like a toilet.

My health problems began with a thyroid that went south. When I came home with the news, Mimi told me that thyroid problems are generally a female thing and that this was a sign of my strong feminine side.

Gout was next, followed by swollen saliva glands in my neck. Gout was chronic but could be controlled by medication. The swollen glands were more disturbing, and just to be safe, my family doctor sent me to a specialist, a young woman who didn't look old enough to have been admitted to medical school.

"We'll need to do a fibre-optic laryngoscopy." She opened a drawer and took out a coil of tubing. On one end was a small probe. The other end was attached to a device that looked vaguely like a pistol with a video screen.

"This is an ENT scope."

"You want to put that down my throat?"

"Actually," she said, "the cable goes in through your nose."

"My nose?"

"We use an anaesthetic spray."

"You want to put that in my nose?"

"You'll hardly feel a thing."

So we're in Prague and it's late afternoon and Mimi has had her fill of show tunes. We wander the food stands, check out the offerings to see if there is anything we recognize. Mimi takes a long look at something called *trdelnik*.

"You think this is the Czech version of fry bread?"

And when we run out of park and bands and food, Mimi consults the map. I can see adventure sparkling in her eyes. I can hear determination lurking in her voice.

"Why don't we explore the river," says Mimi. "See what we can find."

What we find are several giant bronze babies frozen in mid-crawl. I take a picture of Mimi standing next to one of the babies, and I take a picture of Mimi trying to plank on a giant baby's butt.

"See," says Mimi. "This is why we travel."

"They don't have faces."

"It's probably symbolic. I'll bet it has to do with television and the angst of modern existence."

Farther along, we come upon a row of yellow penguins standing in a line on a platform in the river. Mimi consults the guidebook.

"They're made out of recycled bottles. It's supposed to be a comment on global warming."

"Yellow penguins?"

"Thirty-four yellow penguins."

We find a bench and sit down. On the river, paddleboats done up to look like swans and vintage cars drift by. The sun is low, and the light on the water is golden and glorious. I'm tempted to point out that for less money and effort, we could be sitting on a bench along the Speed River with much the same effect.

But I know better.

I've always wondered if doctors are like politicians, if they actually believe the lies they tell. Having a tube shoved up my nose hurt like hell. It hurt going in, and it hurt coming out.

"Did you know you have a slightly deviated septum?"

"What about my saliva glands?"

"They're definitely swollen," the doctor told me. "How would you feel about a biopsy?"

"You want to cut me open?"

"It's the only definitive way to rule out lymphoma."

I said no. Mimi said yes. In the end, medical science removed one of my saliva glands. Day surgery. Home that evening with a drain bag hanging off the side of my neck.

The following week I was back in the doctor's office.

"It's not cancer."

"So, what is it?"

"A swollen gland."

"Why is it swollen?"

"There could be many reasons."

"The other gland is also swollen."

"We could take it out as well," the doctor suggested. "If you like."

"Why would we do that?"

"As a precaution."

"Against what?"

I didn't have the second gland taken out. One round of day surgery and a scar on my neck were enough fun. As well, with the one saliva gland gone, my mouth was as dry as the Okanagan. And for all the probing and the cutting, we still didn't know what had caused the swelling in the first place.

"It's not lymphoma," Mimi told me. "How about we leave good news alone?"

So WE'RE IN PRAGUE and it's evening and now we're lost. Not *lost* lost. Just somewhat confused. We've come away from the river into a web of streets that don't match the streets on Mimi's map.

"It's the right map," she assures me. "It's just that some of the streets have different names."

I wonder if the map that Mimi has was printed before Czechoslovakia was broken up into the Czech Republic and Slovakia. I'm not sure that this would answer the street-name question, but it might provide a historical excuse for any discrepancies.

"Adventure," says Mimi, and she heads down the street towards a row of restaurants, all aglow in evening dress. "Another reason we travel."

We stop at the first place so Mimi can look at the menu that is posted on a stand. We stop at the second one, and Mimi looks at that menu. We stop at the third, and she looks at the menu there as well. Then we go back to the first restaurant, and Mimi looks at the menu again.

Shortly after my adventures with the swollen glands, I had an ultrasound on my bladder. I forget the reason for the test. I just remember the look on my doctor's face.

"You have a growth on your pancreas," my doctor told me. "I wasn't expecting that."

He didn't say "pancreatic cancer." He waited for me to raise the subject. I didn't. So Mimi did.

"Is it cancer?"

The doctor got me an appointment with a specialist in Toronto. I didn't want to go, but Mimi was insistent.

"Better to know," she said.

"Why?"

"So we can plan."

"For what?"

"The future."

As IT TURNS OUT, Mimi already has a recommendation for a restaurant that she got from the hotel, when I wasn't looking.

"If you already had a restaurant in mind," I ask her, "why are we wandering around looking at menus?"

Mimi is unfazed by my attempt at criticism. "Research," she says. "We're going to be in Prague for more than one night. And we're going to eat more than one meal."

Since we don't know the public transit system, Mimi decides that we should walk to the restaurant.

"It's right here," she says, holding up the map in the guidebook.

"That's halfway to Berlin."

"It's out of the tourist centre, but the walk will do us good. Shake the jet lag."

I know objecting isn't going to have much effect, but I object anyway. "That has to be a two-hour hike."

"Not if we walk quickly."

It takes us almost forty minutes to walk to the restaurant. It's a small hole-in-the-wall, ten-table affair. There is no posted menu, and this makes the place feel oddly avant-garde. The interior is austere and feels somewhat martial, as though a squad of Russian soldiers left over from the 1968 invasion might be lurking in the kitchen.

There's an old pommel horse in the middle of the restaurant. So maybe I'm mistaken. Not Russian soldiers. Russian gymnasts.

The restaurant is called Di Mateo, which sounds more Italian than Czech and, as it turns out, it is. I can see that Mimi isn't all that happy about having found an Italian restaurant in Prague, whereas I'm delighted not to have to brave blood sausage and beet soup.

We're seated in a quiet corner when I notice the first of three potential problems. The music playing in the restaurant is not traditional Czech, nor is it traditional Italian. It's Johnny Rivers singing "Secret Agent Man."

Second, our waiter speaks perfect English, a disappointment, as

Mimi was looking forward to doing battle with the cacophony of Czech consonants. His name is Jacob, and he's delighted to discover we're Canadian.

"I'm from Brno," Jacob tells us, "but I did a modern-language degree at the University of Toronto."

Third, not only is there no menu posted outside the restaurant, there isn't a menu inside either. Nothing for Mimi to hold. Nothing for her to read. No chance for her to compare prices.

And this is when we realize that we left our novels back at the hotel. At home, whenever we go out to dinner, we take books with us, so we can read while we wait for the food to arrive. Now we're faced with the real possibility of having to talk to one another.

Jacob explains the choices. Three dishes. Pasta, fish, and meat. He describes each selection, the ingredients, how the dish is cooked, and what comes with it. I choose the pasta. Mimi chooses the fish.

It's only after Jacob leaves that Mimi notices the music for the first time. She looks at me as though I'm responsible.

"Is that . . . ?"

The pasta is excellent, as is the fish. Mimi orders a beer for me and a glass of wine for herself. Both the beer and the wine are from the Czech Republic, and this makes Mimi feel somewhat better.

Jacob comes over to ask if we are enjoying our meal.

"We are," Mimi tells him, "but some vegetables would have been nice."

"Vegetables?"

"Green beans, cauliflower, eggplant?" says Mimi. "That sort of thing."

"There is cabbage," says Jacob, "and we have a wonderful tiramisu."

"What about traditional Czech desserts?"

"You mean like a *medovnik* or a *makovy kolacek*?"

Mimi's face lights up. "Yes," she says, "like that."

"No," says Jacob, his voice repentant, and I can see that Mimi is somewhat sorry she has asked. "Just the tiramisu."

I'm tempted to raise the question of the pommel horse, but I don't.

THE SPECIALIST IN TORONTO was a heavy-set blond man with a ruddy face and a brisk British accent. This was oddly reassuring. His crisp consonants gave him an air of compassion and wisdom. I made the mistake of sharing these thoughts with Mimi.

"And he has a penis."

I protested. "That's not it."

"Remember that specialist you saw for the saliva glands. You didn't trust her, because she was a woman."

"She was young."

"And she was a woman."

"She stuck a tube up my nose and told me it wasn't going to hurt."

The doctor from Britain went over the blood tests and the ultrasound, and I have to admit, I wasn't listening. I was trying to think of all the things I might want to do in the time I had left. It's funny how the anticipation of bad news can drain the life out of you. I mean, you're not dead, but the prospect of having someone tell you that you're dying is exhausting.

"Has anyone explained the situation to you yet?"

Whenever Mimi goes to the doctor with me, she does most of the talking. She asks all the questions. She even takes notes.

"Pancreatic cancer?" Mimi asks, as if this was an option rather than the answer.

"Who told you that?"

No one had actually said "cancer." My doctor had talked around it. A "growth on the pancreas" and "wasn't expecting to see this" and "you'll need to see a specialist" was the way my situation had been framed.

So there I was, waiting to hear how long I had to live, trying to come up with a couple of good jokes to break the tension, when the doctor told me that I didn't have pancreatic cancer.

"I don't?"

"No," said the doctor. "You have a condition called autoimmune pancreatitis, or IgG4."

"And that's better?" said Mimi.

"It's a chronic condition," said the doctor. "It's not fatal."

"Is it a precursor to pancreatic cancer?"

"No, it's not," said the doctor. "However, the IgG4 has damaged the pancreas, which has caused the diabetes."

"I'm diabetic?"

"You are now," said the doctor.

"IgG4." Mimi rolled the diagnosis around on her tongue as though it were an exotic flavour.

"It's a somewhat new condition," said the doctor. "We've been seeing it in Asian and American Indian populations."

I remember Mimi turning to me. "See," she said, "being Native is lucky after all."

So we're in Prague, and after our dinner at the pommel-horse restaurant, we walk the Charles Bridge and pause in the middle to enjoy the river and the lights of the city. Mimi snuggles up against me. I don't know if snuggling is any better in Prague than it is in Guelph, and I don't waste any time thinking about it.

"Did you know," says Mimi, "that women blink twice as often as men?"

Mimi spends too much time on the Internet, and as a result, she's always overflowing with irrelevant information that spills out at irregular intervals.

"And did you know that in the Humpty Dumpty nursery rhyme, there is no mention that Humpty Dumpty is an egg?"

From the bridge, we look down into Kampa Park and see that a movie shoot is in full swing, the crew laying cables, setting up lights, checking cameras. Dozens of tourists press against the barriers, their iPads and cellphones held over their heads.

I have no idea what the movie is about, but one of the actors has a gun.

"Now there's something you don't see in Guelph."

There are sawhorses blocking the stairs to the bridge. Several yellow-and-black sandwich-board signs warn against trespass. Another simply says "MIMO Productions."

"*Murdoch Mysteries* filmed some of their scenes on Douglas Street," I remind her.

"That's television."

A man in a white dress shirt that he hasn't bothered to tuck in drifts through the set, listing to one side, as though he's a tugboat braced against a running tide. Short, heavy-set, bald. Dark glasses, red loafers, no socks. His sleeves are rolled up. His forearms are covered with tattoos.

A tall, flexi-straw woman in a thin yellow dress that billows about her body like a collapsing sail floats along in his wake. She carries a thick red binder, hugs it against her breasts, as though she expects it to save her from drowning.

"Maybe they're making a western," says Mimi, "and they need a Native actor for one of the principal roles."

"Don't think they make westerns in the Czech Republic."

"Sergio Leone made westerns in Spain," says Mimi. "That's how Clint Eastwood got his start."

"I'm a journalist, not an actor."

"Blackbird Mavrias." Mimi holds her hands out and forms a marquee. "*Dead in Prague*. Coming soon to a theatre near you."

We stand around for a bit, and when nothing happens, we make our way back to the hotel. When we get there, we find the front door locked. We try our room key, but it doesn't fit.

"Maybe they lock the front door at night," Mimi suggests, "and you have to ring a bell to get in."

"It's only nine thirty."

"This isn't Toronto," says Mimi. "This is Prague."

I can't imagine that locking tourists out of their hotel rooms is part of traditional Czech culture, so I walk around the front entrance and search for a bell. I knock on the door. And then I knock some more.

Mimi isn't concerned. "Spending the night on the Charles Bridge wouldn't be the end of the world. Remember San Francisco?"

"The Golden Gate?"

"That was fun."

I'm trying to think of something clever to say about Indians on bridges when, suddenly, there's gunfire. And then a scream.

"Come on." Mimi heads back to the movie set at a trot. "Let's go see who died."

A WHILE BACK, Mimi decided that I was depressed. I was sleeping more than she thought necessary, and I was beginning to watch reality shows that involved people shouting at each other and throwing chairs.

"I'm not depressed."

"And the rages?" Mimi held up a hand and began ticking off each finger. "Cellphone companies. Bank fees. Robo calls."

"Nobody likes robo calls."

"Not getting your favourite table at Artisanale."

"That's disappointment."

"You get upset by the little things. I don't think that's normal."

"I like that table."

"As I see it," Mimi told me, "you have two choices."

Most things in life, according to Mimi, involve at least two choices. I know better than to ask what they are. I know she'll tell me.

"You can get therapy."

"What's the second choice?"

"You can get a dog."

At one point in our communal lives, we had had cats. Wesa and Mr. Bean. Two Burmese. They were lovely animals. But having pets was difficult, and when the cats died of old age, even though we were sad and knew we would miss them, there was the sense of relief that a burden had been lifted.

"A dog?"

"I think you have a hole in your heart," Mimi told me. "I think a dog might fill it."

I didn't have a hole in my heart, and I didn't want a dog.

"Why don't we go to the humane society," said Mimi. "Just for a look."

"No."

"Then it's therapy."

So we went to the humane society. The woman at the front desk told us that at the moment, their supply of unwanted dogs was low.

"Let's look anyway," said Mimi. "What can it hurt?"

There were four dogs. In cages. As soon as we stepped into the room, they all started barking. The noise was startling, but it was the smell that stopped me in my tracks. Even Mimi was momentarily immobilized.

"Our dog would be happy," she said. "These dogs are frightened. That's what you smell."

The first cage we came to contained a thirteen-year-old dog

named Muffy. She was a Lab-pointer mix. Her owners had brought her to the shelter because they couldn't afford to get Muffy's teeth fixed.

The minute Muffy heard us, she got off her mat, limped over to the front of the cage, and gave us a sniff.

"She's mostly blind," the volunteer told us, "and deaf."

When Muffy was done sniffing, when she realized that we were not her family come to take her home, she limped back to her mat.

Mimi had been wrong. I had been merely disheartened before. Now I *was* depressed.

So WE'RE IN PRAGUE, on the Charles Bridge, watching the movie crew rearrange the lighting for a reverse shot, when I look back and see that the front door to our hotel is now open.

I point this out to Mimi.

"You do like to catastrophize," she says. "I thought we had agreed to leave Eugene and the Other Demons at home."

There's a woman at the front desk. She speaks fluent Czech, and I speak fluent English, and we rock the languages back and forth until the question is settled.

Turns out there has to be someone at the desk at all times. So, if the desk person has to go to the bathroom, or duck around the corner for a smoke, or nip down the block for a pastry, the front door to the hotel is locked. I want to ask her what happens to the people who might be inside and want to get out, but I haven't the energy.

We walk upstairs to our very hot room, lie on our very hot bed, and roll into the centre like a couple of boulders recently blown out of a volcano.

Still, Mimi is in excellent spirits.

"It must have been exciting."

"What?"

"Uncle Leroy," says Mimi. "Travelling around. Seeing all of those countries. Seeing Prague."

"He didn't travel because he wanted to travel."

"Still. It would have been an adventure."

I get up and turn on the television. Most of the channels are static, but I find a show where a woman points to numbers on a large board and then takes off pieces of clothing until she gets down to her bra. On another channel is a game show of sorts where six adults in diapers try to control an enormous beach ball.

And there's a news channel whose lead story is a demonstration somewhere in the world. Outside an imposing building, police in riot gear are in a confrontation with a grim-faced mob. Men with backpacks and suitcases. Women with babies and cardboard signs. Children holding blankets and toys. All pressed together and milling about like cattle in a pen.

I was hoping for something like *Elementary* or *NCIS* or *Castle*. I wouldn't be able to understand the dialogue, but the plot would be easy enough to follow.

Mimi rolls over. "It's a nice hotel," she says, "but what the hell are those?"

I don't see what she sees. And then I do.

"Are those spiders?"

There is no good answer to this question.

"I'm going downstairs," I tell Mimi. "Maybe the hotel has an electric fan."

"What about the spiders?" Mimi calls out after me. "Ask them about the spiders."

The woman at the desk seems happy to see me. "Fan?"

"For the room. It's hot."

"Hot?"

"Yes, the room is very hot."

"You are to use air conditioner," she tells me.

This is one of the problems with language. I know every word the woman uses, and the sentence makes sense. There is a subject, a verb, an infinitive, and an object. Articles optional. When this happens, I always try to guess at intent, and in this case, I can only come up with one explanation.

"The room has an air conditioner?"

"Yes," says the woman. "Of course."

I had looked for an air conditioner and had not seen one.

"I will show you?"

"Yes," I tell the woman. "Please."

So she locks the front door, and we go upstairs.

"Honey," I call out to Mimi, who is probably still on the bed but who could have slipped into a tub of cold water, "we have company."

Our room has a slightly awkward arrangement. The door to the room opens into a short hall that leads to the sleeping area on the left and to the bathroom on the right. The hallway is a dead space more or less, and this is where the air conditioner is.

In the hallway, above the door to the room.

The woman flips a switch on the wall that looks like a light switch but isn't. As she does, I can hear the whirl of something that might just be an air conditioner.

"There," says the woman, and she points at the grill above the door.

I feel like a fool, of course, but I don't see how an air conditioner stuck in a hallway above a door is going to cool a bedroom that is fifteen feet away and around a corner.

"It feels cooler already," Mimi shouts to me.

I hold my hand up to the grill, and yes, I can feel air coming out. It's the same temperature as the room, but I withhold my comments. It might well cool down in a few minutes.

"Thank you," I tell the woman, who is already heading back down the stairs to unlock the front door.

"Let's not make it too cold," says Mimi.

I hold my hand up to the grill again. There doesn't seem to be much chance of that happening.

"What about the spiders?" says Mimi. "Did you ask her about the spiders?"

OUR TRIP TO THE humane society was a disaster. I was better off not knowing about Muffy.

"It's not your fault," Mimi told me.

It was quite clear that Muffy would die in that cage. She would never see the people who had been her family for all those years. She would die alone.

"And Muffy has nothing to do with residential schools."

"What?"

"I know the way your mind works," said Mimi. "You see an animal in a cage, and you think of residential schools."

"No, I don't."

"Remember that story you did when the prime minister officially apologized for the damage the residential-school system had caused? Remember what you said?"

"I said such apologies were worthless."

"You also said that Canadians treated their pets better than school personnel treated the children in those schools." Mimi gave me a hug and held it longer than necessary. "Okay," she said, "what kind of dog do you want?"

SO WE'RE IN PRAGUE. We've wrapped up our first day in the city and are tucked in our hotel room with an air conditioner in name only and a family of spiders on the ceiling.

"There are sixteen," Mimi tells me. "Eight large, five medium, three small."

Everyone has idiosyncrasies. Balzac drank over fifty cups of coffee a day. John Steinbeck kept exactly twelve sharpened pencils on his desk to make sure he always had writing implements. Flannery O'Connor had a thing for domestic poultry. Benjamin Franklin started each day with an "air bath," which consisted of sitting in the nude and exposing his private parts to the morning breezes.

Mimi counts things. She'll count almost anything, but she's particularly fond of keeping track of bodily functions. She likes to tell me how many bowel movements she's had in a day, how long it takes for her to pee—her record is forty-one seconds—and the amount of mucus she snorts out on her daily jogs.

And now that she's noted the number of spiders and their size, I can't get to sleep. We can hear the tourists outside the window as they walk back and forth across the bridge in the dark, and we can hear music floating on the night air.

Mimi sits up suddenly, slides out of bed, and goes to the window. I stay where I am. I know trouble when I see it.

"It's beautiful," she says.

I imagine that most cities are beautiful at night, when all you see are the lights against a night sky, when everything else is in shadows.

"Look." Mimi drags me out of bed and marches me to the window. The cafés are aglow. Reflections dance off the cobblestones. "Everyone is so happy. Are you happy?"

"Yes," I tell her, "I'm happy."

"Shit, Bird," she says, "can't you lie any better than that?"

Now that Mimi is awake, there's no stopping her. I vote for staying in the room, but evidently, this is not what people on vacation do. So we get dressed and find our way to a café, where a man is playing a guitar and a woman is singing.

Mimi turns to me. "'I'll Be Seeing You'?"

"It was big in the '40s," I tell her.

"Sure, but why are they singing American tunes in the Czech Republic?"

Mimi and I stand off to one side and let the music flow over us. We stick around long enough to hear the woman sing most of the songs that Frank Sinatra and Nat King Cole made famous—"Let's Fall in Love," "Fly Me to the Moon," "Again," "Unforgettable"—and the music makes me somewhat homesick. If I were home, I'd be in front of the television right now with Muffy and a sandwich.

Happy, well fed, safe.

WE DIDN'T GET a dog from the humane society. But a week later, Mimi came home from her weekly jaunt to the thrift stores. She has a circuit that she works, much like a trapper on a trapline.

Salvation Army. Goodwill. Value Village.

And each time she goes, she comes home with a large plastic sack. Sometimes several.

"You'll never guess what I found."

I was watching *Casablanca* and really didn't care what Mimi had found.

"Go on, guess."

I don't know how many times I've watched the movie. And I have no idea why I find it soothing to hear Bogart and Bergman say the same lines over and over.

"It's not candles," said Mimi. "And it's not shoes."

Paul Henreid doesn't do much for me, but Claude Rains as Captain Louis Renault and Sydney Greenstreet as Signor Ferrari are terrific.

"A dog," said Mimi. "I found you a dog."

So we're in Prague, and as we walk back to our hotel, the fog rolls in. We hadn't been expecting this. Before we know it, the city disappears, and we can barely see beyond our hands.

"When you're lost in the woods, you're supposed to stay where you are, so that the searchers can find you."

"We're not in the woods."

"It's the principle," says Mimi.

"And there aren't any searchers coming to find us."

But Mimi's point is well taken. If we try to battle the fog, we could really get lost. I don't know if there are sketchy neighbourhoods in Prague, parts of the city that tourists are advised to avoid, but if there are, I don't want to stumble into them by mistake.

"We could just stand here," Mimi tells me, "and wait for the fog to lift."

"That could be hours. We could be out here all night."

Mimi steps in close and takes my hand. "I had an uncle who went to residential school. Blue Quills in St. Paul. Did I ever tell you that?"

"This the famous Uncle Leroy?"

"No, another uncle. Everett. One time, he ran away from the school with two other boys. They just started walking. Had no idea where they were. Didn't know that Standoff was almost six hundred kilometres away."

"Long walk."

"Made it as far as Killam before they got caught. Said the fog was so thick, they had to hold hands to keep from getting lost. Just like tonight."

"So, this is your excuse for us to hold hands."

"Mum says they had a box of matches with them, but the matches got wet from the fog, and that was that."

"Chanie Wenjack."

"Sure," says Mimi, "that's the story everyone knows. Children running away from residential schools. But it's not the only one."

"What happened to Everett and the other boys?"

"They were taken back to Blue Quills," says Mimi.

"So, they didn't die?"

"No."

"And that's the end of the story?"

Mimi holds my hand a little tighter. "Those stories never end."

THE DOG THAT MIMI takes out of the bag is about the size of a small pillow, with blond fur, floppy ears, and a sweet face.

"Her name is Muffy," Mimi tells me. "And she loves you."

"A stuffed dog?"

"You don't have to walk her or clean up after her or train her." Mimi puts the dog on my chest so her nose nuzzles my neck. "And she loves you."

I'm not sure how I feel about a stuffed dog, but Muffy is cute, and all in all, it's a reasonable compromise.

"And when we travel," says Mimi, "if the two of you become inseparable, we can throw her in a suitcase and take her with us."

SO WE'RE IN PRAGUE. It's two thirty in the morning, and the fog looks as though it has settled in for the night.

"If we find the bridge, we should be okay."

Suddenly, somewhere in the fog, we hear the voices of men singing. At first, they're far away, but then they get closer.

"Come on," says Mimi. "We'll follow them."

"You want to follow drunks?"

I don't know if the group of men are Czech or German or Russian, and I guess it doesn't matter. Mimi swings in behind them, and we wander along blindly, listening to something that sounds martial but could be a sports-team fight song.

"We have no idea where they're going."

"They're tourists," says Mimi. "Tourists always head for the bridge."

This is one of the logical fallacies they teach you to avoid in journalism school, and I'm about to point this out to Mimi when a statue appears in the fog.

"The bridge," she says.

I'm not ready to concede. There are probably statues all over Prague.

"And our hotel," says Mimi, with a condescending wave of her hand, "is right over there."

Mimi doesn't wait for me to object. She leads us down the stone steps and around a corner, and there is the hotel, right where we left it.

"Like an arrow from a bow," she says.

The room is still hot. The air conditioner is still making encouraging noises. The spiders are still on the ceiling.

Mimi crawls into bed and begins snoring almost immediately. I pull a chair over to the window so I can look out at the foggy, foggy night and enjoy the rumour of a breeze.

I'm not sure that I would want to die in Prague, but it's probably as good a place as any. The city has a certain antiquity to it, a certain dignity. Much better than wasting away in a Toronto hospital, laid out on a plastic bed, wired to a monitor that counts down each heartbeat.

Dying here would be more glamorous. In a small hotel on the river Vltava. Looking out at the Charles Bridge.

Pablo Picasso died in Mougins, France. Peggy Guggenheim died in Venice, Italy. Paul Gauguin died in Atuona, French Polynesia.

I slump in the chair, close my eyes, and wait for the dawn.

So we're in Prague. It's morning, and Mimi doesn't want to get out of bed.

"What time is it?"

"Time to get up."

"I need nine hours."

"They only serve breakfast until nine thirty."

"Then wake me at nine twenty-five," she calls out from under the covers.

The spiders have moved into a tight circle in the corner of the ceiling. Outside, the fog has disappeared, and it sounds as though a herd of geese is on the move. But it's only tourists, arrived on the bridge to take photographs of the city in the early light.

"I need to eat," I tell Mimi. "You'll have to get yourself up."

This doesn't even elicit a moan.

I try a different tack. "You wait too long," I say, "and all the good stuff will be gone."

I've stayed at any number of chain hotels in North America—Fairmont, Holiday Inn, Ramada, Hampton—hotels that give you a free breakfast with each reservation. In general, these offerings are breakfasts in name only. Weak coffee, gelatinous yogurt, cold-storage apples, cellophane pastries, toast with whipped butter and strawberry-jam packets, and cook-it-yourself Dixie-cup waffles.

All the nutritional value of a can of Coke.

When I had made the reservations for the Certovka, I had had the option of booking the room with breakfast or without breakfast. Since we had never been to Prague before and since I didn't want to spend the better part of each morning looking for a restaurant, I had gone with the breakfast option.

When I get downstairs, I discover that all the tables are taken.

"Hello, hello."

There is an older man sitting at a table by himself. Short and thin. Dark sports coat. White shirt buttoned up all the way. Silver hair combed straight back. Skin the colour of an old saddle.

"You are the Canadian, yes?" He gestures to the empty chair. "Sit, sit."

I smile politely. "My wife is joining me."

"However, she is still in bed. This is true, yes?"

The man's eyes are different colours. One is blue, while the other one is gold.

"Oscar Zoraster Diggs," says the man with a tilt of his head, so the gold eye catches the light. "But everyone calls me Oz."

"Like the wizard."

"Yes, of course," says the man. "The wonderful wizard."

"Blackbird," I say with a nod. "Blackbird Mavrias. But everyone calls me Bird."

"Mavrias?" says Oz. "This is Greek? Yes?"

"Yes," I say. "My mother."

"And Black? Bird?"

"My father," I tell him. "Blackbird. It's one word."

"This is a Canadian name?"

"Cherokee. North American Indian."

"The pass at Thermopolis," says Oz with a wistful smile. "Little Bighorn."

From the table, I can see the breakfast buffet. Cold meat, fruit, cheeses, breads, and what looks to be some kind of porridge.

"You must eat," Oz tells me. "Before the tourists show up."

"I'm a tourist."

"Yes, of course," says Oz. "But this will be our secret."

I wander the buffet. I pick my way through the things I should eat and the things I want to eat. As a diabetic, I'm supposed to embrace protein and avoid carbohydrates. At least, that's the theory.

Oz is waiting for me when I return. "A Greek god *and* a bloodthirsty savage?"

"Absolutely."

"You must tell me how this could happen."

Oz's ears come to a point. His long nose reminds me of a fox. His English is good, with only the trace of a dancing accent.

I try the cheese. "Are you French?"

"Right now, I am Czech." Oz points to an item on the hot menu. "This you will like."

"What is it?"

"You and your wife are in Prague on vacation?"

"Apparently."

"Ah," says Oz. "Also business?"

I try to imagine how I would explain a lost relative and a medicine bundle to a wizard in Prague. "We're looking for something."

"Something. Yes." Oz leans forward on the table. When he does, I can see that he has a watch on each wrist. "That is for what we are all looking."

There are three choices on the hot menu. When the woman comes by with coffee, I point to the second item.

"There is much in Prague to find," says Oz. "Do you know about windows?"

"Windows?"

"In Prague, they throw politicians out windows," says Oz. "Defenestrations. This is the word, yes? 1419, 1618, and 1948."

I look at the clock on the wall and wonder if Mimi is still in bed.

"In the first defenestration, seven members of council are thrown out the windows of the town hall. They land on pikes. Most unfortunate."

If she's not careful, she'll miss breakfast.

"In the second defenestration, government officials are thrown out windows into a moat." Oz pauses and sips at his coffee. "They land on piles of manure and survive."

I could call the room and remind her of the time constraints regarding morning meals at the hotel.

"In the third defenestration," Oz continues, "Jan Masaryk, the foreign minister of Czechoslovakia, is thrown out a window to his death by Soviet Communists, who claim it is suicide."

Or I could just do nothing. Missing a meal might be an effective object lesson in punctuality.

"Of course, tossing politicians out windows is reasonable, yes?" Oz holds out his wrists. The two watches are about the same size. "Compared to carpet bombings and drone strikes? Sarin gas and napalm? Nuclear missiles and the World Bank?"

One watch has a cream face with numbers the colour of winter ice. The other has a brilliant green face with gold hands.

"Both of these are watches." Oz crosses his wrists back and forth, as though he's running a shell game. "But one is also a state of mind."

I would have added religious intolerance and racism to Oz's list. Though to be fair, religious intolerance and racism aren't the *methods* by which we kill people we don't like. They just provide the narrative and the incentive.

"Can you tell which is which?"

"Does it matter?"

"Ah," says Oz. "A philosopher. Perhaps you can help me. Do you play games?"

"Games?"

"Excellent," says Oz. "Then you will have no preconceived ideas."

"Games? Is that what you do?"

Oz puts his napkin on the table and buttons his jacket. "Take your wife to the Franz Kafka Museum," he says. "It is close. You will enjoy the Cerny sculpture in the courtyard."

The little man is through the breakfast room and gone like a wisp of smoke just as Mimi appears in the doorway, looking slightly dishevelled and lost.

"Over here." I wave.

She waves back but goes directly to the buffet and begins piling food on her plate. There is nothing that the woman won't eat, and she is always hungry. Her mother is the same way. I've seen Bernie Bull Shield go up and down the line of hot trays at the Happy Fortune in Lethbridge like a harvester through hay.

"See," Mimi says when she arrives at the table, "still lots of good stuff left."

I hand her the menu. "In addition to the buffet, you can order one of the hot items as well."

"So, are you all set for our big adventure?"

"You mean putting in time wandering a strange city, looking at old, boring buildings, hoping someone speaks English?"

"That's the one."

MIMI'S MOTHER LIVES by herself in a double-wide trailer on the Blackfoot reserve in southern Alberta. You can sit on her porch and watch the Rockies turn evening purple and wake up to see the Belly River, thin and silver, as it cuts its way through the prairies.

Bernice, or Bernie as she prefers, is a large, sturdy woman who keeps herself well supplied with strong opinions, and every time we visit, she shares them with us.

"Wouldn't hurt you to move back to the reserve," she would tell Mimi. "Traditionally, Blackfoot women brought their men home to live with their mother's family."

"No, they didn't, Mum."

"You remember that story I told you about fishing?"

"God, Mum, not that one again."

"Men are like fish," Bernie would start. "No real skill needed. Drop a line in the water and wait. But just because you catch one doesn't mean you have to keep it."

Sometimes Bernie would try to be helpful. "We should get your man an Indian name."

"I have an Indian name."

"Blackbird is okay, but Mavrias don't sound much Indian to me."

"It's not," I would say each time she brought it up.

"And we're not supposed to be in the same room. If you were Blackfoot, you'd know that."

"It's the twenty-first century, Mum."

"In the old days, you'd have to make amends by giving me a horse."

"Bird is not going to get you a horse."

"But seeing as we're modern Indians, I'll settle for a used pickup."

"Be nice," Mimi would tell her mother. "Remember, it was Bird who insisted that we name Tally after Grandma."

"And if you lived on the reserve, I could help raise my grandkids. Who's going to teach them to speak Blackfoot?"

Our conversation generally followed the same pattern. In the end, she'd remind me that since I was part of the family, I'd need to learn the stories. Which was the way she would always begin the saga of Uncle Leroy and the Crow bundle.

So we're in Prague. In the breakfast room of the hotel. Mimi eats with one hand and works the guidebook with the other.

"What do you want to do?" she asks.

This is a rhetorical question.

"For example, we could go to Old Town Square and see the astronomical clock."

My hot entree arrives. It's a thin slice of ham sandwiched between a piece of cheese and a fried egg on some kind of flatbread.

"We could go to the castle."

I try it, and it's good, especially the cheese.

"There's the Dancing House." Mimi helps herself to my entree. "We could also go to the Prague Zoo, but you don't like zoos."

"Neither do you." I try to fend off the assault on my breakfast. "What about the bundle?"

"We could check out the National Museum." Mimi consults her map. "See if they have ever heard of Leroy Bull Shield."

"Sure."

"Course, you hate museums too."

"They're pretty much all the same."

"Maybe Prague has a typewriter museum. You'd like that. You could buy a postcard and send it to that typewriter friend of yours." Mimi spears a piece of pineapple off my plate with her fork. "What's her name?"

I lean on the table and try to protect my food with my forearm.

"And look at this," says Mimi. "There's a Sex Machines Museum. Tell me you don't want to see that."

"You know you're eating my breakfast."

"You're not eating it." Mimi closes the guidebook. "Stop changing the subject. You know the first thing I want to do?"

"I was taking my time. I don't gulp my food."

"I want to walk the Charles Bridge."

"We walked it last night."

"That was in the dark." Mimi licks her fork. "Come on. Everything always looks different in the light."

LEROY BULL SHIELD was the black sheep of the Bull Shield family, and every time we went to Standoff to visit, Mimi's mother would sit me down at the kitchen table and tell me the story.

"Leroy was real adventurous," Bernie would begin. "Couldn't sit still. Always running off. Those days, you had to have a pass to leave the reserve, but that didn't bother Leroy. He'd get on his horse and just go. One time, he rode all the way to Missoula."

Mimi and I had driven down to Missoula for the big powwow. From Standoff, it had taken us over six hours. I looked up the distance on the Internet and checked it against the speed of an average horse over flat ground.

"You two should try that sometime," Bernice would say. "Borrow a couple of horses from the Goodstrikers."

"Bird isn't really a horse person," Mimi would tell her mother.

"That must be the Greek side."

"I like horses."

"Sure," Mimi would concede. "You just don't like to ride them."

Five days. So far as I could figure, it would have taken Leroy at least five days to make the trip. And that was in the early 1900s, when you couldn't pull over for a coffee in Cardston or bed down for the night at the Red Eagle Motel in St. Mary.

"He'd go to Great Falls as well," Bernie told us. "Man didn't like to stay home."

"Tell Bird about the Crow bundle."

"Why doesn't this husband of yours like horses?"

Mimi and I went to Yellowstone one year. We had been out to Standoff to visit Bernie and decided to drop down into the States to see the park. Those were the days when we were young and fit. We watched Old Faithful erupt, toured the hot springs, jogged up the side of Mount Washburn, saw the Grand Canyon of the Yellowstone, and signed up for a horseback ride.

"Leroy disappeared round the same time those idiot railroad people blew up the side of the mountain and destroyed all those salmon."

"That was later," Mimi would correct her mother. "That happened in 1913. On the Fraser River."

"Who's telling this story?"

The Yellowstone Lodge offered two rides. The Roosevelt and the Canyon. The one-hour ride cost fifty dollars, while the two-hour ride cost seventy-three. Mimi chose the two-hour Canyon ride, which went along the rim of Cascade Canyon and through a series of mountain meadows.

A romantic adventure. Indians on horses under a high Wyoming sky, and for the next two days, I wasn't able to walk.

Bernie liked to come at the story of Uncle Leroy from different angles.

"Back in the day, we had this Indian agent. Name was Nelson or Wilson. Something like that. He lived on the reserve. So he could look after us Indians. You get the picture?"

I would nod and tell Bernie that, yes, I got the picture.

"Nelson or Wilson wasn't all that charming. Some of the people liked him okay, and some of the people didn't. He could be pushy. He liked to order folks around. Some of us didn't mind, and some of us did. You keeping up?"

I would nod and tell Bernie that, yes, I was keeping up.

"And one of the people who didn't much care for Nelson or Wilson and didn't like to be ordered around by some government gasbag was Leroy Bull Shield."

So we're in Prague. On the Charles Bridge.

Mimi already has her guidebook open. "The bridge is famous for its statues of saints."

"Great."

"There are thirty in all."

While Mimi reads the book, I watch the tourists as they crowd around the statues. Some saints are more popular than others.

"There's St. Francis of Assisi and St. Wenceslas and St. Anne."

All of the statues are weathered and black, but some have spots that have been rubbed golden.

"St. Joseph, St. Vitus, St. Christopher."

Evidently, one of the tourist activities in Prague is statue rubbing.

"This is disappointing." Mimi looks up from her guidebook. "It says that most of the statues are replicas."

There are three plaques at the base of one of the statues. The first plaque shows a knight, a woman, and a child, while in the background, a group of soldiers are throwing a figure off the bridge.

"That's St. John of Nepomuk," Mimi tells me. "He's the patron saint of Prague. King Wenceslas had him killed because Nepomuk wouldn't tell him what the queen had talked about in the confessional."

The second plaque is a bunch of writing that I can't read. The third plaque shows a knight petting a dog that has been rubbed golden.

"Touching the falling priest is supposed to bring good luck."

"What about the dog?"

Mimi gives me a hug. "I knew we should have brought Muffy."

At some point in the story of Uncle Leroy and the Crow bundle, Bernie would touch on the drinking.

"Leroy was no drunk," she would say, "but he did drink. And Mr. Nelson or Wilson was one of those born-againers. Man thought he could talk to god when he was really just mumbling to himself. Drinking, according to Mr. Indian agent, led to singing, and singing led to dancing. Man would have banned laughing. Would have made smiling a hanging offence.

"One year, this Wilson or Nelson organized a sports day at the same time as the Sun Dance, to try to lure people away from Belly Buttes. And he ordered the buffalo tongues mutilated, so that the women couldn't use them in the ceremony."

"You never knew the man," Mimi reminded her mother. "You weren't even born yet."

"Stories don't die. Stories stay alive so long as they're told."

Bernie would make another pot of coffee and break out the special chocolate-covered cookies as she worked her way to the heart of the matter.

"There was this bootlegger from around Missoula. Donald somebody. Like the duck. Drug dealer. Back then it was alcohol. Today it's other stuff. So, Donald the Duck would bring his booze onto the reserve, and Leroy would find him or he would find Leroy. Didn't much matter. The result was always the same. Leroy would get drunk, and when he got drunk, he would do something stupid."

"This is where Uncle Leroy paints the guy's house?"

"Stop getting ahead of the story. I raised you better than that."

Sometimes Bernie would tell the story quick, and sometimes she would draw it out.

"Like I said, in those days, you had to have a pass to leave the reserve. Signed by the agent. Leroy didn't pay much attention to that rule, and every time he left the reserve without a pass, that agent would try to have him arrested. And every time Leroy asked that agent for a pass to leave the reserve, Nelson or Wilson would turn him down."

Even if you didn't know the story, you knew that this kind of a situation was bound to go bad at some point.

"Nelson or Wilson had a house. Government issue. It wasn't a big house. The roof leaked a little, and it didn't have no better insulation than a plastic sack. It was painted white, but that didn't last long. Cold winters and hard winds stripped the paint away until there was nothing left but the wood. You need me to draw you a picture?"

"Nope. I can see it."

"So, this one time, Donald the Duck brought his wagonload of booze onto the reserve, and before long, Leroy found him. And not long after that, Leroy got his big idea."

So we're in Prague, and Mimi has me take a picture of her rubbing the dog on the plaque. And then she rubs the guy being thrown off the bridge.

"Rubbing St. John of Nepomuk is supposed to bring you good luck and ensure that you'll return to Prague."

"We just got here."

"Rubbing the dog doesn't do anything."

We walk to one end of the bridge, and then we walk back. The sky is overcast. The water is dark slate. We pause in the middle and watch the tour boats go up and down the river.

"You want to take a boat ride?"

"No."

"You slept in the chair last night."

I take a photo of the river and the stretch of city on both sides. "My stomach hurt."

"I know it's the demons, Bird." Mimi puts her hand on my back. "They can only hurt you if you let them."

We continue walking. The tourists have increased. Small groups stand around each of the statues.

"See that woman with the red-lollipop sign?" says Mimi. "She's a guide. The people around her are part of a tour."

I look up and down the bridge. There are at least a dozen women with lollipop signs, all different colours. Mimi walks over to the red-lollipop tour, and then she walks back.

"I think it's in German," she says. "Let's see if we can find an English-speaking one."

"You want to pay for a tour?"

"No," says Mimi, "but we could stand close enough to hear what's being said."

I lean against the stone wall while Mimi goes off to find her tour, and for the first time, I notice the men lying prostrate on the bridge. Most are on their knees, hunched over with their faces on the ground, their hands cupped in front of their heads.

As though they're praying.

I wonder if they're monks of some sort, but then I see that they're really begging. They're not bothering anyone. In fact, they don't even look up or say anything as the people pass by.

A silent vigil for alms.

If this were Toronto, they would be on their feet, moving back and forth through the pedestrians, stopping people to ask for money. Some would have signs. Others would be making noise on an instrument. The bravest would be working the traffic at the stoplights with a rag and a bottle of water.

The beggars on the Charles Bridge look as though they have come here to die.

In the distance, I can see Mimi. She's found her tour. She has her back to the group and is pretending to admire the sky. Each time the group moves, Mimi moves with them, as though she's dancing with Fred Astaire.

I have a momentary impulse to join the beggars, put my face to the ground with my arms stretched out in front of me. It's a strong urge that I have to work to resist.

I know if I were to lie down, I might not want to get up.

When Bernie tells the story of Uncle Leroy, she closes her eyes so she can see the story, whole and complete. "I told you it wasn't much of a house, didn't I?"

"You did."

"And that all the paint had been stripped off by the weather?"

"You told us that too."

"And that Leroy had had a little too much to drink?"

Bernie would always pause at this point to let the tension build.

"So, Leroy's big idea," she'd begin again, after the proper amount of time had passed, "was that he would paint the Indian agent's house. But he didn't have any paint. And nobody else on the reserve had any paint, either. I'm guessing you can see the problem."

"No paint."

"So Leroy had to improvise."

Just the word "improvise" would set Bernie off, and she'd begin laughing. And we'd have to wait until she stopped.

"In those days, there was a store in Cardston run by this Mormon family. They sold all sorts of used stuff, household and farming. Some of it was okay, and some of it was garbage, and if you didn't know the difference, the Mormons weren't going to tell you.

"So, after Leroy sobered up, he rode over to Cardston to that store and bought an old milk pail, one of those zinc things with a wood piece for a handle. It was a sorry sight, that bucket. There was a story in the newspapers not long ago about a woman who collects junk like that."

"Now they're called antiques," Mimi told her mother.

"So, Leroy took his junk antique and filled it with fresh cow flops. He mixed in some water, stirred it all up until it was brown and pasty, and went to work. He wasn't sloppy either. He took his time and painted every inch of the house with cow poop. From a distance, it didn't look bad at all. And as long as you were upwind, you didn't notice the smell."

So we're in Prague.

Off in the distance, at the far end of the Charles Bridge, Mimi is making her way back through the crowds. I've read the caution in the guidebook about pickpockets, and I pay close attention to the people around her. Not that she has anything to steal. I have the passports and most of our cash.

But thieves wouldn't know that.

When she gets to where I'm standing, she shakes her head. "You were in combat mode again."

"No, I wasn't."

"You were watching me like a hawk, in case someone accosted me."

"I was enjoying the view."

"And then you were going to rush to my aid. Rescue me from the ogre, slay the dragon." Mimi puts her arms around me. "So, which demon is this?"

"We should go to the Kafka museum. Oz said the statues in the courtyard are worth seeing."

"Oz?"

"A guy I met at breakfast."

"You made a friend?"

"He's not a friend."

"If you had more friends, maybe you wouldn't spend so much time with your demons."

When the Indian agent returned and found his house painted with cow shit, he wasn't impressed. According to Bernie, he stormed around the reserve trying to find who was responsible. Everybody knew it was Leroy, but no one said a word.

"Course Leroy wasn't one to leave well enough alone, and each time the agent left the reserve to go to Lethbridge or to Calgary or wherever Indian agents went in those days, Leroy would get out his milk pail and his brush and go to work."

There was, I suppose, a certain poetic justice in painting an Indian agent's house with cow shit. And I have to admit that, in my darker moments, I liked to imagine Uncle Leroy as an avenging angel, riding around the countryside with his bucket and brush, painting the exteriors of residential schools and churches, charging up Parliament Hill and redecorating the walls of government offices.

No, it was not a generous thought.

"So, Leroy painted that house three or four more times. By then, Nelson or Wilson could hardly stand living in it, but everyone agreed that it was a nice shade of brown."

"He ever get caught?"

"Sure," Bernie told me. "That agent wasn't no fool. He pretended that he was going off on a trip, but then he doubled back and caught Leroy with the bucket in one hand and the brush in the other."

There weren't any photographs of Uncle Leroy, so I had to imagine what he looked like, and what I saw was a tallish, slender man with a face like an axe, broad shoulders and no butt, standing next to a clapboard house, holding a beat-to-shit zinc bucket.

"Nelson or Wilson had Leroy dead to rights, and he told Leroy he had a choice to make. One, he could stick around, in which case the agent was going to go to the RCMP post at Fort Macleod and swear out an arrest warrant, after which he'd come back with a couple of officers, throw Leroy in leg irons, and send him to the penitentiary at Stony Mountain."

I tried to imagine what it must have been like to be an Indian in those days with the power that Indian agents, the RCMP, and the church had over your life.

"Or two, there was a Wild West show that had landed in Calgary.

Captain Trueblood's Wild West Emporium. And they were looking for Native performers."

Mimi had gone to the Glenbow in Calgary and found a couple of old posters from the show and a newspaper story. Trueblood's was a modest affair, thirty performers tops. And it spent most of its time in Europe, playing the smaller venues, places the larger shows such as Buffalo Bill and the Miller Brothers didn't go.

"Wasn't much of a choice," Bernie told us. "Go to jail or join the circus."

Bernie was right. It wasn't a choice at all.

"It was only after he left that we discovered he'd taken the Crow bundle with him."

WE DON'T FIND the Kafka museum right away. First, we get lost and wind up walking in a circle.

"You have the map upside down." Mimi turns the map over. "See. The museum is right here."

The place is easy to miss. A white stucco wall. An open gate. A small sign. A courtyard with two copper-green male figures peeing into a small pond. The statues are articulated, and as they pee, their hips move and their penises go up and down.

"This is it?"

"I guess."

"Two guys peeing in a fountain?"

"Cerny," I say. "He's supposed to be famous."

Mimi already has her guidebook open. "Evidently, he's the same guy who did the giant alien babies in the park. Along with a statue of Sigmund Freud hanging by one hand from a roof."

"We haven't seen that one."

"Not yet," says Mimi.

I watch the copper-green men pee in the pond, and I have to admit, the mechanics are impressive. Swivelling hips, moving penises. Mimi circles in for a closer look.

"You know what I don't see?"

These are the kinds of questions I try not to answer.

"Women," says Mimi. "Where are the women peeing in the pond?"

"Women don't pee in ponds."

"No reason why we wouldn't." Mimi walks around the statues several times. "Women can pee in ponds just as easily as men."

I don't try to argue with this.

Mimi undoes the top button of her pants. "Maybe I should demonstrate just how easily it's done."

"Don't."

"Why not?"

"Remember what happened on Santorini. In Oia?"

"When I went swimming at the bottom of the Karavolades Stairs?"

"Skinny-dipping. You went skinny-dipping."

"I left my bra and underpants on."

"Tourists took pictures of you," I tell Mimi, not for the first time. "Those photos are probably somewhere on the Internet. You know how embarrassed Tally and Nathan would be if they saw naked photos of their mother on Facebook?"

"I wasn't naked."

"And then there was that time at Crypt Lake."

"Okay," she says. "There I was naked." Mimi closes her book and fixes her button. "You know, you're only old if you want to be old."

BERNIE WOULD GENERALLY STOP the story at this point and make something to eat. Sometimes it was leftovers, and other times she'd cook a complete meal. And she'd only get back to Uncle Leroy and the Crow bundle after everyone had been fed and the dishes cleared away.

"It was a family bundle. Got opened once a year, so there was the chance it had been misplaced."

Mimi would nod and finish her mother's thought. "But you don't misplace something like that."

"No," Bernie would say, as though she were talking to herself, "you don't misplace something like that."

"And then the first postcard came."

That was Bernie's cue to get the old Hiawatha Tobacco tin out of the cupboard. "The first card we got," she said, "was from Paris."

There was a picture of the Arc de Triomphe on the front. On the back, Leroy had written, "In Paris. Bundle is with me and safe. Home soon. Leroy."

"He doesn't say why he took it."

"Nope."

"Maybe he wanted something that reminded him of home."

Bernie wasn't so forgiving. "Or maybe he thought he needed something to impress the White people in that Wild West show. Something he could use in the show. So they'd hire him. So he wouldn't wind up at Stony Mountain."

I wasn't sure what to say. "It sounds as though he planned to bring it back."

"Sure," Bernie would say, "but whatever he had in mind, the day that Leroy left was the last time we ever saw the bundle."

So we're in Prague, standing in the courtyard of the Kafka museum, watching two articulated sculptures pee into a pond.

"I suppose we should get a picture," says Mimi. "For my mother."

"You could just tell her about it."

Mimi shakes her head. "Don't think words can capture the majesty of the moment."

So I take a picture of Mimi standing by the fountain with her hands on her hips.

"Did you get one with their penises on the upswing?"

I can feel my blood sugars dropping. It's not a pleasant sensation, akin to discovering you're in the middle of Saskatchewan in winter and out of gas.

Mimi moves in closer to the sculptures. "I like the way their hips swivel back and forth."

I recognize trouble when I see it. "Do you know what time it is?"

"Would you be embarrassed if I just touched—?"

"Lunchtime," I say quickly.

Mimi pulls her hand back. "You want to eat lunch?"

"Only if you do."

"You just ate breakfast." Mimi shakes her head. "This is what happens when you don't get enough sleep."

When you're in a strange city, you don't have many options for finding a good place to eat. You can go with a recommendation in the guidebook or you can rely on local knowledge. Guidebooks are notoriously unreliable. Much of the information in them is old and out of date. Chefs change, restaurants close.

Worse, an international conglomerate moves in, buys the place, and uses the restaurant's reputation to sell prepackaged, processed food to an unsuspecting public.

Local knowledge is all well and good, but as we don't speak Czech, this is not an option. In addition, there is always the chance of falling prey to the gangs that work the tourist areas of the world. "Yes," a kindly older man tells you, "there's a restaurant just down this alley. Very good. Very cheap. It's where locals go. Follow me. I'll show you." So down the alley you go, and you turn a corner, and that's the last time anyone ever sees you.

I share these thoughts with Mimi.

"You might want to tell Kitty to keep her ideas to herself."

"I'm not catastrophizing," I tell Mimi. "Do you know how many people were murdered in Prague last year?"

"Do you?"

"No, but I bet it's more than Toronto."

"What about New York?"

"Sure," I say, "but we're not in New York."

Mimi ignores me and consults the guidebook. "How far do you want to walk?"

I don't believe in cosmic laws, but I've come to accept that there is an inverse relationship between good restaurants and wherever we happen to be. The better the restaurant, the farther away we are from it.

Mimi closes the book. "Okay," she says, "I've got the perfect spot."

"So, how far do we have to walk?"

"Not far," she says, and she heads off down the street at a slow trot.

MIMI HAS A THEORY that travel makes time stop. Or at least slows it down. Her reasoning has a simple elegance. When you're home, you fall into routines. These routines are so familiar that you do them without even thinking or noticing the passage of time. You get up, have breakfast, check your emails, go to work, have lunch, finish work, come home, have dinner, watch some television, go to bed. And every so often, you look up and wonder where in the heck the time went.

When you're travelling, everything is new, and every minute is taken up with decision-making.

Tick tock, tick tock.

Exhausting.

Today it's been breakfast, the Kafka museum, articulated men peeing in a fountain, and it's barely noon. We still have most of the day left to fill.

You went to Rome and didn't see the Colosseum?

You stayed in Barcelona and didn't see the Gaudi church?

You spent a week in Amsterdam and didn't go to the Rijksmuseum?

Athens and you only saw the Acropolis from your hotel window?

Tick tock, tick tock.

The first obligation of any vacation is that you experience as much as you can. Wandering the streets, coffee in cafés, sitting on park benches don't count.

Mimi's idea of "not far" turns out to be far enough.

We walk for at least half an hour. If I had been smart, I would have timed it in case I needed to use it as an example later.

"The Nusle district," says Mimi, "and we're almost there."

My hip is beginning to hurt. My toes feel as though the ends have been filed off.

"And here we are."

An ordinary street. It could be anywhere in the world. I could close my eyes for a moment and open them to find myself in Ottawa. Or San Francisco. Or Montevideo.

Or Prague.

I have to shield my eyes to see the sign. It's dark red and white and features the image of a stylized Indian eating an entire pizza.

Baressa Pizza and Pasta.

"This is where you want to eat?"

"The guidebook says 'Baretta,'" says Mimi, "so I'm guessing that those things that look like *s*'s are probably the way the Czechs make their *t*'s."

"There's a headdress in the window."

"Just like home."

"Your mother doesn't have a headdress in her window."

"And while we eat, we can talk."

I step into the shade of the building and wait.

"Eugene," says Mimi. "I want to talk about Eugene and the Other Demons."

"Mimi . . ."

"You can thank me later."

I open the door and stand to one side. Mimi walks in. And because I can't think of anything else to do, I follow.

Eugene and the Other Demons.

Lots of people have demons. I know I do. And my approach to dealing with them is to pretend that they don't exist, to leave them tucked away in the darkness.

Mimi doesn't subscribe to my method, and early on, she decided that we should name them, to call them out as it were, to shine a light into the shadows where they hide.

"Eugene," Mimi began. "Eugene's the main man. Self-loathing."

"Eugene?"

"And you like to catastrophize. That's Cat. Or Kitty."

"This is crazy."

"And then we have the twins, Didi and Desi. Depression and Despair."

I don't mind talking about my medical issues. But personal struggles should always be private. That's what private is all about.

"As well as Chip. For that big you-know-what on your shoulder."

I was not pleased that Mimi had given my demons names, and I was more than put out when she shared them with her mother.

"Eugene?"

"Self-loathing," Mimi told her mother.

"Your daughter is just being silly."

"Seems to me," said Bernie, "every Native person in North America has a Eugene."

"And Bird likes to catastrophize. That's Kitty."

"He's also kinda touchy," said Bernie.

"Chip," said Mimi. "And we don't want to forget the twins."

After that, each time we went to visit, the two of them would have a good time at my expense.

"You still hanging out with that Eugene?" Bernie would ask.

"The two of them," Mimi would tell her mother, crossing one finger over the other, "are like that."

So we're in Prague, and Mimi has walked us halfway across the city to an Indian-themed pizza parlour.

"Totem pole." Mimi gestures towards the front counter. "Over there is a quiver for your arrows."

The inside of the café is dark, on the edge of gloomy, but the place looks friendly enough.

"World is crazy about Indians," says Mimi. "Remember that big festival we went to in Germany?"

"The Karl May festival in Bad Segeberg."

"And the powwow in Denmark?"

"Aarhus."

"And Cafés Indien in old-town Nice?"

There's a buffalo head hanging on the wall. Mimi stands under it so I can take a picture of the two of them. "I guess the Czechs feel the same way."

Mimi reaches up and gives the buffalo a pat. There's a feather hanging off each horn.

"Remember the big raid? Operation Cerberus?"

There's a rattle and a small drum hanging from a hook near a photograph of three Indians on horseback.

"You covered it for *The New York Times*."

Blanding, Utah. 2009. Federal agents raided a number of homes and businesses and recovered more than forty thousand Native artifacts that had been illegally dug up from protected sites. Arrowheads, shell pendants, ceramic pottery, masks.

Mimi looks at the other artifacts on the walls. "Robbing graves and selling culture," she says, "has always been good business. Just ask the Egyptians and the Greeks."

We get a table in a corner. I lean against the wall while Mimi reads the menu. Most of the people in the café are young, but then pizza is a young person's dish. Grease doesn't slow them down. Molten cheese doesn't plug them up. Processed meat doesn't clog their arteries.

Immortal. You have to be immortal to eat pizza.

"We can get a Geronimo or we could try a Crazy Eagle." Mimi hands me the menu. "But we don't have to stay. I just thought we should see the place in case you can use it in the book."

"There is no book."

"That sounds like Didi and Desi to me."

We settle for the Black Bear pizza, which is made with black olives, hermelin, and chicken. Mimi has to look up *hermelin* on her cellphone.

"It's a traditional Czech cheese," she tells me. "Like Camembert, with a coating of white mould."

"Is there anything with pepperoni?"

"We can get pepperoni in Guelph."

"Exactly."

The Black Bear pizza with the hermelin turns out to be excellent. Gooey, but tasty. I'm reaching for my second piece when the cramp hits.

After autoimmune pancreatitis and diabetes, leg cramps were the next surprise on my list of medical staggers. One night, about nine months ago, I was jolted out of a dead sleep with terrible cramps in the quadriceps of my left leg, as though the flesh was being torn away from the bone.

That first cramp came in a series of waves, varying in intensity and lasting for the better part of an hour. At one point, I managed to get out of bed and stand, hoping that the pressure would ease the pain.

It didn't.

I began shaking and sweating until I was exhausted, my body wet and cold. Mimi did all she could. Rubbed the thigh, listened to me scream, offered advice.

"Can you stand up straight?"

"What happens if you stretch the muscle?"

"Maybe we should try singing."

Nothing worked. The cramps finally disappeared on their own. But they didn't leave for long. Two nights later they were back.

The doctor listened to my description with some interest. "Cramps?"

"Yes."

"In the legs?"

"The inside of the thigh to be exact," I said, showing her the spot.

"And you tried standing to relieve the cramp."

"Tried stretching as well."

"Have you injured the leg recently?"

"No."

"Well," she said finally, "it could be a potassium deficiency."

"Potassium?"

"Do you eat bananas?"

"All the time."

"Okay, then it's probably not that."

The cramps generally occurred in the middle of the night, but one morning I was sitting on the edge of the bed, one leg crossed over the other, putting on a sock.

Mimi came in from the bathroom on the fly, a toothbrush in her hand. "Cramp?"

"Yes."

"So it's not bananas."

My doctor sent me to a specialist who made me write down everything I ate of a typical day. There was a series of blood tests that bled me dry, and a fun session with electrodes and voltage.

"Curious case," the specialist told me.

I tried not to hold the electroshock treatment against him. "So you don't know what's causing the cramping?"

He smiled and shook his head. "No idea."

So WE'RE IN PRAGUE, and my initial scream brings the server to our table.

"The pizza," she asks, "it is bad?"

"No," Mimi tells her. "My partner is just having a bad cramp."

"Cramp?"

"In his leg. He gets them every so often."

I'm gripping the table as hard as I can and trying to move into a position where I can brace the leg against something substantial.

Our server is a tall woman, broad at the shoulders and the hips. Blue eyes, a small mouth that gives her the appearance of a large fish. I can see that she is concerned.

"He should eat more pizza," she says. "This is much salt in pizza."

I block my foot against the leg of the table and try to press the cramp out of existence.

"You hear that, Bird," says Mimi. "More salt."

WHEN POTASSIUM DEFICIENCY was ruled out, salt was the next item on the Hippocratic checklist. Low sodium and dehydration, I was told, could cause cramping in athletes. I wasn't an athlete, but at the time, it had pleased me to think that I might share a medical condition with the likes of Alex Morgan and Kawhi Leonard.

The doctor suggested I try a sports drink. "A lot of football and basketball players drink them," he told me. "They're designed to replenish the fluids and electrolytes that you lose through sweating."

I tried to remember the last time I had sweated, but I picked up a bottle on the off chance that it might work. I don't remember the brand, just the colour of the drink.

Iridescent orange.

I had finished most of the bottle before I looked at the list of ingredients.

THE CRAMPS RETREAT, but they retreat slowly. And by the time I'm able to bring my heart rate down to the speed limit, Mimi has eaten most of the pizza.

"Kitty is going to come along any minute and tell you that it's cancer of the muscle," says Mimi. "But there's no such thing."

"There could be."

The buffalo head on the wall looks embarrassed. The drum is covered in dust. Mimi pats my hand. "You going to eat that last piece?"

THE THIRTY-TWO-OUNCE sports drink contained about eleven teaspoons of sugar and salt. Just for fun, I put the same amount of sugar and salt into a coffee cup and showed it to Mimi.

"Nobody cares," she said. "Have you looked at what's in a hot dog?"

I held the bottle up with the Nutrition Facts label facing out. "Heart disease? Obesity? Diabetes?"

"That's why," Mimi reminded me, "the companies spend so much money on advertising."

SO WE'RE IN PRAGUE. We've had lunch, and now Mimi is energized for the afternoon that lies ahead.

"How about the astronomical clock in Old Town Square?"

"You want to see a clock?"

"It's a famous clock."

"Is it close by?"

"Remember where we started?"

I look down the street in the hope that I might spot a taxi. Mimi waits on the sidewalk, her hands firmly on her hips.

"So, were they real?"

"What?"

"The cramps."

"Of course they were real."

"You weren't just trying to get out of our talk." Mimi squeezes a little more sternness out of her lips. "Eugene and the gang?"

I shake my head.

"Because that would hurt my feelings. You not wanting to talk to me about your problems."

"I don't have any problems," I tell her. "And I don't want to talk about them."

It takes a while, but we find Old Town Square without too much difficulty. The astronomical clock is easy to spot. It's an elaborate thing set on the side of a stone building, two giant circles, one on top of the other.

"The top one with the non-concentric circles is the clock," says Mimi. "The four figures at the side are supposed to be Vanity, Greed, Death, and the Pagan Invasion."

One of the figures is holding a mirror, so I guess that this is Vanity.

"Greed was originally pictured as a Jewish moneylender," says Mimi, "but after the Second World War, the figure was altered to reflect more contemporary sensibilities."

Death is easy to spot. A skeleton.

"Each hour, Death rings a bell and turns his hourglass upside down, and the twelve Apostles march past the two windows above the clock. You want to know who they are?"

"Nope."

"You see the gold rooster?" Mimi moves me into place. "It's just above the two windows where the Apostles appear. When they're done marching, the bird crows and that's the hour."

"Fascinating."

"The clock is over six hundred years old," says Mimi. "That has to count for something."

The sides of the clock are draped in scaffolding and blue tarps. A plywood barrier has been thrown up at the base of the building to keep the crowds back.

"Can you read that sign?"

"Nope."

Mimi pushes her way through the crowd. I stand at the back and thumb through the guidebook, which warns that Old Town Square is an area frequented by pickpockets. I've never seen a pickpocket and am not sure what I'd do if I happened to spot one.

Maybe take a photograph. Write a story. Photojournalism at arm's length.

Mimi is back, and she doesn't look happy. "The sign says that the clock is under repair."

"It doesn't work?"

"No idea."

"So, all these people are standing around, waiting for nothing to happen?"

"Maybe part of it works," says Mimi. "Maybe the clock doesn't tell time, but the Apostles still walk past the windows."

I check my watch. "It's twenty minutes to the hour."

"Then let's wander the square," says Mimi. "Check out the crafts market."

"We have a crafts market in Guelph."

"And then when it's near the top of the hour," says Mimi, "we can come back and see what the clock does."

It was bad enough when my demons were just shapeless emotions and unpredictable moods, but as soon as Mimi named them, they began to take physical form.

Eugene, for instance.

Dark hair, dark eyes, full lips. Stupid smirk on his face. Frog butt. Reflective sunglasses and a dirty-white straw on his head.

Eugene likes to hang out with Didi and Desi, fraternal twins who aren't all that easy to tell apart. Self-loathing, Depression, and Despair. Your popular power ménage-à-trois.

Kitty is tall and thin, blond, brittle, with sharp edges and a voice that can make cars pull to the side of the road.

Chip shaves his head and spends too much time at the gym.

They don't look like demons. They don't look scary at all. They look like people you pass on the street every day.

At first, they were easy enough to ignore. But then Mimi named them.

And then they started to talk.

So WE'RE IN PRAGUE, marking time in a crafts market while we wait for the famous astronomical clock in Old Town Square to do something. Mimi sorts through scarves and leather handbags while the vendors follow us around with discounts and deals.

At times such as these, I tend to retreat into myself and drift. A mistake. And before I know it, Eugene is standing beside me, his hat pulled down over his eyes, as though he's worried someone might recognize him.

How's my favourite loser? he says.

Kitty doesn't waste any time joining in. *Do you know how many tourists are killed each year in Prague?*

Killed? says Didi.

We should have stayed home, says Desi.

Bring it on, says Chip.

You got nothing to worry about, Eugene tells me. *One look at you, and the crooks won't bother to waste their time.*

Mimi turns and holds up two bags. "Which one do you like?"

It takes me a moment to recover. "You want a purse?"

"Not for me," says Mimi. "For you."

"I don't want a purse."

"It's not a purse. It's a messenger bag."

"I don't need a messenger bag."

You don't deserve a messenger bag, whispers Eugene.

The vendor is a short, fat man with a thicket of a moustache and dark, curly hair. "Feel the leather, sir," he says. "Feel how soft it is."

I look at my watch. "It's almost time," I say. "We can come back after we see what the clock does."

"The clock is every day here," says the vendor. "But soon this bag is gone."

Eugene throws a hand over my shoulder as we head back. *You don't even deserve to be alive.*

A substantial crowd has gathered in front of the clock. Everyone has their cellphones and their tablets out at the ready. I check the crowd for pickpockets. Now would be the time for them to move in.

I try to imagine that I'm a thief. What would I look for? The open purse hanging off the shoulder of the woman in the blue pantsuit? The bright foil shopping bag the teenager has set on a stone abutment while she sends a text to a friend? The wallet sticking out of the back pocket of the old man in the Bermuda shorts and the canvas hat? The young man in a wheelchair with the day pack hooked over the push handles?

Mimi takes my hand and leads me through the crowd. "We can see better from back here," she says.

"Don't think there'll be much to see."

"You ready with the camera?" says Mimi.

We stand there in Old Town Square and wait. The hour comes and goes. At one point, there is a shout and something on the clock moves, but it's nothing more than a mechanical twitch, a fidget, as though the mechanism is trying to wake up from a bad dream. The Apostles don't make an appearance. The rooster doesn't crow.

"Well," says Mimi, "that wasn't as exciting as it might have been, but just seeing the clock was worth the walk."

I agree that it's an impressive clock.

"It's supposed to have been built by Jan Hanus," says Mimi. "The story goes that when the clock was finished, some of the city fathers decided to blind the clockmaker, so that he couldn't make another clock like it."

"The guy builds a great clock, and in appreciation, they blind him?"

"With a hot poker," says Mimi. "After he was blinded, he made his way to the clock, and before anyone could stop him, he sabotaged the mechanism."

"Can't fault him for that."

"It's a good story," says Mimi, "but the clock was really built by Mikulas of Kadan and Jan Sindel. And there was no eye gouging involved."

"So why doesn't it work?"

"No idea," says Mimi. "What about that messenger bag?"

One of the problems with travel is that once you start, you can't get away from it. If I were home, I could take a break and go out to my workshop, or I could sit in the backyard and read a book, or I could curl up on the bed with Muffy and take a nap. These aren't options when you travel, since one of the demands of travel is that you keep moving.

"What do you want to do next?"

We are standing in the middle of Old Town Square, next to a massive monument composed of creepy guys dressed in long robes. One of them is reaching out with a claw-like hand, as though he is going to snatch up a passing child and eat it.

"Surprise me."

"The old Jewish cemetery in Prague," says Mimi, reading from the guidebook, "has more than eleven thousand gravestones."

"You want to spend the afternoon looking at gravestones?"

"You know who's buried there?"

"Elvis."

"Are you tired, Bird? Is that the problem?"

"I wouldn't mind an espresso."

"You just had pizza."

"We're on vacation," I say. "People on vacation sit in cafés and drink espresso."

I'M NOT SURE why we travel.

The default response is that we travel in order to see new places, to meet new peoples, to broaden our understanding of the world.

Whereas I tend to see travel as punishment for those of us who can afford such mistakes.

Travel does allow us to collect new adventures, gather up new stories we can share with family and friends. The problem is that travel stories are only interesting if something untoward happens, if trouble makes an appearance, if a disaster is survived.

No one cares that your trip to Turkey went off without a hitch, that your plane was on time, that your room was lovely and had a view of the Aya Sofya, that the food was marvellous and cheap, that everyone spoke English, and that you weren't robbed, mugged, or annoyed in any way by the locals, the police, or other tourists.

The first expectation of a good travel story is that something went wrong. No one wants to hear about the perfectly uneventful time you spent in Istanbul. Not even you.

Next time, try harder.

When we were younger, before we had children, Mimi went on the Internet and found a seven-day, all-inclusive vacation to Costa Rica for next to nothing. There were colour pictures of large white birds and scary-looking crocodiles and trees filled with howler monkeys, along with a young couple walking hand in hand on a sun-drenched beach while a dark-skinned man in a white jacket followed them around, in case they needed a towel or another drink.

I came home from the trip with a sunburn, a great story about Mimi having the top of her swimsuit ripped off on a jungle water-slide, and a dozen photographs of some very large iguanas.

But I don't remember feeling that my social conscience had been improved.

The resort had been a sanitary bubble designed to shield you from the realities of culture and to limit your interaction with the local people. They were there to serve you, and you were there in your role as an ATM with a camera.

So WE'RE IN PRAGUE, walking down a street that looks a great deal like many other streets in the world.

"Besides the Jewish cemetery," says Mimi, "there's also a couple of famous churches."

After years of travelling the world with Mimi, looking for the Crow bundle and trying to find out what happened to Uncle Leroy, the last thing I want to do is go into another church.

Of any sort.

To be sure, the things are historic, and the architecture is remarkable. But all I see are monuments to indulgence and power.

"How about we skip the churches."

Mimi sighs. "Okay," she says. "Let's check out the cemetery, and then we can stop at a café."

So we walk over to the Jewish cemetery, but when we get there, we discover that there is a long line of tourists outside the ticket booth.

"We have to pay to get into a cemetery?"

"You check the prices," says Mimi. "I'm going to take a peek."

Taking a peek is one of the things that Mimi does best. When we moved to Guelph and were looking for a house, Mimi would march onto porches and look in windows. Once, she leaned a ladder against a house and climbed up so she could check out the kitchen.

Today, she ambles over to an iron gate and peers through the grating. I pretend to price the tickets. Mimi waves me over.

"You can see some of the gravestones from here."

What I can see of the cemetery is disturbing. I don't know what I had expected, but this wasn't it.

"Why are all the gravestones so close together?"

Mimi checks the guidebook.

"Looks like a salvage yard." I hold out my hands by way of apology. "And the wait time to get in is at least an hour."

"Really?"

"No less than forty-five minutes."

Mimi decides we should at least walk the perimeter. The graveyard is surrounded by a thick stone wall, but every so often, there's a small portal that you can look through.

"You can't see much," Mimi tells me. "The gravestones are stuck in the ground at all sorts of angles. It looks as though someone dropped them out of the sky and just left them where they landed."

I don't bother looking. Graveyards are graveyards.

"I'd like to be able to read the inscriptions on the stones."

"They're probably in Yiddish."

"Probably."

"Or Czech."

"Rabbi Loew is supposed to be buried here," says Mimi. "According to legend, Loew is the guy who created the Prague Golem."

I know the story of the Golem. A brute made out of mud. Brought to life to defend the community. The desperate fantasy of a desperate people. Gods and angels, Wonder Woman and Superman. Every culture has heroes and talismans that it looks to for protection.

Mimi comes away from the wall and brushes herself off. "The problem with creating monsters is that, in the end, it's impossible to control them."

At the Battle of Hattin, the Christian army under the command of Guy of Lusignan carried the True Cross into battle and was slaughtered by the Muslim army under the command of Saladin. At Wounded Knee, the people put on Ghost Dance shirts in the hope that they would stop bullets.

"Let's get that coffee," says Mimi. "And while we're at it, maybe we can figure out what we want to bring home from Prague to put in the new bundle."

One of the first places we went when we started following Uncle Leroy's trail was Paris. When we got home, we went out to Alberta to visit Mimi's mother and to give her the initial report.

"Where are the children?" was the first thing Bernie wanted to know.

"They're grown, Mum. Tally is working in Ottawa, and Nathan is finishing up at UBC."

"No reason you can't bring them along."

"I'll tell them to call you."

"I don't want a phone call. I get all sorts of phone calls. People call to tell me about my tax problems and my dirty ducks."

"Ducts, Mum. And you don't have a tax problem. Those are scams."

"I know they're scams," said Bernie. "I tell them I don't have any dirty ducks but that I got a bunch of geese that could use a good scrubbing. You know what they say?"

"They hang up."

"So, did you find out what happened to Leroy?"

Mimi shook her head. "You have to remember, Uncle Leroy was in Paris more than a hundred years ago."

Bernie took a deep breath and closed her eyes. "So what? You see a Blackfoot warrior hanging around the Eiffel Tower, and you're going to forget it? Probably made all the newspapers."

"Leroy was a Blackfoot warrior?"

"Close enough," said Bernie. "So, where are you two planning to go next?"

"Follow the postcards," Mimi told her mother. "We'll just follow the postcards."

Sometimes, Bernie would pick up Chinese takeout in Lethbridge. Pork fried rice, chicken with black beans, teriyaki beef, and steamed dumplings. I would set the table, while Mimi's mother caught her daughter up on the local gossip.

"So, I have this idea," Mimi said. "And I don't want either of you to say anything until I'm done explaining. Can you two do that?"

"Probably not," said Mimi's mother. "You want a fork or chopsticks?"

"What do you guys know about medicine bundles?"

I helped myself to some of the chicken before it disappeared.

Mimi didn't wait for an answer. "They're mnemonic devices."

Bernie waggled a chopstick at her daughter. "Someone's been on Google again."

The teriyaki beef looked good, but I knew it had too much sugar for me.

"Bundles contain things like feathers or stones or bones," Mimi explained between bites. "Each of the items could have some spiritual significance, or it might have been attached to a specific story or to a song."

"And someone's been reading Wikipedia."

"But not all bundles are sacred." Mimi scooped most of the pork fried rice onto her plate. "Some are secular. Family bundles. Bundles that are a living history."

"Crow bundle was a family bundle," said Bernie.

I watched Mimi take the last dumpling. "So, what's your idea?"

Mimi picked a piece of *gai lan* out of her teeth. "What do you think our chances are of finding out what happened to Uncle Leroy or to the bundle?"

"What's less than zero?"

Mimi sat back in the chair. "So," she said, "assuming that we will never find either of them, what do you think we should do?"

"We should stay home."

"Or?"

"We should stay home."

Bernie kept a ready supply of ice cream and chocolate syrup in the house. Mimi and I cleared the table, while Bernie got out spoons and bowls.

"What we should do," said Mimi, after the ice cream had been allotted, "is continue to follow the postcards around Europe and look for Uncle Leroy and the bundle. At the same time, we should create a new bundle."

"Make our own bundle?"

"They don't just fall out of the sky," she told me. "People put them together. Someone put the Crow bundle together, and we could do the same thing."

"You want to get a piece of leather and put stuff in it?"

"Not just any stuff," said Mimi. "It would be things we find on our travels."

Bernie thought about it and nodded. "Honour Leroy's memory."

"We could call it the Travel bundle."

I got the smallest bowl of ice cream with no syrup. "This in honour of the guy who ran off with the old bundle?"

"I got just the thing." Bernie pushed away from the table. "Just make sure he doesn't touch my ice cream."

She came back a few minutes later with a black case. "Here we go," she said. "Ballistic nylon. And it has a zipper."

"I was thinking more along the lines of a piece of elk hide," said Mimi.

"Sure," said Bernie, "if this were the nineteenth century."

"You want to make a medicine bundle out of a zippered nylon case?"

"Used to belong to your auntie Helen."

"The chef?"

"She carried her knives in it," said Bernie. "When she quit and went back to singing, she gave me the case."

"Doesn't seem all that authentic," I said.

"Authentic is overdone," said Bernie. "Authentic is one of the ideas Whites use to hold us in place. It's one of the ways we hold ourselves in place."

"I got no problem with a nylon medicine bundle," said Mimi. "And the zipper will make it easier to put things in and take them out."

"If you're concerned about authentic," said Bernie, "I can always get Ester Fox to do a little beading on the case. Maybe a floral design."

"Okay," said Mimi, "so let's get started."

"Sometimes," Bernie told her daughter, "starting is how we continue."

So WE'RE IN PRAGUE. Mimi finds a coffee shop. I have an espresso, which comes with a cookie. Mimi has something called an Italian hot chocolate. Once I sit down, I don't want to get up. Mimi is wrong about travel. It doesn't slow time, it just wears you out.

"Are you tired, Bird?"

"I'm tired."

"But not too tired."

"I'm very tired."

"Then we'll go to the castle tomorrow." Mimi sips her hot chocolate. It's quite thick and looks as though it would be better managed with a backhoe.

I sink into the chair. If I sink down far enough, I may disappear altogether.

"What do you want to do for the rest of the day?" Mimi slides the guidebook across the table, in case I need help with the right answer. "Your choice."

She doesn't mean this, of course, but it's sweet of her to offer. I take a moment to contemplate all the things we could do and see in Prague, City of a Hundred Spires, Rome of the North, Mistress of Bohemia.

And then I sink into the chair even further, flag down the server, and order another espresso.

IV

I wake up in the middle of the night to find my left eye swollen shut. This is the very newest of the medical bruisings.

Kitty catches me on the way to the bathroom. *Cancer*, she whispers. *Intraocular lymphoma*.

I close the door and stare in the mirror. Eugene is standing behind me shaking his head.

Death warmed over, he says.

Didi and Desi stand quietly next to the toilet, holding hands.

My eyelid and the surrounding soft tissue look like the leading edge of a mudslide.

"Shit." I can feel moisture leaking out the sides of the eye and trickling down my face. I get a piece of toilet paper and dab at it. "Shit!"

I listen for any movement in the bedroom.

Louder, says Eugene. *She can't hear you*.

Screw sympathy, says Chip. *Fight through it*.

There is the momentary impulse to get dressed, go onto the bridge, and throw myself off. I have no idea how far it is to the water, or if the fall would kill me or just get me wet and cranky. I'm sure there's a formula. Height, velocity, the degree to which water will compress.

Don't worry, says Eugene. *We can look it up on the Internet*.

"Bird?" Mimi sounds sluggish and far away. "You all right?"

"Fine."

"Who you talking to?"

When I get down to the breakfast room, Oz is waiting for me. Today, he is dressed in a dark suit jacket with a bright yellow T-shirt. The T-shirt has da Vinci's *Vitruvian Man* on the front with a caption that reads, "Give Chimps a Chance."

Considering the successes of human evolution, this seems a reasonable request.

"Ah," says Oz, and he comes to his feet. "Blackbird Mavrias. Here you are."

"Here I am."

"Your eye is unhappy."

"Allergies."

Oz spreads the napkin on his lap. "Today, the special is the same, but first, you must tell me of yesterday."

I pull up a chair and sit. "We saw the statues. In the courtyard."

"Kafka." Oz cocks his head to one side. "And the pond? Did you notice the pond?"

"What about the pond?"

"In the shape of the country," says Oz. "The statues are pissing on the Czech Republic."

"Ah."

"In Prague, we have a great sense of history and of humour," says Oz. "Not long ago, either would have got you shot."

I check the menu. Oz is right. The choices are the same. "And we saw the big clock."

"Of course," says Oz. "Everyone who comes to Prague goes to the clock."

"It wasn't working."

I tell Oz about the pizza place and the Jewish graveyard and the wasted afternoon we spent at the Dripstone Wall and wandering a farmers' market.

"Good, good," he says as I tick off the attractions. "So today, you must go to the castle and see Zlata ulicka."

"Okay."

"It is also called Golden Lane."

And, that in the evening, Mimi found us a restaurant near the KGB Museum that served *koleno*, which turned out to be pig knuckle marinated in beer, served with a heavy, dark bread and vegetables soaked for much too long in vinegar.

"I think it's on Mimi's list of places to see."

"Near the entrance to Golden Lane," says Oz, and he closes his eyes for a moment as though he is trying to look at something inside his head, "there is a statue of a naked boy. Tourists rub his penis, and now it is golden."

"And that's why it's called Golden Lane?"

"No," says Oz. "Of course not. Golden Lane was the street where goldsmiths used to live. The boy has a golden penis because the tourists will not leave him alone."

I try to imagine people taking time out of their vacation to rub a statue's penis.

"The saints on the bridge and the men peeing in the pond are symbolic," says Oz. "But with the boy, the rubbing is for fun."

I wonder if more women than men rub the boy's penis.

"Blackbird Mavrias." The little man wags a finger at me. "You are famous. I find you on the Internet. Yesterday, I read many of your stories. My favourite is 'Words on Rock.'"

"Writing-on-Stone," I say. "It's a provincial park in Alberta."

"We have such camps in the Czech Republic. Weekends and the summer."

I turn the handle of my coffee cup to the right.

"But in our Indian camps," says Oz, "there are no Indians."

And then I turn it to the left.

"Littlechild." Oz bows his head. "A sad story. Story after story you write. Then, there is nothing. Why is this? Will there be a book?"

"So, you design games?"

Oz cuts a piece of pineapple into triangles. "Justice. Always you write about the need for justice."

I've never been much for games. In a past life, I made the mistake of getting a PlayStation. Tally and Nathan had loved insanities such as Uncharted and Gran Turismo. For me, being lost in a computer-generated jungle and shooting at anything that moved, or sitting in front of a monitor for hours, crashing cars into one another, had been a mind-numbing, soul-sucking experience I never want to repeat.

"Did you stop writing because you could not find justice in words?"

Not that board games were any better. Roll the dice. Spin the wheel. Leave everything to chance. No skill required.

"When you look at the world, what do you see?" Oz closes his eyes. "A peaceable kingdom? A calamity of the absurd?"

I ignore Oz and his mutterings and concentrate on my fruit bowl. The strawberries look fresh. The pear is from a can.

"Corporations, governments, profit, and war. The planet as commodity."

"Video game? Board game?" I poke at the blueberries. "Does it have a name?"

"My friend's game," says Oz. "He may call it 'Bees and Bears.'"

I stop poking. "Bees?"

"Bees and Bears." Oz begins chuckling. "A long time ago, the Bees made the mistake of sharing their honey with the Bears. The Bears were delighted, and having discovered the pleasure of sweetness on the tongue, they began roaming the land, searching for Bee trees. And each time they found one, they would destroy it in order to get the honey. You can see the problem? Yes?"

"Bears as weapons of mass destruction."

"This was, as you might imagine, a disaster for the Bees. And they quickly came together to discuss what could be done about the unacceptable behaviour of Bears. Of course, the answer is easy enough."

"And this is the game? Bees and Bears?"

"But look at the time." Oz stands suddenly and holds out both wrists. "I will be late."

"So what's the answer?"

"Golden Lane," Oz calls out as he hurries past the buffet. "It is not to be missed."

Mimi arrives in the breakfast room just as breakfast is being cleared away. She sees the danger immediately, grabs two plates, and plows her way through the staff and the food as though she is clearing snow off a sidewalk.

"You didn't wake me." Her hair is wet, and the label at the back of her shirt is sticking straight up in the air.

"Not my job."

"I could have missed breakfast."

"Then get up earlier."

"I need nine hours," says Mimi. "You know I'm no good without nine hours."

I seldom sleep more than four hours a night. Some nights I don't sleep at all.

Mimi blames Eugene and the Other Demons, but I've never been able to sleep for more than six.

"You know what happens when you don't get enough sleep."

"You get more work done."

"A lack of sleep leads to problems with the immune system and early onset dementia."

"I thought you told me that as you get older, you need less sleep."

"The Institute to Confound and Demoralize," Mimi tells me, "has decided that that is no longer true."

The Institute to Confound and Demoralize is something that Mimi has made up to deal with the contradictions that seem to arise with alarming frequency.

Coffee is bad for you. Coffee is good for you.

Red wine helps blood health. Red wine reduces your ability to fight infection.

Exercise is essential for general fitness. Exercise contributes to inflammation of the joints.

Kale, the silent killer.

Mimi is the only person I know who can eat and talk at the same time. "So," she says, "what shall we do today?"

"Fly home?"

"The castle," says Mimi. "We could see the castle."

"We've seen more castles than anyone should have to see," I say. "The Loire Valley?"

"Those were mostly châteaux."

"Mont Saint-Michel? Neuschwanstein? Alcazar? Versailles?"

"Versailles is a palace."

"Sleeping Beauty Castle?"

"Disneyland Park? In Paris?" Mimi shakes her head. "I hope you're being ironic."

"We don't have to travel to see castles," I remind Mimi. "We have Hatley Castle in Victoria and Casa Loma in Toronto."

"Prague Castle is older," says Mimi, "and it's one of the top ten things to do when you're in Prague."

"So?"

"So we're in Prague," says Mimi. "It's going to be sunny. You should wear a hat."

A FEW YEARS BACK, we had gone to the south of France. Uncle Leroy had sent the family a postcard from Nice, and Mimi thought we might find the Crow bundle in the Picasso Museum in Antibes, which was just up the road.

I didn't have much hope. "The big Picasso Museum is in Barcelona," I reminded Mimi, "and we looked there already."

"Picasso was influenced by African art," Mimi had countered. "Good bet he would be interested in something like the Crow bundle."

"Picasso was in Antibes for less than a year."

"More than enough time to talk Uncle Leroy out of the bundle."

Of course, there was no way that this could have happened. Leroy would have been in Nice around 1904. Picasso didn't get to Antibes until 1946. By the time the artist took up residence on the second floor of Château Grimaldi, the Indian would most likely have been dead.

But we caught the train from Nice to Antibes and spent an afternoon at the museum. Mimi liked *La Joie de Vivre*. I liked *The Goat*. We both enjoyed the view of the Mediterranean from the sculpture garden.

Afterwards, we wandered the town.

"Nikos Kazantzakis's house is around here someplace," Mimi told me. "Maybe we can go in, and you can channel your Greek side."

"Kazantzakis?"

"According to the guide, Kazantzakis wrote *Zorba the Greek* while he was living here."

"In Antibes?"

"And there's a square named after him just off the Rue du Bas Castelet."

We wandered around some more, until Mimi found the house.

"Do you feel any Greek literary zeal swelling up inside you?"

There were no signs to indicate that we could tour the place, and I was just as happy to stand outside. Mimi walked up the path to the front door and looked in a couple of windows.

"'I hope for nothing. I fear nothing. I am free.'" Mimi took my hand, and we strolled back to the port. "That's the epitaph on Kazantzakis's grave in Heraklion. What do you want on yours?"

"'Dead,'" I told Mimi.

"Bird, that doesn't sound like an epitaph. That sounds like a complaint."

Port Vauban in Antibes is the home of the Yacht Club d'Antibes. It's the largest marina for luxury boats and yachts in the Mediterranean. Mimi and I took our time walking around the outer ring of the harbour.

I had Mimi stand by the seawall so I could take a photograph.

"Any one of these yachts," she said, "could feed a small country."

At the top of the harbour was a sculpture by the Catalan artist Jaume Plensa. A seated figure with his knees drawn up against his chest, made up of white letters knitted together into a transparent skin.

From a distance, it looked for the world like a mound of bleached coral.

"It's called *Nomade*," Mimi told me. "Plensa is supposed to be suggesting the constructive potential of an alphabet. As a writer, you should understand that."

The sculpture was hollow. You could stand inside or climb up on the letters.

"What do you think?" Mimi asked me. "Does the world seem different when you look at it through language?"

Even from halfway up the structure, the sky over the sea didn't look any less blue. The town in the distance didn't look any less touristy. The flotilla of sailboats, cabin cruisers, and mega-yachts stacked up in the harbour didn't look any less ostentatious.

"You see that?"

There was an enormous yacht parked in the harbour with a coal-black hull and a bright white superstructure. On the side of the hull at the water line, someone had spray-painted, "Know Me for What I Am" in sloppy red letters.

"Someone was determined."

I thought about it for a moment. "You'd have to have a boat to do that."

"Yacht graffiti." Mimi wiped an imaginary tear from her eye. "Another heartbreaking First World problem."

The ship sat high in the water, so you couldn't see if there was anyone on deck. All the windows were blacked out, so you couldn't tell if there was anyone home. I suspected that the ship had a helicopter pad, possibly two, and a complement of swimming pools, but you would have had to have been in the hills above Antibes, looking down on the marina, to be sure.

So we're in Prague. We debate whether to walk up to the castle or take the tram.

I vote for the tram.

"Exercise wouldn't hurt us," says Mimi.

"It's too hot," I counter. "You were right about the hat."

The hill is steeper than I thought, and I'm glad we're taking the tram. It reminds me a bit of the cable cars in San Francisco.

When we get to the castle, I point to a sign at the entrance. "Three hundred and fifty to get in?"

Mimi snorts. "Bird, that's 350 Czech crowns. It's about twenty dollars Canadian. And that's for Circuit A. There's also Circuit B and Circuit C, which are cheaper."

"So, we get the cheap tickets?"

"If we get the cheap tickets, we could miss something."

"Such as another church."

"That's the spirit." Mimi tucks the guidebook into her pack and heads to the ticket booth. "Let's get going before the tourists show up."

St. Vitus Cathedral is just inside the main entrance. There is an Asian couple on the front steps, getting their picture taken.

"What do you think," says Mimi. "A wedding?"

The woman is wearing a white ball gown. She holds the sides of the skirt out like a fan and turns one way and then the other as the photographer follows her with a camera. The groom stands behind her as still as a statue, his tuxedo jacket open, his thumbs tucked into black suspenders.

"Remember Santorini?" says Mimi. "The little blue domed church in Oia with the couples lined up to have their photographs taken?"

Suddenly, the man begins dancing around his bride, stopping every few steps and freezing in an action position that doesn't seem to have anything to do with a wedding. The woman continues swaying from side to side, her dress floating around her like a soft breeze.

The man stops and strikes a pose, his arms crossed, one foot in front of the other, his chin up, his eyes fixed on the sky. The woman slides in behind him and drapes herself over his shoulders.

As though she were an accessory.

Mimi leans into me. "You want me to dress up in a wedding gown and wrap myself around you?"

According to the guidebook, Prague Castle is the largest castle in the world.

"Where do you want to start? There's the Old Royal Palace, St. Vitus Cathedral, St. George's Basilica, along with the Picture Gallery and the Powder Tower." Mimi looks at the flyer she got when she bought the tickets. "But the tower is closed right now."

"Too bad."

"And there's Golden Lane."

"That's where Oz said we should go."

"Oz?"

"He's the guy I talk to at breakfast," I tell Mimi. "When you're still asleep."

Mimi looks at me sideways. "This Oz," she says, "he happen to be a friend of Eugene?"

"Oz is real." I don't try to keep the annoyance out of my voice. "Eugene and the Other Demons are something you made up."

"They're real enough," says Mimi. "I just gave them names."

"If you would get up in the morning, I'd introduce the two of you."

"This is what happens when you don't get enough sleep," says Mimi. "You get cranky."

The good news is that the castle is not all that crowded. The bad news is that it's boring.

"This is Vladislav Hall," Mimi tells me, as we stand on a vast stone floor with a web of arches overhead. "They used to bring horses in here for many of the celebrations."

"Horses? How?"

"There's a special ramp called the Knights' Stairway."

"What did they do with the you-know-what?"

"The hall is sixty metres long by sixteen metres wide." Mimi stretches out her arms to show me the scale. "The arches are twelve metres off the floor."

Wandering through old buildings is not my idea of a vacation. Sure, there's history here, but most of it revolves around state-sponsored mayhem and gratuitous violence. Assassinations, expulsion of ethnic groups, court intrigue, occupation by Nazis, Russians, and the International Monetary Fund.

Blood and money.

All reduced to postcards, flags, garnets, Mucha posters, and beer cosmetics.

[illegible] the same thing about Toronto," says Mimi. "Or New [illegible] out trying to find something positive about the place."

[illegible] ns."

[illegible] takes my hand. "You're not going to make a fuss about that [illegible] are you?"

"I just don't see why they can't provide tourists with restrooms."

All of the major tourist destinations in Europe have washrooms. But you have to pay to use them. And for as much as we've travelled, I've never gotten used to coin-operated toilets or bathrooms with sentinels at the entrance who take your money and dole out slivers of thin toilet paper, as though each piece were a sheet of hammered gold.

"Charging to use a bathroom is just wrong." I can feel myself warming to the task. "Remember the restaurants in Italy where they brought us bread at every meal? The bread was terrible, but they charged us for it anyway, even when we said we didn't want it."

Mimi puts her arms over her head and stretches from side to side. "Maybe that's why we travel."

"So we can pay for bread we don't want and rent time in a toilet?"

"To complain." Mimi stops stretching. "Maybe we travel so that we can complain."

Frankly, I don't need to travel in order to complain. I can find plenty of things to criticize without stepping out of the house. Big box stores such as Walmart that treat their employees like indentured servants. The religious right that can always find someone to hate. Politicians who acknowledge global warming but take no actions that would affect corporate profits. The gun lobby that believes thoughts and prayers are the proper response to the killing of schoolchildren.

I can even complain about where I live.

Guelph, Ontario, is a lovely place. University town. Couple of rivers, the Speed and the Eramosa, running through it. Eric the Baker. Artisanale. The Bookshelf. Wyndham Art. In the summer, when they lower the floodgates, you can canoe the Speed up past the Boathouse, all the way to Victoria Road, before you begin to run out of clearance.

But my idea of paradise is the Northwest Coast. Somewhere like Tofino. Open ocean. Fog. Rain. Where it's never too hot, never too cold. Goldilocks country. And grey. Where the dominant colour is grey.

When Mimi and I were both working, our jobs controlled our landscape. Now that we're retired, we could live wherever we wish.

"Bird, all your friends are in Guelph."

"I don't have any friends."

"What would your friends think, if they heard you say that?"

"I bet my health would improve if we lived on the coast."

"Didn't we decide that the geographical solution never works?"

"Why don't we try? You like the coast."

"For a vacation, sure. But I like sunshine."

"Sunshine is overrated," I tell Mimi every time we have this discussion. "If you die before me, I'll move to the coast."

"We could compromise and move to Alberta. Mom would like me to come home. And we could ride horses. Remember how much fun that was."

I tried to imagine myself on the prairies.

"Sure," I would say every time the discussion got to this point. "Hot summers. High winds. Rampant racism. Religious intolerance. Right-wing politics."

"I need sun, Bird. I don't like being cold."

I don't know for sure if living on the coast would improve my outlook on life, but I'm convinced that it's worth a try.

"If we moved to the coast, I'd leave Eugene and the Other Demons in Ontario."

Mimi is skeptical about this. "That a promise?"

"Absolutely," I tell her. "I'd be happy on the coast. Happy, happy, happy."

So we're in Prague, walking around the grounds of an old castle, looking at old buildings, when Mimi stops me.

"Bird, did you know you're sweating?"

"It's hot."

"It's not that hot," says Mimi. "Are you okay?"

I always like it when Mimi is concerned about me.

"Is it your blood sugars?"

Eugene is standing in the doorway of St. George's Convent. He has his camera out. *Smile*, he shouts. *For the obituary.*

"I'm fine," I tell Mimi. "Nothing a house on the coast wouldn't cure."

"Jesus, Bird," says Mimi. "I did tell you to wear a hat."

Golden Lane is at the far end of the castle complex. The statue of the naked boy that Oz had told me about is in a small square just before the entrance to the lane. There are a number of tourists standing around the statue, taking pictures.

Mimi squints into the sun. Then she walks over to the crowd. Then she walks back.

"The tourists," she says, "you want to guess what they're doing?"

I don't know what I had expected, but Golden Lane isn't it. The lane is a long, narrow street of brightly painted cottages all stuck together, the kind of long, narrow street you can see in almost every city in Europe. Not to mention North America. Petit Champlain in Quebec City, Maiden Lane in San Francisco, Government Street in Victoria, Acorn Street in Boston.

We stroll along with the rest of the tourists while Mimi gives me all the details.

"The houses were originally built to quarter the castle guards."

"Why are there only houses on this side of the street?"

"The other side was torn down in the nineteenth century."

"Why?"

"No idea," says Mimi. "Ottla Kafka had a house at number 22. Her brother, Franz, stayed with her and wrote some of his short stories there."

I can see that the place has history, but whatever Golden Lane used to be, it is now a tourist trap.

"A famous fortune teller once lived at number 14. Madame de Thebes. She predicted the fall of the Third Reich." Mimi shakes her head. "She was arrested and tortured by the Nazis."

The Kafka house is now a souvenir shop.

"Number 12 was the home of film historian Josef Kazda. You can see a recreation of his workspace."

"Can't wait."

At the far end of the street is a museum of sorts. Weaponry for the most part. Swords, spears, axes, pikes, along with shields and suits of armour. Everything you would need to kill people. We make our way up a narrow staircase that only has room for one person at a time.

"Look, Bird." Mimi points to a sign. "You can shoot an authentic crossbow."

"Pass."

"I'll be the damsel in distress," says Mimi, "and you can save me from the dragon."

"Pass."

"I'll take your picture." Mimi tries to keep the smile off her face. "Indian with crossbow."

So I shoot the crossbow. I get three shots. I hit the target twice.

"Tell me that wasn't fun."

"The bows weren't full strength," I tell Mimi. "The arrow barely stuck in the target."

Mimi nods. "They probably don't want a bolt to ricochet and hit a tourist."

The weapons museum seems to go on forever, and it doesn't take long for the second wave of boredom to set in. And then Mimi finds the torture room.

"Is that what I think it is?"

In addition to a rack designed to stretch people and tear them apart, an iron cage with spikes, and an assortment of wood stocks, pliers, manacles, and chains, there is a wooden chair covered in nails. There are nails on the seat, on the back, on the armrests, and on the neck support.

Along with thick leather straps that can be cinched down to hold every part of you in place.

Mimi is impressed. "What kind of sick mind would think up something like this?"

I suggest the Department of Indian Affairs.

"The chairs at residential schools weren't nail chairs," Mimi reminds me. "They were electric."

You might imagine that you can still hear the cries of the people who were tortured with the devices in the Golden Lane museum or that you can taste the blood and smell the bodily fluids that would have soaked the floor.

But you can't.

"And during the reconciliation hearings," Mimi says, her voice hard as flint, "school officials were adamant that the chairs were never used at full power."

« »

So we're in Prague. At the castle. We've just toured Golden Lane, and now we're both cranky.

"I have to find a bathroom."

"Are you going to make a fuss?" Mimi crosses her arms and looks at me sternly. "How much did the airline tickets cost us to come to Prague?"

"Is this one of your irrelevant analogies that tries to compare the high cost of international air travel with the trivial cost of European bathrooms?"

"Yes."

"The plane had free bathrooms."

"People make their living looking after the bathrooms. It's probably a traditional activity."

"And they never give you enough toilet paper."

Mimi shrugs. "We can always buy a roll and carry it around with us."

There are no washrooms in Golden Lane, but we find one near the Supreme Burgrave's house.

"Any idea what a supreme burgrave is?"

Mimi consults the guidebook. "Evidently, he looked after things when the king was away."

"Like the bathrooms."

"Bird, it's only ten Czech crowns. About fifty cents Canadian. I think we can afford that."

The bathroom is not very large, and it's on the filthy side. There's toilet paper, but it's thin. I arrange strips of it on the seat.

Are you crazy? says Kitty. *You're going to sit down on that?*

I try not to move or rock back and forth.

Home, sweet home, says Eugene.

Chip and the twins are waiting for me when I come out of the stall. Chip is not happy.

What a rip-off, he says as I wash my hands. *You call that stuff toilet paper? They saw you coming.*

I ignore him.

Kitty tries to look sympathetic. *Now your fingers are going to stink for the rest of the day.*

I CAN UNDERSTAND MIMI'S reluctance to move to the coast. No sunshine. No friends. Having to start over again without the ignorance and enthusiasm of youth. Moves, in the abstract, might look to be wonderful adventures, but they're really more akin to a life-threatening disease or the death of a spouse. Most people recover. But it takes at least two years to get back on your feet.

Some of us have that kind of time. Some of us don't.

"I can write anywhere," I tell her. "You can paint anywhere."

Whenever I bring up the possibility of moving to the coast, Mimi reminds me that when we built our house in Guelph, we were making a commitment to stay there until we died.

I don't remember agreeing to this, and Mimi has nothing in writing.

The most telling argument that Mimi employs against such a move is, what happens if we move, and then I die? I have nothing to counter this, because she's right. With my health situation, I could die. And then she would be stuck where she did not want to be, in a house that was not as nice as the one we had before we went chasing after my dream.

You try to move to the coast, says Kitty, *and she's going to leave you.*

Which is just what you deserve, says Eugene.

I don't like packing, says Didi.

We're packing? says Desi.

Just go, says Chip. *You don't need her.*

Moving from one place to another would be easier if you could just go to your new location, pick out an apartment or a house, hit an app on your cellphone, and presto, the next day all your belongings were somehow transported and arranged without your ever having to unpack a box or go searching for the toaster.

In that perfect world, your bank accounts would all have been transferred, your new health card and driver's licence waiting for you on the kitchen table. Along with the name of a good doctor and a dentist. All the utilities hooked up, cable television and Netflix ready and waiting.

Your mail properly forwarded.

But what if you don't like the new location as much as you thought you would? What if the one neighbour restores motorcycles and the other is a musician? What if there are no good coffee shops or bookstores in the area? What if after all the anguish and trouble of a move, you discover that you have made a mistake?

To her credit, Mimi always tries to find the compromise.

"How about we go to the coast every other year or so and rent a place. You could walk the beach, get all cold and clammy, commune with the fog. I could manage without sun for a few weeks."

"Every year or so?"

"Okay, every year."

"A few weeks?"

"We don't need to be prescriptive."

I appreciate that Mimi tries to come up with a compromise, but visiting the coast isn't the same as living there. Sure, it can be cool and damp and grey. And, yes, some people might find it depressing. But there is also a cumulative effect that comes about over time, a calming, a slowing, a feeling of being in a soft bed with a warm lover, of being hidden away, safe from the glare and the clank of modern life.

Mimi is waiting for me when I come out of the bathroom. She gestures to the line that has formed at the entrance to Golden Lane.

"Good thing we got here when we did."

"Sure," I say. "We might have missed the nail chair."

The castle grounds have filled up. I retreat to the shadows of St. George's Basilica and watch the tourists flow past us like a river in flood. Mimi stays in the sun.

"Of the places we've been," she says, "which one did you like best?"

"They all run together." I lean against the stone of the church. It's surprisingly cool. "They're sort of like malls."

"Amsterdam and Venice had lovely canals," says Mimi.

"So does Ottawa."

"Barcelona and Cologne had great churches."

"Saint Joseph's Oratory of Mount Royal in Montreal is pretty impressive."

"How about the Eiffel Tower. Or the Acropolis. They were certainly memorable."

"As are the Rocky Mountains."

An athletic woman with a tour group in her wake steams past us. She holds a green umbrella high in the air, a rallying point for her small flotilla.

"You want to follow that group around?" I ask. "Maybe it's in English."

"No," says Mimi. "I think I'd like to go back to the hotel."

"You okay?"

"A little tired," she says. "I wouldn't mind a nap."

I glance at my watch. It's only three. Way too soon for Mimi to be giving up on the day.

"What's wrong?"

"You wear me out, Bird," says Mimi. "I love you, but sometimes you wear me out."

We have to push against the crowds in order to get to the exit. I'm hoping that we'll take the tram down the hill, but Mimi wants to walk. All the way back to the hotel, Mimi is silent, and I'm left with the certain knowledge that I've done something wrong.

Again.

When we get to our hotel, nothing has changed. The air conditioner is still going, our room is still hot, and the spiders are still on the ceiling. Mimi lies on the bed and pulls the blanket over her body. I sit in the chair by the window and wait.

Outside, in the shade of the Charles Bridge, a solitary musician begins playing "Yesterday" on an unhappy sax.

I don't remember falling asleep, but when I wake up, my neck is stiff. My mouth is dry, my head hurts, my eye feels even more swollen than before.

And Mimi is gone.

At first, I think she's in the bathroom. I shift into a more comfortable position and wait. Then I think maybe she went downstairs to see if anything could be done about the spiders.

So I stay in the chair and wait some more.

No Mimi.

I don't wait too long. I get up and walk down to the front desk.

No Mimi.

I step outside. The musician is still standing in the shade of the bridge. Now he's playing "If Ever I Would Leave You."

Chip slaps a hand on my shoulder. *Don't these assholes know anything but old show tunes?*

I wander through the food and craft stalls in Kampa Park, and then I walk back to the hotel and check the room. Just in case.

Still no Mimi.

I'm not worried. She has probably gone to find a market. We

don't have a refrigerator in our room, but there are lots of things that could sit out, provisions for a late-night snack. Bananas and grapes, crackers and cheese.

Or perhaps she wanted to see a particular church. A heritage site recommended in the guidebook. "I thought I'd let you sleep," she'll tell me. "You don't like churches anyway."

And there's the bridge itself. She could be on the bridge. A stolen moment standing against the stone wall, watching the boats as they pass beneath her.

I decide to start there. I take Didi and Desi by the hand, and we walk the length of the bridge. The tourists are still in numbers, and there's the chance that we might have missed her on the first pass, so we do it again.

As we search for Mimi, I'm reminded of those comic situations in movies where the heroine goes missing, and the hero hurries off to find her. In the meantime, the heroine returns, finds the hero missing, and goes out to find him. Back and forth they go, each time missing each other by the smallest of margins.

With musical cues, so you know when to laugh.

If we were home, there would be all sorts of possibilities. She could have gone to the library. She could have had a doctor's appointment that she had forgotten to mention. She could have met friends for coffee.

But when you travel, when you're on the road, these possibilities vanish. No library, no doctor, no friends. No routines to fill your day. There's just the two of you, alone in a strange city.

I stand at the window. Every so often, I see someone who could be Mimi, but isn't. Where would she go without me? Why would she leave without telling me? It's been a couple of hours now. How long do I wait before I do something? And then the question will be, do what? Go to the police? Check the hospitals? Not so easy to do in a country where you don't speak the language. It's true that English is understood, to some degree, throughout the world, but finding a missing person is more complicated than ordering a coffee, asking directions, or buying a souvenir.

Eugene and the Other Demons sit quietly on the bed. They know when to keep their mouths shut.

MIMI AND I MET in San Francisco. She had come to town for an art exhibition. I had just started working for the *Examiner* and had been sent to cover the show, to write a piece for the Sunday edition.

I had been able to make a hit-and-run meal out of a table awash with vegetable spears, squares of cheese, and crackers, and was standing in front of a canvas that was painted black when Mimi found me.

"You look lost."

"Baffled."

"You an artist?" she had asked.

"Journalist."

"So, you're thinking, why would anyone paint a canvas black?"

On the far wall were three paintings that had succeeded in capturing the surface of water. "I like those a lot better."

"Those are mine."

At first, I thought she was kidding. "Mimi Bull Shield," she said.

"Bull Shield?"

"Blackfoot. You know anything about art?"

"Nope."

"But they sent you to do the story."

"Rookie assignment."

"What do you normally write about?"

"There is no 'normal' yet," I told her. "I take what the editor gives me."

"What would you *like* to write about?"

No one at the paper had ever bothered to ask me that. "Not sure," I said.

"Okay," she said. "Then you can begin with me."

MIMI ARRIVES BACK at the hotel a little after five.

"I lost track of time," she shouts and dashes into the bathroom. "God, but I have to pee."

I sit in the chair and practise looking unconcerned and nonchalant.

"Thirty-eight seconds," she calls out. "Almost a new record."

I cross one leg over the other, and I lean a little to the right so my head touches the edge of the wingback.

"Why didn't you join me?"

I hadn't been expecting a question, and if I had been expecting a question, this wouldn't have been it.

Mimi frowns. "You're upset."

"No, I'm not."

"You are upset." Mimi continues to frown. "Didn't you see my note?"

Another question I wasn't expecting.

"You were sleeping in the chair, and I didn't want to disturb you, so I left a note."

"A note?"

"On your lap." Mimi shakes her head. "You thought I had left you?"

"Never crossed my mind."

"Really? In Prague?"

I slide my hand between the arm of the chair and the cushion. I try to do this so Mimi doesn't see me do it. But she does.

"Is it there?"

The note is on a small slip of paper, the perfect size to get lost.

"And what does it say?"

I hold the note out as though I'm examining a clue in a television mystery. "Went to Vltava beach to see swans. Join me."

Mimi gestures at the end table next to the chair. "I even left the guidebook so you wouldn't get lost."

I hold the note a little higher.

"And you jumped to conclusions, didn't you."

Eugene and the Other Demons look at each other and shrug.

"I was worried about you," I say.

Chip winks and gives me a thumbs-up.

"And I'm just fine." Mimi takes the note, crumples it up, and drops it in the wastebasket. "So, where do you want to eat?"

MIMI LED ME AROUND the gallery, introduced me to the other artists. I took photographs, got several quotations about the importance of art in a materialistic world, and listened to a short talk on the *giclée* as a way to increase sales and exposure.

After the show, Mimi and I went out for coffee.

"Cherokee." She had looked me up and down. "Mother? Father?"

"Father."

"Georgia? North Carolina?"

"Oklahoma."

"You ever been to Oklahoma?"

"Once."

"Sounds like there's a story there."

"More like a footnote."

"And Greece?"

"My mother," I told her. "Her father came from there. He always planned to return, but he never did."

"What about you?"

"Go to Greece?"

"Yes."

"Maybe. One of these days."

Mimi was in town for the week. We had lunch together. Then we had dinner. Then we had lunch and dinner. Somewhere in the middle, we began talking, and once we started, we didn't stop.

WE LEAVE THE HOTEL and head out across the Charles Bridge. Mimi takes my arm and lets her body sway back and forth as we walk. "Would you like to *flaner*?"

"What?"

"It means to stroll or wander. If we walk slowly, as though we don't give a damn, people may think that we're French."

Mimi runs her hand along the stone wall. "I met a woman at the beach. From Scotland. She just got in from Budapest."

I'm still a little annoyed with Mimi for running off and leaving me. After all, it wasn't my fault that the note got lost.

"It's only six hours from here by train."

I would have liked to have seen the beach, to have seen the swans, to have that experience in common with her, so that when she told the story, I could add some little detail to make the moment come alive.

"What do you think?"

"About?"

Up ahead, a large, blond woman in a blue cape is having her caricature done by a street artist. The woman sits on a stool with one hip cocked up and a shoulder thrown back, as though she is posing for a movie poster from the '40s.

"Budapest. Just for the day," says Mimi. "We could catch an early-morning train and then come back later that night."

"You want to go to Budapest?"

The artist has accentuated the woman's eyes and lips and chin, so it looks as though her face is going to explode. Her hip is the size of a truck tire.

"That Scottish woman I met? Carol? She said you can still see bullet holes in some of the buildings in Budapest from the 1956 invasion."

"You want to go to Budapest to see bullet holes in buildings?"

"And there are cast-iron shoes along the Danube, a memorial to the Budapest Jews who were killed and thrown into the river."

"Lovely."

"The victims were ordered to take off their shoes before they were shot."

"In Budapest."

Over Mimi's shoulder, I can see Kitty climb onto the stone wall and get ready to throw herself off.

"And, if we go to the university, there's a memorial that's not in the guidebooks."

Eugene just stands there and watches as Kitty leans out over the water. The twins are yelling at her, but I can't hear what they're saying. Chip has his cellphone out and is taking pictures.

"Carol says that between the bricks on one of the buildings, there is a narrow copper strip with the names of the professors and students who were sent to concentration camps."

"What happened to going to castles, churches, and museums?"

Mimi doesn't break stride. "There's Buda Castle, some famous hot baths, and the Parliament building, which Carol says is amazing at night, but we won't have time."

"We won't have time for anything."

"Budapest is close, Bird. It's so close."

I wait. Sometimes, when I wait, a problem goes away. Sometimes, it doesn't. "It's only for the day," says Mimi. "Think of it as research."

"Research for what?"

"Life," says Mimi. "Think of it as research for life."

MIMI DID NOT HAVE an easy childhood. When she was eight, her father was killed. Martin Bull Shield was on his way back from Waterton Lake when he had to stop to fix a flat tire.

"Hit and run," Mimi told me. "Guy drove off and left Dad to die."

Mimi's mother buried her husband and moved the family to Lethbridge.

"Why didn't you stay on the reserve?"

"I think Lethbridge was a way to get away from the blame and the pity."

"Why would anyone blame your mother for your father's death?"

"Bad luck," Mimi told me. "People tend to see bad luck as contagious."

"The guy who killed your father? Was he drunk?"

"Probably."

"They ever catch him?"

"Rob or Bob somebody. Real-estate developer in Calgary. Showed up in court with a couple of lawyers, his wife, two kids, and the pastor of his church. Man was real remorseful. Talked about his personal life and how his business had been doing poorly and how financial anxiety had left him depressed."

"So he got drunk, jumped in his car, and killed your father?"

"Cried when he got off."

"Hit and run, and he got off?"

"Judge didn't want to destroy the life of a good man."

The night Mimi told me about her father, we went walking on the

Golden Gate Bridge. The sky had been clear, but you couldn't see the stars because of the lights of the city.

"At Standoff, you can see the stars."

"Canada sounds nice."

"Maybe you'll come and visit."

"Maybe."

"How do you feel about sex?"

I had never had a woman ask me that question before.

"Did I shock you, Mr. Blackbird Mavrias?" Mimi leaned in and kissed me on the cheek. "What do you think we should do about it?"

We find a small café on the Old Town side of the bridge. We share an order of beef sliders. We each get one, and Mimi cuts the third one in two and eats both halves.

"So, we get up early tomorrow and go to the train station."

"What about breakfast?"

"We'll get something at the station or on the train."

"What if we can't get tickets?" I wipe my hands on the napkin. "Maybe everyone is going to Budapest to see bullet holes in walls and the train is booked."

I can see that Mimi's mind is made up, so there's little to be gained by trying to stand in her way.

"And seeing as it's Hungary," she says, "we're going to need another guidebook."

After our stroll on the Golden Gate, Mimi and I went back to her hotel room. She didn't wait for me to make the first move. She simply unbuttoned her blouse and took it off.

"What are you thinking?" she said.

"You mean like, now?"

Then she took off her bra.

Afterwards, as we lay in bed, I told Mimi about my father. He hadn't been killed by a drunk driver. I was three when he simply walked away from a wife and two kids, and never returned. For years, I was sure that it was my fault. Then I blamed my mother. By the time I got out of high school, I realized that I had never known him at all. That he was just a handful of old photographs.

"You never saw him again?" Mimi stuffed all the pillows under her side so she could watch my face. "He never came back?"

Mimi's mother had had five kids. My mother only had two.

"Don't know that numbers mean all that much," Mimi told me. "For a woman, critical mass is generally achieved with one."

Neither of our mothers had remarried, even though in those days, that was the thing to do. Protection, security, support, companionship. A man was supposed to provide all that. Maybe after the death of her husband, Bernice Bull Shield had figured out that the only shelter she would have in her life would be of her own making.

Maybe after my father left, my mother had come to the same conclusion.

It wasn't that men didn't try. Several were even persistent. One guy bought me a bike, an end run around my mother's defences.

"He bought you a bike?"

"He did."

"What kind?"

"Think it was a Schwinn."

"What'd he buy your brother?"

But she hadn't let any of the men any closer than the kitchen table and a cup of coffee. I don't know that I would have liked having a stepfather, and my mother never asked me. Maybe after trusting one man, she wasn't about to make that mistake twice.

Nor had she been willing to lose time over a situation she couldn't control. She took back her maiden name, fiddled with mine and my brother's, got a job with the Southern Pacific, and raised two boys.

"So, your father taught you that men can just walk away whenever they feel like it?"

"He didn't teach me anything."

"But the example is there."

I had always wondered what happened to my father, if he married again, had more children, or if remorse had overpowered him and he had lived the rest of his life with regret.

Probably not.

But I liked to think that his betrayal had scarred him in some way.

Mimi snuggled in against my chest. "I never had a bike."

"What did you have?"

"Horses. There were always horses."

The hotel bed was overly soft, and I had to prop myself up on one elbow. "You think I could have a pillow?"

"Why? You thinking about going to sleep?"

So we're in Prague.

It's almost midnight. We walk back to the hotel. The room is hotter than before, and even with all the windows open, I can see that it's never going to get cool. The air conditioner is still making encouraging noises, and the spiders are still moving about on the ceiling.

Mimi sheds her clothes and crawls into bed. "We have to get up early," she says. "The train leaves just before eight."

"This is a bad idea."

"You'd rather stay in Prague and go to the Museum of Chamber Pots and Toilets?"

I ease into the chair by the window and open my book.

"Could you turn off the light?"

"I can't read without light."

"It's too late to read." Mimi begins rolling herself up in the blankets. "You can read on the train."

I turn out the lights and move the chair closer to the window. There is some illumination that finds its way into the room from the light standards on the bridge, but not enough for reading. Sometimes, when I can't sleep, I'll close my eyes and try to imagine what I might do to make the world a better place.

And because I like easy answers, I generally blame greed and racism, arrogance and sexism. I blame individuals and corporations. I blame the social norms and political structures that allow such destructive ideas and behaviours to breed and flourish.

Line them all up against a wall.

Of course, this is not an answer.

Still, I figure it's better than doing nothing.

So that's where I start my evening, sitting quietly in the chair, indulging my rage. And in no time at all, I'm able to turn my anger back on myself.

What have I done to make the world a better place? I write stories. I take pictures. At least I did. Now, I don't even do that.

Nobody read your stuff anyway. Eugene leans against the radiator, his hands jammed in his pockets. *Bleeding-hearts crap*.

He almost got shot at Oka, Desi reminds Eugene.

Sure, says Eugene, *but they missed.*

And he did get death threats for his piece on the Kinder Morgan pipeline.

Death threats? says Kitty. *We're getting death threats?*

The twins sit together on the bed. *How about we talk about something happy?* says Didi.

How about you stop feeling sorry for yourself, Chip barks at me, *and start kicking some ass. That'll make you feel better.*

Sometimes when Eugene and the Other Demons gang up on me, I fight back. Blackbird Mavrias, I begin, First Nations photojournalist. Winner of a National Pictures of the Year award and an Aboriginal Achievement award.

That and a buck fifty will get you a cup of coffee at Timmy's, says Eugene.

What about the death threats? says Kitty.

As well as an award from the Canadian Association of Journalists for outstanding journalism.

You kick some ass, says Chip, *and they'll pay attention.*

Old news, says Eugene. *You're old news.*

I leave Eugene and the Other Demons to their own devices. Chip picks an argument with Eugene, and Kitty tries to scare the twins with her disaster tales. I go back to saving the world from the safety of a comfortable chair with the potent power of my imagination.

Mimi and I lay awake in that San Francisco hotel room the entire night. "So, what do you know about Canada?"

"*Rose Marie.*"

"Rose Marie?"

"It was a film," I told Mimi. "My mother took my brother and me to see it."

The film was awful, but I remember being impressed with the Canadian landscape. Especially the untamed rivers. I could imagine wolves haunting the banks, cougars stalking the treeline above the white water, grizzly bears crouching in the shadow of a cascade.

Mimi was amused. "That's it? A movie?"

We didn't have anything in Roseville to match the wild rivers in the film. We had Dry Creek, a brown, sluggish ditch of a watercourse that staggered along through valley oak and scrub, home to a scruffy gang of muskrats and a lazy flotilla of overweight carp.

In *Rose Marie*, Canada looked clean and fresh. I didn't see any of the actors sweat or slap at a single mosquito.

"Actually, it was a musical. Set in Canada. Mountains, forests, Mounties."

"Singing Mounties?"

"Mounties don't sing in Canada?"

Mimi began laughing. She was still laughing when the sun came up.

MIMI WAKES ME at six the next morning. I'm still in the chair and, once again, my neck is stiff, and the world is no better for all my efforts.

"Do you have your diabetic supplies?"

"Yes."

"Needles, insulin, test strips?"

"Yes."

"Money, camera, dark glasses, hat?"

I hold up the items in turn, so Mimi can check each one off her list.

"You're going to love Budapest."

"No, I won't."

"Remember when you didn't want to go to Athens," she says. "Remember how well that turned out?"

The train station is crowded; streams of commuters flow off in all directions. Mimi pauses on the bank for a moment and then plunges into the currents and steams straight ahead to the ticket window. I hang back, hoping that the train to Budapest is full or that the woman at the wicket doesn't speak any English.

After Old Town Square and the Charles Bridge, I had expected that the station would be housed in a crumbling relic, and there is an older part that is historic and ornate, but Praha hlavni nadrazi proper is modern and shiny with bright red pillars and blue accents. There are wide ramps that take you up and wide ramps that take you down. Quick and efficient, so long as you know where you're going.

Mimi appears out of the crowd, holding a fistful of brochures. "I got the tickets and a map," she says. "No guidebook, but these will tell us what we should see while we're in Budapest."

"We won't get there until mid-afternoon."

"That is correct."

"So, we're going to get off the train, look at bullet holes, and then get back on the train? That's not much time to see the place."

"Staying overnight isn't going to kill us."

"Overnight?"

"I found an interesting hotel in downtown Budapest." Mimi hands me one of the brochures. "Hotel Astoria. The Nazis used it as their headquarters in World War II, and the KGB took it over when Russia invaded Hungary."

"We can't stay overnight in Budapest."

"Stalinist chic and centrally located."

"We have a room here in Prague."

"And we'll still have the room when we come back."

We're really going to Budapest? Kitty wraps her arms around herself. *Do you remember what the Russians did to Imre Nagy?*

There's a large screen in the middle of the station that shows the trains and the platforms. Our train is not on the list.

"They don't give you the platform in advance?"

"It's announced about fifteen minutes before the train leaves."

Kitty is turning around in tight circles. *Why don't we just go to Chernobyl or Fukushima while we're at it?*

"We don't even know where the platforms are."

The train doesn't leave until just before eight, which gives us time to find something to eat. Mimi already has the Prague guidebook out and is going through the choices.

"There's Salanda and Burger King, but neither of them gets very good reviews." Mimi turns the page. "We could eat at Café Coffee Day, but it looks as though they only have coffee and muffins."

"Any restaurants nearby?"

"Restaurant Zvonice is just outside the station," says Mimi, "but they don't open until eleven thirty."

"Grocery store?"

Mimi turns more pages. "Billa. Let's try Billa."

THE LAST NIGHT that Mimi was in San Francisco, we grabbed dinner at Tad's Steak House on Powell.

"Steak, garlic bread, salad, and baked potato." I opened the door for Mimi the way gentlemen did in the movies. "Best meal deal in town."

"And cheap," said Mimi. "I like that in a man."

"How about tomorrow we go out to Cliff House?"

"Can't. Tomorrow I fly back to Toronto."

I had forgotten about that. "You live in Toronto?"

"Guelph."

"Guelph?"

Mimi handed me a business card. "I teach art at the university."

"Thought the Blackfoot were in Alberta. And Montana."

"My mother lives in Alberta. On the reserve at Standoff."

"But you're in Ge . . . Gel . . ."

"Guelph," said Mimi, with only the hint of annoyance in her voice. "Do you live with *your* mother?"

"So, if I want to see you again, I'd have to go to Guelph?"

After dinner we went to a street dance in Union Square. There was a trio playing, guitar, bass, sax. I wasn't much of a dancer, and neither was Mimi, so we just stood in one place and swayed back and forth, until the band stopped and everyone went home.

I HAVE THIS RECURRING expectation that when we go to fascinating places, we'll be surprised and amazed by what we find. It's a misconception, of course, and as we walk into Billa, I can see that the grocery store in the train station will not be an exception to the rule.

"We can get yogurt for breakfast," says Mimi as we wander the aisles, "and sandwiches for lunch."

"Just like back home."

"Bird, if the food was exotic and unusual, you wouldn't eat it."

"Slightly unusual would be okay."

"Look, they have ham and cheese."

Mimi gets a yogurt and two sandwiches along with a couple of bananas. I slide past the containers of lunch meat floating in jelly, displays of Kinder eggs, and the rack of candy bars in bright colours.

Mimi picks up a coconut and weighs it in her hand. "What do you think?"

"You want to buy a coconut for the trip to Budapest?"

How about we buy the coconut, says Kitty, *and stay in Prague.*

"You'd need a hammer to break it open."

Didi and I would like an ice cream, says Desi. *Ice cream always cheers us up.*

I don't see much protein here, says Chip.

"Or we could just hit it against something hard or drop it on the sidewalk," says Mimi.

Where it will splinter into a million pieces, says Kitty, *and put someone's eye out.*

We leave the coconut in the basket and pay for our purchases. Mimi walks back into the main terminal and stands in front of the digital display. Every so often, the train times shuffle and change. At 7:45, the platform still hasn't been announced.

"Maybe the train has been cancelled." I try to sound concerned rather than hopeful, but I'm not successful.

At 7:53, our train number pops up. Platform twelve. Boarding right now. All aboard.

"This way," says Mimi.

Eugene gives Kitty a push. The twins skip ahead. Chip brings up the rear. I have the backpack, and Mimi has the tickets and brochures.

And just like that, we're off on our Hungarian adventure.

VI

So we're in Prague.

And while we don't know the Prague train station at all, Mimi finds platform twelve on the first try.

Even Kitty is impressed.

We do make the mistake of getting on at the wrong end of the train and, as a result, have to squeeze our way past passengers and step over luggage stacked up in the aisles. And we're still walking from car to car when the train lurches out of the station, tossing me against a large man who is not all that friendly, especially when he discovers that I don't have the language and can't appreciate the full extent of his grievance.

But eventually, we do find our seats.

Mimi settles in next to the window. I take the aisle. When we travel in a country where we don't speak the language, it doesn't matter if the train is crowded or empty. We're on our own, and unless dumb luck intervenes and drops an English-speaking tourist in our laps, the only person we'll be talking to for the next six hours is each other.

"Are you hungry?"

"No."

"Sometimes when you're hungry, you get grumpy."

"I'm not grumpy."

"But you don't think going to Budapest is a good idea."

"It's an adventure."

"Here," says Mimi. "Eat a banana."

"I don't want a banana."

"Eat it anyway."

The train from Prague to Budapest is not as well appointed as the train in the 2017 remake of Agatha Christie's *Murder on the Orient Express*, with its ornate and opulent carriages all tucked up with brocade upholstery and heavy draperies, soft surfaces and shaded spaces.

A Victorian parlour on wheels.

Our train is iron and steel, cold and brutal, a Trans-Siberian prisoner transport on its way to a gulag.

"It's not that bad," Mimi says. "Beats driving the 401 at rush hour."

Twenty minutes into the trip, an older woman steps into our carriage and sits down. I smile. She smiles. I look out the window with a practised nonchalance and begin my Sherlockian deductions.

WE WENT TO GREECE after the financial collapse and before the big fires. Mimi spent a good month planning the trip.

"First we'll go to Crete," said Mimi.

"Crete?"

"Then we'll stop in Santorini. We can't go to Greece without seeing Crete and Santorini."

In Chania, we stayed in the Palazzo di Pietro on Agion Deka, a small hotel run by a daughter and her father. We toured Old Town, wandered the narrow streets, stopped at the shops and the open-air craft booths, ate at small restaurants recommended in the guidebook.

We walked the seawall that protected the harbour and got an Australian couple to take a picture of us in front of the Venetian lighthouse.

In Oia, we rented an apartment that turned out to be less than advertised. It was supposed to have a view of the caldera, and it did, if you leaned out over the edge of the roof. The rest of the panorama was blocked by a grocery store with a second-floor restaurant. From our bedroom, we could see tourists enjoying the view we had been promised.

I was cranky about that, but Mimi had been undeterred. "It's not a big deal," she said. "If we want to see the caldera, all we have to do is walk along the main street."

We toured Oia. We wandered the main street, stopped at the shops, ate at small restaurants recommended in the guidebook. We walked the three hundred steps down to Ammoudi, dodging tourists mounted on mules and stepping around piles of mule shit. We caught the bus to Fira and hiked the trail along the edge of the volcano.

"Athens won't be as touristy," Mimi promised. "We'll check on Uncle Leroy and the Wild West show, and then we'll go up to Kymi and look for your grandfather."

We weren't going to find my grandfather. He had died when I was three. I only knew him through the stories my mother told.

The time I tried to follow him up the ladder.

The day I put on my cowboy hat and robbed him at gunpoint.

The afternoon I sat with him in the garden and ate tomatoes right off the vine.

"Maybe you'll find a great aunt," said Mimi. "Or a cousin once removed."

"He left Kymi in the early 1900s. We're not going to find anyone who remembers him."

And even if we did find relatives, what was I going to do? They would be strangers. Family is not just about blood. We wouldn't have any stories to share. We wouldn't have any memories to polish. We would have a single individual in common, loose change in a pocket, and nothing more.

"Are you excited about going to Kymi?"

"It's a fool's errand."

"And we're just the fools to do it."

THE WOMAN SEATED ACROSS from us is wearing a light wool suit, windowpane plaid, the lapels too wide to be current, a faint smell of moth balls floating on the fabric, something she's had in the closet or a trunk for a while.

I wonder if Mimi notices these sorts of things.

I decide to call her Olga. She's middle-aged. Her skin is clear, her hair neat, her teeth straight. A fastidious person.

And then there are the contradictions. Her clothes would suggest a woman who does not have a great deal of money, while her presence in a first-class compartment would argue against such a conclusion. The fact that she's travelling to Budapest with no luggage leads me to believe she is a widow on a pension, a Hungarian returning home from visiting a daughter or a son in Prague, a grateful child who purchased a first-class ticket for their mother.

I want to share my findings with Mimi, but there is the remote chance that the woman can speak English and would not like her impoverished life aired in public.

Through the window, I can see the Czech countryside fly by. There's nothing to distinguish it from other places in the world. We could be travelling from Guelph to Toronto or through Central Valley, California.

Mimi leans against my shoulder.

"It's amazing," she whispers. "Last week we were in Guelph, and now here we are on a train to Budapest."

I don't notice the man until he is at the entrance to our compartment. A large man, blond hair, sweaty face, slacks, blue polo shirt, dark windbreaker. He's dragging two large suitcases behind him.

"Next time," he says to my Hungarian pensioner, "we fly."

As far as Uncle Leroy and the Crow bundle were concerned, Athens was a bust. There was no record of any Wild West show having passed through within Leroy's time frame and nothing to suggest that a Leroy Bull Shield had ever been to the city.

"We have the postcard," said Mimi, "so we know he was here."

We went to the Acropolis, strolled by Hadrian's Gate, checked out the Acropolis Museum and the National Archaeological Museum, and made our way through the anarchy of Athens traffic to a *komboloi* shop on Amerikis.

"You should buy a set."

"An Indian with Greek worry beads?"

"You're not just one thing, Mr. Mavrias," said Mimi. "'I am large, I contain multitudes.'"

I had never much cared for Whitman, but I was tempted by a particular string of ebony beads with bronze inlay.

"We can take them to the next powwow," said Mimi. "Blackbird Mavrias. Drumstick in one hand, *komboloi* in the other."

So I bought the beads, and the guy at the shop showed me how to swing them around my finger and catch them in my hand.

"Look at that," said Mimi. "You're a natural."

We stayed in Athens for two nights. The drive to Kymi was only about two and a half hours, but after watching the motorists and the pedestrians play chicken all along Andrea Syngrou, I arranged for a car service to take us there. I could have rented a vehicle, but driving unfamiliar roads and trying to read signs in Greek while listening to Kitty in the back seat making disaster noises would have been unsettling.

The next morning, our driver was waiting for us when we came out of the hotel. He was holding a handwritten sign that said "Mavrias."

"I'm Mavrias."

"Good morning, good morning."

"Car service to Kymi?"

"Kymi. Yes."

"How long is the trip?"

"Kymi. Yes."

When I booked the service, I had asked for an English-speaking driver. I just hadn't specified the degree of fluency.

"So, you speak English?"

"Kymi. Yes."

I would have preferred someone who could have pointed out any sights along the way, someone who did not spend most of the trip talking on his cellphone.

"It's his girlfriend," Mimi whispered to me as we drove north. "Or his wife."

"You don't speak Greek."

"Don't need to," said Mimi.

Looking at the map, I had thought that Kymi would be right on the Aegean. But it wasn't. It was in the hills above the port, a village of about two thousand, built into the slopes and angles of a rocky landscape.

"It would have been smaller when your grandfather was a boy," Mimi told me as we drove along the main street. "But I'll bet it hasn't changed all that much."

I had booked a room at the Archontiko Kymis, with a view of the village and the ocean.

"It's only four thirty, but I'm hungry."

The woman at the hotel spoke enough English to give us a recommendation, a place called the Kapitsalio, just down the street and around the corner.

"It's the restaurant we saw when we came into town. The one with the sign of a guy holding a beer and a fork," said Mimi. "Let's hope they have an English menu or something with pictures."

The Kapitsalio was in a yellow stucco building with a small covered patio at the front.

"You want to sit outside or in?"

"Outside," said Mimi. "We're in Greece."

I wasn't sure what "Greece" and "outside" had to do with each other, but the weather was pleasant, and we could sit and watch the cars go by.

The menu was all in Greek. My Greek wasn't completely nonexistent. I could ask to borrow the car, and I could sing "Christos Anesti" from the Greek Orthodox Easter service.

"*Signomi, milate agglika?*" I asked the woman who had brought the menus.

"*Okhi,*" said the woman with a shake of her head.

"So, we're going to have to guess?" said Mimi. "That could be exciting."

"*Perimene ena lepto, parakalo.*" The woman held up a hand, then turned and went back into the restaurant.

"What do you want to do?"

"I say we close our eyes and point to something on the menu," said Mimi. "Put our fate in the hands of the gods."

"There are no gods."

"If you made a noise like a chicken, we might get an egg dish."

I studied the menu hoping that I would see a word that looked vaguely familiar. I was going through the menu a second time when a motorcycle pulled up to the restaurant and a tall man with a beard jumped off.

"Hello, hello," he said with only the trace of an accent.

"Hello," said Mimi.

"I am Nikos," the man said, spreading his arms out as if to embrace the world. "I am your English menu."

Nikos, it turned out, owned the restaurant, and to Mimi's great delight, he sat down at the table and took us through our options. Mimi ordered spaghetti and chicken. I went with a pork dish in a creamy white sauce with fries.

"I worked in New York," Nikos told us. "My English is from there."

"Mimi Bull Shield," Mimi told Nikos. "Blackfoot from Alberta, Canada."

"Blackfoot?"

"And this is Blackbird Mavrias. He's Cherokee."

"Mavrias?"

"Yes."

"But this is a Greek name."

"Bird's grandfather was Greek," said Mimi. "Matter of fact, he was born and raised here in Kymi."

"No!"

"Yes."

"Your *pappou*?"

Pappou. Another word I knew. Grandfather.

"He is from Kymi?"

"Yes," I said. "I'm hoping to find some relatives."

"Yes, of course," said Nikos. "But Mavrias, this is not a name I know in Kymi."

"No?"

"But there are villages there, there, and there," said Nikos, indicating several directions at once. "Very close. It is possible that he is from one of those."

The food was excellent. The kind of homemade that was really homemade. I had a taste of Mimi's chicken. She ate most of my pork.

"Androniani," Nikos told us over coffee. "And there is Vitala, and Maletiani as well."

"My mother told me he was from Kymi."

"What you must do is to go to the town hall. They have all the records there. If he was born here, they will have his name in a book."

"You hear that, Bird," said Mimi. "Town hall has the records."

"You are fortunate that it is your *pappou*," said Nikos. "If it had been your grandmother, the records would be more difficult to find."

I wasn't about to ask why. I had already figured it out. I was sure that Mimi had too, but she asked the question anyway.

"Why?"

"Well," said Nikos, "until the 1930s, no one keeps track of the women."

"Unless they married." Mimi wasn't smiling, but to someone who didn't know, what was on her face might have *seemed* to be a smile. "And they had children."

"Exactly," said Nikos. "Of course, now such a thing would be . . ."

"Sexist?"

Nikos shrugged. "But back then . . ."

We sat around the Kapitsalio well into the evening, while Nikos alternated between his other customers and tales of his time in Manhattan.

"Busy. Noisy. Anything you want, you can get. Many things you don't want, you can also get."

Mimi had never been to New York. "Why did you go?"

"All Greeks wish to go to New York. Big Apple. New York Yankees. Statue of Liberty. Central Park. My uncle went to New York. So did two of my cousins."

The bill came to less than fifteen dollars.

"That's where Bird's grandfather landed." Mimi paid the bill and left a generous tip. "Ellis Island."

Nikos walked us up the street to the corner. The lights of the village were soft and warm. Overhead the stars filled the sky. I wondered how much had changed since my grandfather had been a boy.

"Town hall," Nikos called out as he headed back to the restaurant. "Tomorrow. Town hall."

THE WOMAN ON the train is Trudy. Her husband is Jim. The Blunds, from Orlando, Florida. Trudy taught elementary school. Jim was a sales representative for Nestlé. Both retired.

"Just sold our home," Trudy tells us, "and here we are."

"Goodbye, Orlando," says Jim.

"We had a very nice home," says Trudy. "Golf course. Community pool. Tennis courts."

"Twenty-four-hour security," says Jim, "for all the good that did us."

"Six months ago, we had a break-in." Trudy straightens her jacket. "Took both televisions, bunch of jewellery, a stereo, and Jim's laptop."

"Turned out to be one of the security guards," says Jim. "Wouldn't give you two cents for gated communities."

I'm willing to let the conversation die and sit quietly in silence the rest of the trip, but I can see that Mimi is intrigued with Trudy and Jim.

"So, you don't have a house to go home to?"

"Nope."

"Where are you going to live?"

"Well," says Trudy, "first we're going to take our river cruise, and then we'll decide."

"From Budapest to Amsterdam," says Jim.

"Friends of ours did it last year," says Trudy. "Said it was spectacular."

"Except for the problems with the water levels."

"They had to get off the boat in a couple of places and take a bus."

"Not much of a cruise, if you have to take a bus," says Jim.

"So, I researched all the cruises that go from Budapest to Amsterdam," says Trudy, "and found a company with shallow-draft boats that can manage low water."

"You think you'll go back to Florida?" says Mimi.

"I don't think so," says Trudy. "Florida is filling up."

"With all the wrong people," says Jim. "We've lost control of our neighbourhoods."

"Our daughter lives on the Oregon coast," says Trudy. "I wouldn't mind living on the ocean."

"Wouldn't give you two cents for the ocean."

"Our son lives in Colorado," says Trudy. "But it's hard to know where you'll be comfortable, until it's too late."

"We should look at Texas." Jim gives Trudy a squeeze. "Bet you can find some decent clothes in Dallas."

Trudy opens the jacket, so we can see the label. "I have a thing for vintage clothing."

Jim grunts. "Dresses like my grandmother."

Trudy smiles and pats Jim's knee. "He doesn't mean to hurt my feelings. He just does."

"Bull in a china shop." Jim hunkers down in the seat and splays his legs out as though he has all the room in the world. "That's me."

"But he's my bull," says Trudy. "So, you two are from Canada."

"We are," says Mimi.

"Metric system?" says Jim. "Two languages? Free health care?"

"That's right."

"Wouldn't give you two cents for socialized medicine."

I lean back and close my eyes. Mimi can deal with Trudy and Two-Cent Jim. I want to save my energy for Budapest. If I know Mimi, she's going to want to try to walk the entire city.

"So why are you two going to Budapest?" says Trudy.

"You know, Hungary's got a serious refugee problem," says Jim. "Serbs are pouring into the country."

"Syrians," says Trudy. "We saw it on the news."

It takes me a moment, and then I remember. The story of television. The men with the backpacks, the women with signs, the children with toys, the police in helmets with shields and guns.

It hadn't been a riot.

Jim takes his cellphone out of his jacket and holds it up. "I get all the travel advisories. There's one for Budapest."

"What did you do at Nestlé?" says Mimi.

"Bottled water division," says Jim. "I looked after most of the East Coast."

My hand is on Mimi's thigh in an instant, but I'm too late.

"In Canada," she says, "there's a debate around bottled water."

Jim rolls his eyes. "Let me guess," he says. "Bottled water should be banned. Plastic bottles are a blight on the environment. It takes seven hundred years for the plastic to break down. Eighty percent of the bottles are never recycled. Each year, over 38 million plastic bottles wind up in landfills." Jim pauses and squares his shoulders. "How am I doing?"

I squeeze Mimi's thigh a bit harder.

"You forgot about the amount of oil and fresh water it takes to make the bottles in the first place," she says. "Or that ninety percent of the cost of bottled water is in the bottle itself."

Jim holds up his hands. "I confess. I'm the devil incarnate."

"Bottled water is very popular," says Trudy. "If people want it, they're going to get it."

"Tried to ban alcohol back in the 1920s and look how that turned out." Jim pulls his legs back and gets to his feet. "Going to find the little boys' room. If you hurry, you can have a gallows built by the time I get back."

I keep my hand on Mimi's thigh. She doesn't say anything. And then she does.

"I'm sorry if I upset your husband."

Trudy sits up straight. "He's not a bad man. But he's not particularly flexible."

"Neither is Bird," says Mimi.

Two-Cent Jim doesn't return right away. Trudy and Mimi talk about vintage clothing for the next hour, and when Jim still hasn't returned, Trudy goes looking for him.

"They're not coming back," I tell Mimi, after Trudy leaves.

"Their luggage is still here."

"They'll pick the bags up when the train gets to Budapest."

"It's sad not having a home," says Mimi. "But it's probably for the best."

"Best?"

"It's obvious that they're not going to stay together," says Mimi. "Not having a house will make the divorce easier. You really should try to pay more attention."

The next morning, we set out to find the town hall. Kymi wasn't all that big, but the town hall proved to be more elusive than I would have supposed. The directions came in pieces. Up this street. Down that one. Behind the church. Above the bus station. Just past the statue.

But we weren't in any rush, and it gave me time to practise with my *komboloi*.

"This is the way you see a place," Mimi told me after we had circled one particular block for the third time.

We did finally find the town hall, a building we had walked past several times. It was Mimi who noticed the flag.

"Greek flag," she said, pointing to the building. "Town hall."

"You sure?"

"They're not going to fly a flag over a fish market."

Most guidebooks do not tout the town halls of the world as holiday highlights, and for good reason. The town hall in Kymi was no exception. It was an older structure, not exactly falling down, not exactly standing up. It was the sort of government building you could find almost anywhere on the planet, from Havana to Missoula, Lethbridge to Limerick, Quito to Chengdu. Dull white on the outside with a dim interior of soft light and shadow. Not a gloomy place and not murky. Well worn. Your grandmother's house with the windows sealed and the shades pulled.

"You're going to have to do all the talking," Mimi told me.

"Sure."

"Is your Greek good enough for that?"

"You bet."

"You want the phrase book?"

The first thing any traveller needs to learn when going to a foreign country is how to ask the question "Do you speak English?" in the resident language. In Greek, this all-important phrase is "*Signomi, milate agglika?*"

To which the answer is generally "*Okhi.*"

But if you ask the question enough times, you're bound to find someone who will say "*Nai.*"

And I did.

A man in his fifties who looked as though he had been born in the building and had never left.

I explained my situation as best I could.

"Your *pappou* is born here?"

"Yes."

"But he goes to America?"

"To join his older brother," I said.

"And does not return."

"Right," I said. "He went to California, met my grandmother, and had four children."

"But you come back to Greece," said the man.

"I'm the first in the family to return," I told him.

The official took this in for a moment, went to a computer, hit a couple of keys, looked at the screen. Then he went to the shelves and pulled down a large ledger.

It was one of those books you see in the movies. Something out of an episode of *Harry Potter*. Large, gilded, dusty. A book that had been around before the Egyptians began building pyramids.

"Mavrias?"

"Yes," I said. "That is correct."

He opened the book and began running a finger down columns of exquisitely handwritten entries. Then he turned a page. And another. And another.

"Here," he said, stopping his finger at a name. "Mavrias. Giannis."

"That was my great-grandfather's name."

"His wife is Eleni?"

"Yes. Giannis and Eleni Mavrias."

"And your grandfather?"

"Thomas."

"Yes," said the man. "He is here. And a brother, Georgios."

I hadn't expected to find any trace of my grandfather. And yet there he was. A name in a book that was older than me. My grandfather and his brother. My great-grandparents. Alive again.

"But," said the city official, "he is not born in Kymi. The family is from Maletiani."

"That's one of the villages Nikos mentioned," said Mimi. "This is great."

"Four kilometres is Maletiani," said the man.

"You hear that, Bird? Four kilometres." Mimi put her arms around me. "We can walk that."

I WAS RIGHT. The Blunds don't reappear until we pull into Keleti station.

"One of these days," says Trudy, "I'd like to visit Canada."

"Watch yourself in Budapest," says Jim as he begins dragging the bags down the aisle. "Desperate times. Desperate people."

Mimi doesn't get up right away. She waits in her seat as the other passengers file by us.

"I'm sorry we had so little time," she says.

"Time?"

"With Jim. I was really looking forward to talking to him about baby formula."

Television likes to turn simple misfortunes into major catastrophes, and as Mimi and I make our way along the platform, I'm expecting to find the station itself empty and quiet, the refugees having moved on.

Mimi is in high spirits. "What do you want to do first?"

"Do you really want to stay in Budapest overnight?"

Normally, train stations are busy and noisy. Union Station in Toronto is always abuzz with public announcements and the sounds of people on the move. But as we come off the platform and into the station proper, the world erupts, and for once, it appears that the press hasn't exaggerated the situation.

The lower level of Keleti station is awash in blankets and tents, boxes and backpacks. Men stand around in tight groups, while women sit on the floor with babies and younger children. The older children race through the mass of people, pushing each other, playing a makeshift game of soccer with a paper coffee cup.

A little girl huddles against a wall, holding a stuffed monkey.

Mimi stops. I wait for a moment and then try to nudge her forward. But she doesn't move.

"I don't think we want to stand here."

"Are you seeing this?"

Young women in safety vests are passing out bananas and bottled water, while men in combat gear form a corridor so that the commuters and the tourists can get through the camp quickly and efficiently. I don't know if the men are military or police, and I'm not sure I care. I can see that they're armed, as though they expect that the refugees might conjure up tanks and fighter jets out of their backpacks.

"Babies."

One of the security guys waves at Mimi. It's clear he wants us to keep moving.

"*Honem!*" the man shouts at Mimi.

Mimi holds her ground.

"Move!" the man shouts in English.

Mimi drags me back against the wall, out of the way. "We should stay and help."

"How?"

"Jesus, Bird. They brought their babies."

The man cuts through the crowd to where we're standing. "American?"

"Blackfoot," says Mimi, which is what she says when she crosses borders or has to deal with arrogant government officials.

"Canadian," I say.

"Ah, Canada," says the man in accented English. "You stand on guard, yes?"

I've never liked that line. The song is a bit too far on the militaristic side for my taste. With the ease that nations go to war, I don't think we need musical encouragement.

"We stand on guard also," said the soldier. "Very difficult the situation. You can see. Too many people. Everyone is upset. So, you must move."

"What's going to happen to all these people?"

The soldier shrugs. "No one knows. More come all the time. So, you must move."

"We'd like to help."

"Yes." The man resettles the rifle on his shoulder. "But now you must move. You cannot stay here. Here is not the place for the tourists of Canada."

Mimi pushes off the wall, and we start to work our way through the crowd. The soldier stays with us until we get to the stairs.

"No one likes this," says the man. "I have three children. No one likes this."

The refugees have taken over the top level of Keleti as well, and they've spilled out onto the street and into the park across the boulevard. I'm not good at estimating, but I'm guessing that there are several thousand people camped around the station.

I try to put a good face on it. "At least they have good weather."

Mimi walks around in a circle. Which is never a good sign. "Let's go."

"Where?"

"Back to Prague."

"I thought you wanted to stay the night and see Budapest."

"Now I don't."

Mimi goes back into the station to find a ticket counter. I wait outside in the sunshine. I know how she feels. It's not easy to see people in distress, to walk by them as though they don't exist, as though they don't matter.

Of course, I do it all the time. Young men who wait outside shops and ask for change. Young women who sit on street corners with cups and dogs. Older men who stand at traffic lights, holding signs. I don't even pause to wonder how they got to where they are. Drug abuse, alcohol, mental illness. Bad luck.

And I really don't care.

So why would I care about the people in Keleti station?

Mimi doesn't come back, and after twenty minutes, I begin to worry that she might have gone down into the bowels of Keleti to do battle with the forces of injustice and indifference, that she is, even now, rallying the refugees to her banner.

People have broken out signs and flags, and there's singing and chanting and yelling. A knot of young men has started an argument that threatens to break into something serious.

We could be shot. Kitty huddles at my shoulder. *Or worse.*

Eugene has retrieved a piece of cardboard that says "I am a human being." Chip and the twins are in the crowd somewhere, but I can't see them.

I slip my camera out of my pocket. I don't know why I feel hesitant about taking a photo of the refugees. Almost everyone has a camera or a cellphone. There are several television crews at work. Very young women, buffed and lacquered, roam about with microphones, looking for good visuals—children holding each other, an old man with blood on his face, three animated teens waving a Hungarian flag at the refugees, a mother comforting a crying child.

Eugene raises the cardboard sign high over his head. *Here I am*, he shouts.

The last time this happened, Kitty whispers, *they sent in tanks.*

Mimi has been gone long enough, and I push back into the crowd to find her.

"Bird!"

And there she is, at the entrance to the station, looking no happier than when she left.

"There's a train at five forty," she says. "It gets to Prague just after midnight."

I don't feel like arguing.

"That is," she says, "if the trains run. They're talking about closing the station."

"Because of the refugees?"

"So, we have a little under four hours." Mimi tucks her hair behind her ear. "What do you want to do?"

"Save the world."

"You want coffee, don't you."

"Sure, coffee now, save the world later."

So far as I could tell, Vogiatzi was the main street in Kymi. Kymi Square, with its statue of Georgios Papanikolaou, the man who developed the Pap test, was on Vogiatzi. So was the church and most of the stores.

"Small world," said Mimi.

There was a taxi parked at the curb, and standing next to the car was the same guy who had picked us up in Athens.

"Our English-speaking driver."

There was a teenage boy in the car. As soon as the man saw us, he began talking rapidly to the kid.

"Good morning," said the boy. "How are you today?"

The boy's English wasn't great, but it was considerably better than my Greek.

"Hi," said Mimi. "We need a taxi."

"I am Talos," said the boy. "My father is Stavros. He is very good driver."

"*Poso tha kostisei na paei Maletiani?*" I said, exhausting all of my Greek.

Talos quickly consulted with his father. "*Exi*," he said.

"Euros?" I flip my *komboloi* a couple of times, in case there's a discount for fellow Greeks.

"Yes."

"Both ways?"

I tried to imagine what Talos would do with his life. Good manners. Good looks. He could be an actor. Or a musician.

"*Okto*," he said. "Eight. Both ways."

"Will you come along and translate?"

"Sure, yes, *deka*. Ten. You understand?"

A lawyer. The kid had all the makings of a lawyer.

The ride up to Maletiani took a little over ten minutes. I wanted to learn as much as I could about Kymi, and Talos wanted to talk about Toronto.

"Toronto is very big."

"It is," I told him. "So is Athens."

"Yes," said Talos, "but no jobs in Athens."

"Were you born in Kymi?"

"Yes," said Talos. "The family goes to Athens. Two years. But no jobs, so we come back."

The road to Maletiani was windy and slow, with tight turns around granite outcroppings and tough, stringy trees.

"Why are you to Maletiani?"

"My *pappou* is from Maletiani."

"Your *pappou*? You are Greek?"

"My mother's side."

"You are here to buy the village?"

"What?"

"Maletiani," said Talos, "is small. *Ekato*. One hundred persons."

"In Maletiani?"

"Yes. Very old."

"The people?"

"You should buy the village."

Mimi was intrigued. "Why would we buy a village?"

"Americans. American dollars," said Talos. "They come to Ellada and buy, buy, buy."

"We're Canadians."

"If you buy Maletiani," said Talos, "then you could fix."

"I don't think we're going to buy a village."

"If you fix," said Talos, "the people will love you. Then you will be king."

MIMI AND I STAND on the sidewalk in front of Keleti station and ignore the people pushing past us.

"Here we are," I say, making sure my voice is filled with artificial enthusiasm. "Budapest."

Mimi ignores me and digs the brochures out of the pack.

"We could catch a cab, have coffee, walk around a bit, see the bullet holes and the shoes, and be back in time for the train." I wait to see if this is an idea whose time has come. "We could even pick up some pastries for the refugees."

"Pastries?"

"Not for everyone," I say, "but we could give them to a family, as we're going to the train."

"Pastries."

I know it sounds a little condescending, but it's something we could do, and maybe a slice of cake or a piece of chocolate would brighten their day.

Every major city in the world has at least one great place for coffee. Café El Escorial in Havana, Spella Caffe in Portland, Capital Espresso in Toronto. And every major city in the world has at least one famous coffee house. Café Brasilero in Montevideo, Caffè Florian in Venice, Le Procope in Paris, Caffe Reggio in Manhattan.

Sometimes, the famous places, cafés where history and ambience are the draw, don't serve the best coffee, and sometimes, the places that serve great coffee, cafés where the quality of the beans and the roast bring people in, are housed in storefronts with all the character and atmosphere of a chicken coop.

"Okay," says Mimi, sorting through the material she collected at the station in Prague, "we've got the New York Café. Opened in 1894 and was a place where writers and artists hung out. Very ornate and opulent."

"Sounds good."

"However, in 2006 it was linked to the New York Palace, a luxury hotel, and now it gets a lot of upscale tourist traffic."

"Pass."

"Then there's the Café Astoria in the Hotel Astoria."

"Isn't that the place you wanted to spend the night? Nazis, Russians, Stalinist chic?"

"I did."

"Also pass."

"Which leaves Central Café," says Mimi. "Famous meeting place for writers such as . . ." Mimi turns the brochure over. "Frigyes Karinthy and . . . Lorinc Szabo. Evidently, the place was a hotbed for art and politics. It says the Communists closed most of the coffee houses, but that after the fall of the dictatorship in 1989, Central Café was one of the first to be reopened."

"Let's go there."

"And it's near the university." Mimi puts the brochures back in her bag. "Fancy yourself a dissident writer, do you?"

"Just hope the coffee is good."

STAVROS AND HIS SON dropped us off at a three-way intersection, each street no wider than an alley.

"Maletiani," said Stavros.

"This is it?"

"Yes." Talos handed me a small card with a phone number on it. "Maletiani. When you are done buying, call and we come."

The building in front of us had a sign on it that said "*KOINOTHTA MAΛETIANON.*" I was pretty sure that *koinothta* was the word for "community," and the second word probably was the village itself, Maletiani.

"Well," said Mimi, "here we are."

The building was closed. Nothing to suggest that it had ever been open or was planning to open anytime soon.

Mimi peered in through the glass door. "It feels like a government office of some sort."

I had assumed that there would be a shop or a store in Maletiani, some place you could step into and begin a conversation about a lost relative and a prodigal grandson. But in a village as small as Maletiani, there were just houses.

"Maybe it's only open so many days a week. Or maybe it's only open one day a week."

Mimi walked around to a window, but it was too high off the ground.

"You know, like the old West with the travelling judges on a circuit and the dentists who worked out of a covered wagon."

Villages set in the hills tend to be hilly, and Maletiani didn't disappoint. We wandered up one street that rose rapidly and then slalomed back down the next. Up and down we went, weaving our way through the village.

"We could take a photo of a nice-looking house and pretend that that was where your grandfather was born and raised."

On the third run, we turned a corner and ran into a cart drawn by a donkey. The cart was filled with various vegetables, tomatoes, potatoes, peppers, and onions, and standing around the cart was a group of men and women, all older than me.

"All right," said Mimi. "Show me what you got."

THE UNNERVING PART of arriving in a new city is that you have no idea as to the layout of the place, and after the first five minutes in the taxi, neither Mimi nor I have any idea where we are. We had said Central Café, showed the driver the address, but we could be on our way to Bratislava for all we knew.

"American?" asks the cab driver.

"Blackfoot," says Mimi.

"Canadian."

Mimi elbows me in the ribs. "I wish you wouldn't do that."

"He's not going to know who the Blackfoot are."

"And he's certainly not going to know if we don't tell him."

"Movies," says the cab driver. "Bruce Willis. Bang, bang. Tom Cruise. Bang, bang."

Given its history, I expect that Central Café will be in a sketchy part of Budapest, one of those down-the-next-dark-alley establishments, a small, smoke-filled hollow frequented by poets, spies, and the secret police. So it is a minor disappointment to find the café sitting on the edge of an upscale shopping mall. The building looks old enough, but when it comes to coffee shops, ambience is everything, and Central Café looks as though it has walked away from its colourful history and gone shopping for Zegna and Ferragamo.

"This is it?"

"Very famous," says the cab driver. "Number one for tourists."

Central Café is in a stone building with arched windows and

doors. Inside are tall ceilings, hardwood floors, and red leather. Everything polished and sparkling. We find a seat at the front where we can see the display filled with Hungarian pastries. I try, but I can't imagine spending a day in such affluent surroundings, writing poetry, drinking espresso, eating tortes, working on political intrigues with friends.

"Not exactly bohemian," I tell Mimi. "You want a pastry?"

"I want to go to the bathroom." Mimi stands up. "If the waiter comes, order me a cappuccino and something chocolate."

There are photographs on the walls. Mostly men in suits that are fifty years out of date. I guess that these are the artists who frequented the café in its heyday, but they could just as well be plumbers and truck drivers. On the back wall is a large portrait of a young man staring out at the customers. There's something disturbing about the painting. One eye is in shadow, and the man's mouth is drawn as though he is anticipating something unpleasant. Or cruel.

When the waiter arrives, I ask him about the portrait.

"Ah," says the waiter, in perfect English, "this is Endre Ady. Do you know his work?"

I have to admit that I don't.

"He was a poet and a journalist. Very famous."

I check the menu one more time, but I know what I want.

The waiter takes out his pen. "American?"

As SOON AS THE people standing around the vegetable cart saw us, they stopped talking, and they stopped moving, as though someone had hit pause on the remote. I smiled and waded in with my exceptional Greek.

"*Kalimera*."

The man at the town hall had copied the page in the ledger that showed my grandfather's birth along with the names of his parents and his siblings. I pulled the page out of my pocket and held it out.

"My *pappou*," I said, pointing to the entry.

One of the older women came around the side of the cart and looked at the paper.

"*Pappou?*"

"*Nai.*" I pointed to my grandfather's name. "Maletiani."

The woman pointed to the ground at her feet. "*Pappou*? Maletiani?"

"*Nai. Milate agglika*?"

This was greeted with head shaking and a chorus of "*okhi.*" I pointed to my grandfather's name again. "*Pappou.* Thomas. *Athanasios.* And then I pointed to my grandfather's brother's name on the Xerox. "Georgios. *Adeltos.*"

This sparked a lively conversation among the villagers at the cart, with the women taking the lead and the men chiming in every so often.

Mimi pressed against me. "What are they saying?"

"No idea."

"What happened to 'I speak Greek'?"

"Different dialect."

"Right. So, do they know your grandfather?"

"Not sure."

And just as quickly as the conversation began, it stopped, and the villagers went back to sorting through the vegetables. Mimi and I stood by the cart for a moment and pretended to admire the produce, and then we quietly slipped away.

At the top of the street, we stopped and looked back down.

"This is how life used to be," said Mimi. "Simple. Uncomplicated."

"Life has never been simple."

"You know," said Mimi, "it wouldn't hurt if you tried to look at things positively every now and then."

"Quiet," I said. "The place is quiet."

"There," said Mimi. "Was that so hard?"

Not that the quiet was all that encouraging. While there were no cars and trucks rumbling up and down the streets, no emergency vehicles with their sirens, no loud music, neither were there any sounds of children playing or the voices of neighbours talking.

As we walked up and down the streets of Maletiani, the only sound was the wind.

"How about this?" Mimi stopped in front of a house with a grape arbour in the yard. "This look like your grandfather's kind of place?"

Tomorrow the car service would take us back to Athens and the airport for our flight home. This was the one day I had to see where my grandfather was born, to close one of the unfinished circles of my life.

"Or maybe that one."

I shook my head. "Not the way it works."

"You're a journalist," said Mimi. "So, pick a house and make up a story about it."

Mimi had a point. One of these houses was the house in which my grandfather was born and raised. The records at Kymi town hall had confirmed that. How many houses were there in the village? What was wrong with picking one and laying claim to it? The odds of being right were infinitely better than buying a lottery ticket or putting quarters into a slot machine at the casinos in Niagara.

"You stand in front of a house you like," said Mimi, "and I'll take a picture."

I was about to explain why this was a bad idea when an old man came out of one of the houses and hurried towards us.

"*Herete.*"

Followed by a flood of Greek that I couldn't follow.

The man was probably in his eighties. Maybe older. Short, powerful, the kind of man my grandfather had been in the handful of photos I had of him.

"Mavrias." He waved a hand at an old stone house across the road, its door chained, its windows boarded. A wire fence and an iron gate guarding the property. "Mavrias."

It took me a moment. "Mavrias?" I said, pointing at the deserted house.

"*Nei, nei,*" said the man. "Georgios Mavrias."

"Mavrias," I said. "*Pou einai?*"

"Ah, ah," said the man, laying his face against his hands in a sleeping gesture. "*Nekros.*"

"*Nekros?*" said Mimi. "Is that like necropathy? As in . . . dead?"

"*Athina,*" said the man. "*Nekros. Athina.*"

"Athena?" Mimi raised her voice, in case volume was going to lead to understanding. "The goddess of wisdom and war?"

"I think he means Athens. They're either dead or they went to Athens."

"*Nei, nei.*" The old man hurried to the iron gate and held it open. "Mavrias," he said again, with emphasis. "Mavrias."

The house was a square two-storey. It sat by itself on a piece of land with a view of the valley to the west. There was a large tree in the yard that had probably been there when my grandfather was a child. To the side of the house, on the second floor, was a balcony that looked out at the church in the distance.

The old man stood by the fence and gestured me forward with his hands.

"Look, Bird," she said, "he's telling you that this is yours."

"Maybe."

"The family pile," said Mimi. "Your grandfather's house. Come on, Bird, that's got to make you feel good."

"Sure."

I stood in front of the house and looked out across the land. There were clouds in the distance that weren't going to reach us anytime soon. The air was warm and filled with the smell of dry grass and olive trees.

Mimi reached down, picked up a grey and white stone and handed it to me. "Thomas Blackbird Mavrias," she said. "Lord of the manor."

BY THE TIME MIMI returns to the table, her cappuccino and chocolate cake are waiting for her. I've already tried a bite of her cake, and this is the first thing she notices.

"You ate my cake."

"You always eat mine."

"That's different." Mimi sips her coffee. "So, how is it?"

"It's okay."

"Are you depressed again?"

"Just tired."

"It's the refugees, isn't it?" says Mimi. "You don't like seeing children in distress."

I can't imagine that anyone likes to see anyone in distress, but as soon as I think this, I remind myself that I'm wrong. For the most part, no one much cares what happens to other people, just so long as it doesn't happen to them. We have the capacity for compassion. We simply don't practise it to any degree.

It's more an ideal that we hang on a wall where it's easy to see and almost impossible to reach.

"The cake is good," says Mimi. "You should get your own piece."

"Not hungry."

"Then I could have a bite of yours."

"We should head back to the station." I check the clock on the wall. "You want to try to find the university and that copper strip?"

"What about the refugees?"

I don't see the rage until it's on me. "Maybe we can talk Two-Cent Jim into donating a couple pallets of bottled water."

"That's not nice."

"Or better yet, we could pack a couple of the families into our luggage and take them home with us."

"Bird . . ."

"You know, like souvenirs. Nothing Canada loves better than a bunch of refugees."

"Stop it!"

"Or we could just shoot them and be done with it."

Mimi sits back and stares out across the room. I cradle my espresso and listen to each breath I take.

Slow. Deliberate. Slow. Deliberate.

"The portrait," I say, after I get myself under control, "is of Endre Ady. He was a poet. And a journalist."

Mimi has tears in her eyes. She pushes her cake to me. "Here," she says.

We sit there in silence until the waiter brings the bill. The two of us, in the heart of Budapest, in the middle of a summer afternoon. There is probably something I could say, something I should say, but in the end, we simply leave the café and catch a cab back to the station.

VII

The train back to Prague is an uneasy truce, a silent passage. I sit and look out the window, watch the land rush by, hum show tunes in my head.

"The Impossible Dream" from *Man of La Mancha.*

"If I Loved You" from *Carousel.*

"Some Enchanted Evening" from *South Pacific.*

This is dangerous and not recommended. Musicals tend to make me emotional, and there's no telling when the humming will get out of hand.

Mimi passes the time reading an English-language book she bought at the station. The cover suggests that it's a gathering of porn stars in a hospital. It's not what Mimi normally reads, but then she'll read anything with text.

It's my fault. I understand that. It was probably the "just shoot them" remark. Which was supposed to have been satiric. At least, that's what I tell myself, now that the fury has faded.

But I'm more inclined to hold the refugees responsible.

If they hadn't been trying to escape the devastations of war, they wouldn't have been in Keleti station. And if we hadn't gone to

Budapest to see the sights, we wouldn't have seen the children. And if we hadn't seen the children, Mimi wouldn't be angry with me.

The logic is somewhat flawed and self-serving, so I don't repeat it out loud.

By the time we pass through Bratislava, I've run out of show tunes.

"Good book?" I ask, to try to break the impasse.

Silence.

Out the window, the land is flat, and I can see that there is no pardon on the horizon.

So we're in Prague.

We pull into the station before midnight and take a cab back to our hotel. The air conditioner is still going, the room is still hot, the spiders are still on the ceiling, the tourists are still walking back and forth across the Charles Bridge.

I go directly to the bathroom, and when I come back out, Mimi is already in bed, wrapped up in a fortress of blankets and pillows.

I sit in the chair and watch Czech television shows with the mute button engaged. That's the beauty of television and life in general. You don't need sound to understand what's happening.

I'm still in the chair the next morning. I check my watch. The breakfast room has just opened. I could wake her, but I leave Mimi sleeping and head downstairs. She'll find me soon enough. After Budapest, it's probably best if we begin the day in public and on neutral ground.

The table in the corner is free. I sit with my back to the wall and do a slow review of my life and what I've accomplished.

Photojournalist.

That's about it.

The Indian expert. My great claim to fame. The man who covered all the major contemporary events. Alcatraz, 1969. Trail of Broken Treaties, 1972. Wounded Knee, 1973. The Seminoles and

Native gaming controversy, 1979. Oka, 1990. Ipperwash, 1995. Idle No More, 2012. Elsipogtog fracking protest, 2013. Dakota Access Pipeline protest, 2017.

If it had feathers and a drum, I was there.

For over forty years, I took the pictures, wrote the stories. And then I walked away.

Mark Twain said, "It takes your enemy and your friend, working together, to hurt you to the heart, the one to slander you and the other to get the news to you," but I know better.

I don't need any help. I can do the job all by myself.

One day I was covering major news events with my own byline, and the next I was sitting at home watching *Murder, She Wrote* reruns and *Murdoch Mysteries*.

I didn't use the word "quit" when I told Mimi.

"Retiring? From what?"

"Work."

"Thought you wanted to save the world?"

"Can't save it from people," I told her.

"That sounds like despair."

"And I'm tired."

"And that sounds like depression."

WRITING-ON-STONE PROVINCIAL PARK.

Just north of the Alberta-Montana border. Sunday, July 10, 2016. A makeshift camp had materialized on the Milk River. Four tipis, seven men, six women, five children. They had been there for about two weeks when a group of tourists hiking through the park noticed the smoke from the cooking fire and reported it.

The camp was the idea of Annie Littlechild, a Cree from Wetaskiwin. She had left a clerical job with Shell Canada and decided to try to live as her ancestors had lived. The rest of the encampment consisted of a mismatched assortment of Natives from Rocky Boy and Wetaskiwin, Siksika and Bella Coola, along with a German university professor who had written a book on Karl May.

The *Toronto Star* had commissioned me to write a story about the camp, take photographs, a human interest piece for the Life section. I remembered coming in off the trail that morning and seeing the camp for the first time. It wasn't going to win any authenticity awards. The tipis were new, unbleached canvas, fresh out of the box. Someone had strung a clothesline between two cottonwoods. The line was so loaded that the jeans in the centre were touching the ground. There was a beat-to-shit gas generator off to one side and a crude firepit made out of river stones.

Even if you squinted and suspended your disbelief, it wasn't a nineteenth-century diorama.

I did interviews, took pictures of the adults in front of the tipis, followed the kids when they went to the river in search of bugs and minnows. I helped with the chores, ate with the group, listened to their stories. I had expected that these would be sad narratives of alcohol and drug abuse, of poverty and desperation, but for the most part, the people in the camp were ordinary, working class, from offices and factories.

They weren't looking to change the world, Littlechild told me that first night. They were just trying to make sense of their lives and how such lives could be lived.

I was more skeptical than I needed to be. How were they going to manage basic water and sanitation? Where would they get their food? What would they do when winter arrived and turned the land to ice?

I had asked much the same questions when I covered the occupation of Alcatraz years before. There had been a lot of bravado on the Rock, clenched fists and drums, political speeches and visits from celebrities. Press coverage and the prison's proximity to the amenities of San Francisco had turned the protest into a media romance that helped to hold the occupation together long after it had fallen apart.

Here on the Alberta prairies, out of sight of television cameras, movie stars, and sound bites, the Writing-on-Stone camp looked to have as much a chance of surviving as a picnic in a thunderstorm.

I DON'T SEE Oz until it's too late. The little man appears in the doorway and is across the room in a flash.

"Hello," he says. "You are here."

"I am."

"You are not here yesterday."

I don't feel like talking, but that is not going to stop Oz. "We went to Budapest."

"Budapest?"

"Early in the morning," I tell him. "Then we came back."

"The same day?"

"Yes."

Oz rubs the side of his nose. "What good luck."

"Luck?"

"Today, there are no trains." Oz arranges his knife and fork so they are parallel to each other. "They have closed the station in Budapest."

"The refugees closed the station?"

"No, no," says Oz. "The government closed the station. There are too many refugees, and there are too many angry people."

The server comes by, and I decide that I'm hungry after all and won't wait for Mimi. I order the ham dish. So does Oz.

"You saw the refugees?"

"Yes," I say. "It was sad."

"To see them is sad," says Oz. "To be one is . . . *bouleversant*, but this is not strong enough."

"Shattering?"

"Yes," says Oz. "Shattering. Moria. Zaatari. Calais. Mae La. Dadaab. To be a refugee is to be shattered."

I follow Oz to the buffet. There is a good selection of fruit today and some small pastries with raisins.

"So, what will you do today?"

"I don't know. You have any suggestions?"

Oz takes two of the pastries. "You have seen the clock?"

"We've seen the clock and the Kafka courtyard and the castle and the statue of the boy and we've been to Golden Lane."

"And, of course, the bridge."

"We walked through the old Jewish quarter and saw the cemetery, but we didn't go in."

Oz stops in front of the yogurt. "Have you been to the KGB Museum?"

I'm tempted to tell Oz about the medicine bundle and Uncle Leroy.

"When you were in Budapest, did you go to the castle?" Oz waves a serving spoon in my face. "There is a museum. In the basement of the castle. The Hospital in the Rock. Filled with wax figures. My favourite is a German officer sitting on a toilet with his pants around his ankles."

"Wax Nazis?"

"Doctors, nurses, patients, soldiers," says Oz. "A history lesson in wax."

We finish with the buffet and go back to our table. It's only eight thirty. I don't expect to see Mimi for another hour. Now that I have food in front of me, I'm no longer hungry. What I really want to do is go back to the room, crawl into bed, and stay there for the rest of the day.

Instead, I sip my coffee and wait for Oz to finish his meal. Through the window, I can see the sun in full throat, and I can hear the sounds of motor scooters as they zip up and down the narrow streets.

"Tell me," I ask him as he eats the last of his pastry, "what do you know about Wild West shows?"

THE SECOND DAY I was at the Littlechild camp, park rangers, with their official voices at the ready, showed up and told the people that they would have to leave or face a fine and jail time. Littlechild was friendly but firm. This was Indian land, she told the park people. They weren't bothering anyone. And they weren't going to move.

Oh, and would the rangers like to join the camp for lunch?

The next morning, I had walked to high ground so I could get a good shot of the camp and the river and the sky floating above the land. I had just finished setting up the camera when the RCMP arrived in four patrol cars, trailed by a rented cube van. Everything was much too far away for me to hear what was being said, but you could tell that the cops had not come to negotiate a treaty.

There was a brief confrontation, after which the officers moved in quickly and arrested everyone. Littlechild tried to take refuge in one of the tipis. I watched as she was dragged out, handcuffed, and shoved into the back of one of the cruisers.

Then, quickly and efficiently, the police moved on the camp itself. They broke down the tipis, gathered up the sleeping bags, the folding chairs, the barbecue, and the generator, and threw everything into the back of the cube van.

The raid lasted less than an hour.

There was little I could do. So I did nothing. And, in the time it took the police to arrest everyone and dismantle the camp, I didn't move.

SOMEWHERE IN MY CAREER as a photojournalist, I had written a feature story about Wild West shows for *Saturday Night*, and what I had enjoyed most about the research were the photographs.

I had used four in the article.

One had been a candid shot taken during the 1901 Pan-American exhibition in Buffalo, New York. It showed Indians on horseback, sporting full feathered headdresses, getting ready for a race.

Or a raid.

The second photograph, taken in 1905, was a re-enactment of the death of Custer. This image was staged and probably shot in a studio. Custer is standing upright with a raised sword in one hand and a pistol in the other. At his feet are three dead Indians, the inference being that George Armstrong did not go down without a fight. A fourth Indian stands in front of the lieutenant colonel and is in the process of driving a knife into Custer's chest.

It wasn't Sitting Bull. Not that it mattered.

In any case, whoever the Indian was, he had a full feathered headdress just like the riders in the first photograph.

The real Sitting Bull was in the third photograph I used. It had been taken earlier, in 1885, and showed him standing side by side with Buffalo Bill Cody. Cody has one hand over his heart, as though he's in the middle of making the Lakota chief a promise, while his other hand rests on his rifle. Sitting Bull stands next to the famous frontiersman, in full headdress, his eyes closed as though he's asleep or simply bored with the whole process of myth-making.

The last photograph I used, which was undated, showed a group of thirty or so Indians in full headdresses standing with Buffalo Bill in front of a backdrop of tipis and tents. There were two Native children in this one. They were wearing feathered headdresses as well.

In all four of the photographs, the feathered headdresses were the markers, the sign that these were Indians and not Chinese workers at the Three Gorges Dam or coal miners on a coffee break in West Virginia.

A few of the Indians in the Wild West show photographs didn't have headdresses, and I had to conclude that there had been only so many headdresses available, that if you came late for the shoot, you'd have to settle for a single feather or a leather headband.

The story of Uncle Leroy and the medicine bundle delights Oz. "He paints the house with cow shit?"

"He does."

"Then he must join the Wild West show?"

"Captain Trueblood's Wild West Emporium."

"And comes to Europe?"

"Paris, Athens, Amsterdam," I tell him. "We have the postcards."

"And he comes also to Prague?"

"Yes."

"And he sees the astronomical clock?"

"Probably."

"So far from home. But he returns?"

"No," I say. "He never returns."

"To be a refugee." Oz shakes his head sadly. "A very hard life."

I had never thought of Uncle Leroy as a refugee. But, of course, that is exactly what he was. Forced off the reserve, dragged through an assortment of countries and languages. Homeless.

The old man in Keleti station with the vacant eyes. The women huddled in the corner. The child with her stuffed monkey. The young men with angry faces, ready to fight.

"But tell me more about this bundle."

"What do you want to know?"

"What is inside the bundle?"

I had never seen the bundle, and neither had Mimi. Not even Mimi's mother had been alive the last time the bundle had been opened.

"Could be anything," I tell Oz. "A stone, a tooth, a feather, a piece of cloth, a bone of some sort."

"And this is sacred?"

"No," I say, "it's more a family history, a collection of stories."

"Bones and stones?"

"They remind us of stories."

"And now you make a new bundle."

"My wife's idea."

"To replace the bundle that has been lost."

"Yes."

"Nylon? With a zipper?"

"One of the women on the reserve did some beadwork on the pouch," I tell Oz. "It looks pretty nice."

"Of course," he says, "of course. Cultures are living things. They must continue to change or they will die. This is true, is it not?"

I don't disagree with Oz, but there is still something about a nylon medicine bundle that bothers me.

"And what do you put in this new bundle?"

I run through some of the items that Mimi has gathered so far. A piece of honey nougat wrapped in gold foil that she bought at a shop in old-town Nice. A glass button we found in Venice in Piazza San Marco after an *acqua alta*. The stone from my grandfather's village in Greece. A cork from our first bottle of wine in Paris.

"I have a friend," says Oz, "in Copenhagen. She makes a scrap-book of the places she visits."

"Sort of the same idea."

"But for the bundle, there is a ceremony?"

"Don't know," I say. "Probably."

"A song?" says Oz. "A dance? The burning of sage?"

"You'd have to ask my wife."

"I should tell my friend," says Oz. "A ceremony would please her."

I check the doorway. Mimi is going to be late for breakfast again.

"But there is much to do." Oz stands and buttons his jacket. "And I have promises to keep."

I'm tempted to finish the stanza, but instead I smile and wish the little man a good day.

"Tomorrow," he calls back to me from the doorway. "Tomorrow, the Bees and the Bears."

LITTLECHILD'S CAMP WASN'T the first such attempt to get back to a simpler life. In June of 1971, just as federal marshals were removing the last of the protesters from Alcatraz, I flew in to Edmonton to do an article on a bush camp that had been established in 1968 on the edge of the Brazeau Canyon Wildland, in the shadow of the Rockies.

The Mountain Cree Camp.

Cree elder Robert Smallboy and 140 people, more or less, from the Ermineskin Band just down the road from Wetaskiwin.

The camp was large and well established. I took pictures, talked with the leaders, ate with the people. The idea for the camp was a simple one. To sidestep the contemporary world and the havoc of alcoholism and drug abuse. To try to stem the epidemic of suicide.

Which is pretty much what Littlechild had wanted.

But unlike the Littlechild camp, the Mountain Cree Camp was larger and much more isolated. Even though the Crown claimed the Kootenay Plains as federal land, officials chose not to move on it. The Littlechild camp was much smaller, but it was in a provincial park, and the potential threat that a small band of Indians posed to the sensibilities of tourists was not to be tolerated.

And 1971 was a world away from 2016.

Not that Robert Smallboy fared much better in the end. On a trip to Banff in the winter of 1984, he was forced to spend the night in the snow after hotels in the tourist township decided that, while Indians on horseback riding in the Banff Indian Days parade were tolerable, a single Indian wanting to rent a room for the evening was not.

The night was cold, and he wound up with frostbite in his toes. The toes turned gangrenous, and by the summer of that year, he was dead.

I GO TO THE BUFFET and get a second pastry. I doubt that these are recommended for diabetics, but they're small, and the trick is to eat them slowly. With coffee. Mimi's mother read an article that suggested coffee inhibits the rapid absorption of sugar.

I don't believe this. More than likely, it's the Institute to Confound and Demoralize hard at work. Nevertheless, the possibility is a comfort.

The breakfast room is empty now, and as I sit alone at the table, I imagine that I'm back in Guelph, sitting on the sofa watching football. The little girl from Keleti station is sitting next to me, her monkey in her arms. Muffy the Wonder Dog is on my lap. Together, we watch the Toronto Argonauts lose another game. The girl wants to know why the players don't have guns, and I tell her that football is a game and that if the players had guns, they would kill each other, and that would be war.

Maybe, the girl tells me, we should take guns away from soldiers and give them footballs instead.

I have these moralistic daydreams from time to time. They never last long, and they have little lasting effect.

Eugene sits down next to me with a thud. The twins stand near the window with their hands linked, rocking back and forth, as they sing "Row, Row, Row Your Boat."

So full of good intentions, says Eugene. *As long as you don't have to do anything.*

I watch the staff as they clear away the breakfast buffet.

Didi comes over and leans against the chair. *You want to sing Row-Row?*

Singing always makes me feel better, says Desi.

Kitty doesn't say a word. She fidgets in the doorway and chews off her fingernails.

It's going to be a nice day, a day for walking around and seeing the sights. I stand up, leave a tip, and head for the stairs.

I bump Eugene with my shoulder as I go by. Just because I can.

Mimi is sitting in the chair by the window. She sits very still, and at first, I think she might be asleep.

"You know what I'm thinking?" she says.

"You missed breakfast."

"I'm thinking that this is what it feels like to be rich."

I sit on the bed and wait. Mimi looks out the window at the bridge and the tourists and the river.

"We can fly anywhere we want, stay at a nice hotel, eat at a decent restaurant, see the sights, and fly home. Bada-bing, bada-boom."

"Budapest isn't our fault."

"And if we see something upsetting, we can just ignore it."

"You're going to have to eat."

"How many times?"

"How about we leave the guidebook behind for the day."

I go to the bathroom and inject myself with insulin. Eight units. Because of the pastry. In case coffee therapy is a myth.

"How about we just wander?"

Mimi is waiting for me when I return. She stands by the bed, her jacket in hand. "How many times?"

"Arabic." I slip the camera into my pack. "I looked it up. The Syrian refugees speak Arabic."

«»

Mimi's right. How many times have we walked around an injustice? Ignored intolerance? Rewarded bigotry and racism with silence? By the time we walk downstairs and step out of the hotel, I've already come up with more than a dozen instances without even trying.

"I'm not angry," Mimi tells me as we come onto the bridge and work our way through the crowds. "I'm just disappointed. That's all."

Up ahead, a tour group is gathered around a saint, while a guide explains why martyrs matter.

When we get to the middle, Mimi stops and looks out at the river and the city. "With all that we could do," she says, "we do this."

The world being what it is, I have, on a number of occasions, contemplated suicide. But I've never been able to come up with a good note. Once, I went on the Internet to see if anyone had had more success with this than me.

The poet John Berryman had written "I am a nuisance" on the back of an envelope. Vachel Lindsay, another poet, had left the message "They tried to get me—I got them first," while the actor George Sanders wrote three suicide notes, the pithiest of which said "Dear world, I am leaving because I am bored. I feel I have lived long enough. I am leaving you with your worries in this sweet cesspool. Good luck."

None of these is particularly impressive. I would have liked to have come up with the line from the Gloria Shayne Baker song.

"Goodbye, cruel world, I'm off to join the circus." Short and clever.

But Baker had beaten me to it. However, she didn't commit suicide. She died of lung cancer at age eighty-four, so the line might still be available.

In one of my weaker moments, I shared my dilemma with Mimi.

"You want to commit suicide?"

"I was thinking about it."

"But you were worried about the note?"

"I think it would be important."

"Bird," Mimi had said, "if you're that concerned about the quality of your prose, you're not suicidal. You're just having a bad writing day."

"Okay, what would you do?"

"Me? Suicide?"

"Yes."

"Book a room at a nice hotel with a large tub," said Mimi without much thought. "Dark chocolate. Some wine. Hang a sign on the bathroom door that said 'Do Not Enter, Suicide in Progress.'"

"I'm serious."

"What makes you think I'm not?"

AFTER THE MOUNTIES LEFT, I had walked down to what remained of the Littlechild camp. There was a child's toy in the grass, along with a plastic container blown into the water by the wind. A spoon and a fork lay next to a tipi stake that had been pounded flush to the ground.

The only thing still standing was the firepit.

In the end, Writing-on-Stone wasn't much of a story. The people who had been at the camp were taken to Lethbridge, where they were reprimanded and released. Littlechild was charged with trespassing. She was given a year's probation and was barred from setting foot in any provincial or national park.

There was a protest by Native students at the University of Calgary in support of the short-lived camp. Littlechild was supposed to speak at the event, but she didn't appear, and no reason was given as to why she didn't show.

By then, I was back in Guelph.

Safe and sound. No worse for wear.

A couple of months after the incident, there was a story in the *Calgary Herald* about a family who had wandered onto the abandoned campsite. One of the kids took a picture of the firepit and put it on her Facebook page. It showed thin wisps of smoke rising out of the ground.

That day at Writing-on-Stone, I had watched the police douse the fire with water and turn the ashes, but in spite of their best efforts, the coals had persisted and continued to smoulder.

So we're in Prague.

The sun is shining. The day has gotten hotter than I find comfortable, but as Mimi loves heat, I'm hoping that the warmth will cheer her. With any luck, she'll forget about Budapest and the refugees before the day is out.

I try to do my part. "Are there any churches you want to see?"

Mimi cocks her head and narrows her eyes. "Who are you, and what did you do with my sweetie?"

"Today's your day," I say quickly. "We do what you want to do."

"What happened to 'let's just wander around'?"

"We can wander around and see a church."

"We saw a church the other day," says Mimi. "Up at the castle."

"There must be more than one church in Prague."

"Maybe I'd rather go shopping."

I stop in my tracks and wait.

"Prague must have one or two thrift stores."

For me, thrift stores are in the same category as the garbage bins behind fast-food joints. For Mimi, they're gold mines just waiting to be quarried.

I try to maintain a neutral tone. "You fly all the way to Prague to go to thrift stores?"

"What's wrong with recycling?"

I've got nothing against recycling. I separate plastics from organics. I use hemp shopping bags. We have several solar panels on the roof of our garage. We're thinking about buying an electric car.

"I don't know why you dislike the idea of used clothing," says Mimi. "You get a wider variety of choices at a thrift store."

"Yesterday's fashions at today's prices."

"You sound like a snob."

"Used underwear?"

"Everything is washed," says Mimi, "and you can wash it again when you get home."

"A thong. Tell me you would buy a used thong."

"We all can't buy new clothes, throw them away, and buy more new clothes." Mimi has her hands on her hips. "Maybe we could find you a shirt."

"What's wrong with my shirt?"

We get across the bridge in good order. At the first major intersection, we have to make a choice.

"Does the guidebook even mention thrift stores?"

"It does," says Mimi. "But none of the stores is close." Mimi makes a right-hand turn at the first intersection and stops. "We can walk or take a cab."

"Farther than that pizza restaurant?"

"Maybe," says Mimi. "So, what do *you* want to do, and don't hurt my feelings and say that you want to go home."

Two men in suits pass us. One guy takes a quick look at his wrist, and I see a flash of gold and remember Oz that first morning.

"Watches," I say before I have a chance to think it through. "I'd like to look at high-end watches."

"You want a high-end watch?"

"Maybe."

"You don't even like watches."

"There are lots of things I do that I don't like."

Mimi nods. "Such as follow me around thrift stores."

"Maybe if I had a nice watch, I'd feel better about myself."

"I don't think that's going to work," says Mimi, "but I suppose there's no harm in looking."

The store Mimi wants to visit is the Prague Thrift Store on Budecska in the Vinohrady district. She's in through the door and immediately disappears into the racks of clothing. I have not been in all the thrift stores in the world, but the ones I have been in all smell the same. And they look the same. The one on Budecska could be Value Village on Silvercreek. Or the Mission Thrift on Victoria. Or St. Vincent de Paul on Elizabeth.

Same smell. Same look.

Akin to being trapped in a laundry hamper.

On the surface, donated clothing looks to be a simple proposition. You donate clothing to a charity. The charity sells the clothing in their stores. The profits help people in need.

And if that's the way it worked, it would be a no-brainer. But it's not.

Charities get more clothing than they can possibly use, and they get clothing they can't possibly sell. Of the tons of donations they receive from a caring public, thrift stores manage only a small percentage. The rest is shipped to developing countries such as India or Kenya or Chile or Tunisia, where it competes with developing textile industries in those countries, or is thrown into landfills, or is taken out into fields and burned.

In 2016, Uganda, Tanzania, and Rwanda tried to ban all imports of second-hand clothing, as a way of protecting their textile industries, as a way of keeping North America's refuse out of their landfills. Almost immediately, the US stepped in and threatened sanctions if anyone tried to close down the free world's favourite garbage dumps.

I've mentioned this to Mimi on a number of occasions, and she agrees that the matter is problematic.

Still, it's hard to pass up a Dolce & Gabbana organza blouse for $6.50.

I wander through the store trying not to touch anything. All the usual suspects are here. Jeans, tops, purses, belts, hats, children's clothing and toys, jackets, books. Everything arranged in tight rows with no room to pass.

A cornucopia of First World detritus.

The store is not all that large, but Mimi has vanished. Some thrift stores have dressing rooms. Some have curtains pulled across a dent in the wall. Some force you to hold the article up and guess.

Men's clothing is at the back of the store. To keep boredom at bay, I flick my way through the T-shirts on the off chance that something catches my eye.

Mimi and I have different ideas about T-shirts. Mimi doesn't like them. Doesn't matter the colour or the image. For her, a shirt without a collar and buttons isn't a shirt.

It's a paint rag.

For me, a T-shirt is the daily default, provided it's a black crewneck with no breast pocket.

There are a dozen black T-shirts on the rack. Only three in my size, which makes a decision easier. One shirt says "There's a 99% Chance I Don't Care." Another has a Nike swish symbol, which kills any chance of my ever being caught alive wearing it. The last black shirt has an image of a stylized Indian on a horse racing across the prairies.

I'm holding it up against me, looking for a mirror, when Mimi turns the corner.

"That's worse than the one you're wearing," she says.

"I sort of like it."

"How about 'sort of' putting it back on the rack?"

"Did you find anything?"

It's a rhetorical question. Mimi has her arm draped with clothing. "I'm still thinking."

I hold the T-shirt up again. "I could wear it on special days."

Mimi closes her eyes for a moment. And then she opens them. "Remember that White guy who was selling T-shirts at the Toronto powwow?"

"The guy who was dressed up to look like Buffalo Bill?"

"Remember that one T-shirt?"

In addition to the standard run of "Homeland Security," "Red Nation," "Warriors," and "Native Pride" T-shirts, the guy had shirts in several different colours that said "Will Dance for Booze!"

"This shirt is almost as bad," said Mimi. "Plus, it's black."

I wander the store while Mimi tries on the clothing she isn't going to buy, and I wonder, not for the first time, if the majority of the junk has arrived here courtesy of death.

Someone dies, and whoever is left standing has to deal with the accumulations of a life. Jerry gets the piano. Thelma gets the silverware. Angela gets the painting hanging over the sofa, which the parents bought when they went on that cruise. The dining room table and chairs go to a niece who just got married, and the TV winds up in the basement of a nephew who is working on a man cave and just needs a neon beer sign to finish off the room.

The rest is sent to a thrift store, because it's cheaper than renting a Dumpster. This is not, strictly speaking, recycling. It's more a version of abandonment.

When Mimi finds me, I'm holding a kitchen implement of some sort that looks as though it could double as a sex toy.

"Don't get excited," she says. "It's for pasta."

"You find anything?"

"I talked to one of the clerks," says Mimi. "She gave me the name of a street."

"A street?"

"Near the clock."

"We've seen the clock."

"Watches," says Mimi. "Parizska is *the* place for watches."

"You want to go watch shopping?"

"No." Mimi rolls her eyes. "*You* want to go watch shopping. *I* want to watch."

The clerk's exact instructions were to go to the clock, walk around the square, find the rich people, and follow them. This proves to be easier than it might seem. And Parizska is lousy with watch shops.

"You get to pick one store," says Mimi, "and one store only."

"I am the master of my fate."

"So, choose well."

We walk along Parizska for a few blocks in each direction. And then we do it again. I look at the watch shops, while Mimi reads the menus posted at the restaurants along the way.

"Okay," she says, "who's the lucky winner?"

I choose the shop with the security doors and the armed guard, the shop with the dark wood and polished brass. I have to ring the bell and wait for someone to let us into the small foyer. There we have to wait for the door to close behind us before the door in front opens and lets us into the shop proper.

By the time I step into the shop and clear the guard, I'm feeling important.

I had expected that I would be free to roam the store, stroll past the cases, look at the watches, nod my head appreciatively as I go by, but this is not what happens.

As soon as I make my way to the first case, a tall, elegant woman floats over as though she's a sailing yacht coming into harbour.

"Good day," she says with a soft British accent. "American?"

"Canadian."

"Even better." Her smile is quite impressive, full lips and bright white teeth, and I'm glad that I did not buy the T-shirt. "How may I assist you?"

"Watches," says Mimi, who tries a smile of her own, just for fun. "The master of his fate and the captain of his soul would like to examine watches."

"'Invictus,'" says the woman. "William Ernest Henley."

I know a little about Henley. When he was about sixteen, he lost a leg to tuberculosis. And then, less than ten years later, he was told that he might lose his other leg. Instead, he got a famous English surgeon to work on the remaining leg, and after multiple surgeries, the leg was saved. He wrote "Invictus" while he was recovering.

"Invictus" was one of my mother's favourite poems. I had always thought of it as an ongoing quarrel that Henley had had with medical science. She used it as a buffer for misfortune and poverty and the desertion of a husband.

"My name is Sophia. Are you interested in any particular brand?"

"Something expensive," says Mimi. "My captain is feeling the clutch of circumstance."

"Bird," I say. "Just call me Bird."

"Mr. Bird, how good to meet you and Mrs. Bird."

"Bull Shield," says Mimi, the smile all but gone now.

Sophia is tall, with auburn hair and blue-grey eyes. She's dressed in a fitted black shift with a string of pearls, and looks as though she should be stepping out of a limousine at a film opening in Cannes, rather than showing watches to a couple of senior citizens from Canada.

"Bull Shield," says Sophia. "Is that Blackfoot?"

Even Mimi is surprised.

"My husband is German," says Sophia. "He's crazy mad for Indians. His big dream is to attend a powwow in Alberta. He will be very jealous."

"What's your most expensive watch?" asks Mimi.

"Right now," says Sophia, "we have a Patek Philippe on consignment from a collector for 3.6 million euros."

A deep silence fills the shop.

"But you are going to wear this watch," says Sophia. "Yes?"

"Of course," says Mimi.

"So, I would not recommend the Patek. That is a watch you put in a safe and hold for appreciation."

As I sit in the chair, I realize that Rolex is the only brand of expensive watch that I know.

Sophia shakes her head. "You do not want a Rolex. Everyone has a Rolex. Do you drive a Chevrolet or a Ford?"

I don't drive a Chevrolet or a Ford, but I'm not sure I want to tell her that I drive a Subaru.

"Then you must not buy a Rolex." Sophia pushes away from the desk. "Wait here, and I will bring you several excellent watches to consider."

As soon as she leaves, a young man comes over. He could be Sophia's younger brother.

"May I bring you a coffee or a glass of wine?" he asks. "A bottle of sparkling water?"

I'm enjoying myself. I try not to look at Mimi. "Wine would be great," I say.

"And you, madam?"

"Water," says Mimi, her voice military grey, as though she's just ordered the bombing of a small village.

Sophia is back almost immediately with a velvet tray and five watches spaced equidistant from each other. At first glance, they all look disappointingly like the Citizens and the Seikos that decorate the malls of the world.

"Fine watches are a very personal acquisition."

I try to read the brands off the faces of each watch in the hope that the name will trigger something in my subconscious, but the print is much too small.

"I don't know." I glance at Mimi. "You see anything you like?"

Mimi isn't biting. "Oh," she says, "I like them all."

Sophia moves in quickly. "Let's start with the Audemars Piguet," she says, and holds the first watch up to the light. "This is an example of Audemars Piguet's Royal Oak collection."

"Of course," I say with authority.

"Pink gold. Thirty-seven millimetres. Crocodile strap. Note the distinctive case and the extraordinary work on the face. This is a watch that is immediately recognizable."

"Price?" says Mimi.

"23,700 euros," says Sophia.

"And this one?" asks Mimi.

"Ah," says Sophia. "This is a favourite of mine. The Jaeger-LeCoultre Reverso. Pink gold again. Rectangular case. But whereas the Piguet is an automatic, the Jaeger is hand wound."

Sophia presses on the side of the case with her thumb, and the face comes loose and flips over, revealing a second face.

"Two faces," she says. "In essence, two watches. One black face. One white face."

"For day and night," I say, not wanting to be left behind.

"Exactly," says Sophia. "And only fifteen thousand euros."

"What about the silver one?"

Sophia picks up a rather ordinary-looking watch. "This is not silver," she says. "It's platinum."

"Another Jaeger?"

"Because of the rectangular case?" says Sophia. "No, this one is an A. Lange & Söhne."

"A. Lange & Söhne," I repeat, so I don't forget how to pronounce the name.

"You have an excellent eye," says Sophia.

"That's my captain," says Mimi.

"This is one of their Cabaret Tourbillons. A hand-wound masterpiece. 210,000 euros."

I do a quick calculation of the cumulative value of the five watches lying in front of me on their velvet bed. Over 300,000 euros. Half a million Canadian.

"May I ask, is this watch for society or for psychology?"

I smile.

"Many of our customers are in business situations, where an expensive watch is part of the, how would you say, uniform?"

"Yes," says Mimi, "I can picture Bird in a uniform."

"While others buy watches for personal reasons."

"To try to make themselves feel better about themselves?"

"There is nothing wrong with this," says Sophia, "but it is seldom successful."

"Hear that, Bird?" says Mimi. "Seldom successful."

I hold my glass up to the light and marvel at the rich burgundy colour.

"And, of course, one can buy a prestigious timepiece simply because of the fine craftsmanship," says Sophia. "If you have the money, the reasons are endless."

The rest of the day, we wander Prague. We stroll through the small artistic neighbourhood of Novy Svet, have lunch at Café Louvre, where Einstein and Kafka had hung out. We find the Sigmund Freud sculpture hanging in space over the street, and we check out the memorial to the victims of Communism, a disturbing series of human figures coming down a set of steps, metal men who appear to have been ripped apart by an unexpected blast.

And we walk up to Letna Park. This is high ground above the river and the city. At one point, when the Soviets held Prague, there had been an enormous monument to Joseph Stalin on the site, which dominated the skyline. Shortly after Stalin's death in 1953, Nikita Khrushchev, no great fan of Uncle Joe, ordered the seventeen-thousand-ton statue blown up. The site sat vacant until 1991, when Vratislav Novak designed and built a giant working metronome on the spot.

Today, Letna Park is a showcase for graffiti artists and skate-boarders.

Mimi and I watch the kids slide their boards along the railings and bounce them off the stone walls and down the steps.

"Did you ever try skateboarding?"

I had been on a board once. It hadn't been pretty. "Are those shoes?"

Hanging from a thick power cable that connects the metronome to a hydro pole are dozens of shoes, their laces tied together.

"Why would anyone do that?"

"Maybe it's a protest."

Mimi is unconvinced. "So, what are they protesting?"

"Or maybe it's like that bridge in Paris."

"The one with all the locks?"

A tour group has gathered around the metronome. About a dozen men and women clustered around a tall woman with a bright yellow umbrella. I can feel Mimi lean towards the sound of the tour guide's voice.

"English," Mimi says.

"Go ahead."

"You sure?"

"I'm going to sit down."

"Are you all right?" asks Mimi. "Not a problem with low blood sugar?"

I find a bench, and Mimi hurries off to do her dance with the tour. Chip pops out of a group of skateboarders. He's practising ollies and kickflips.

Hey, old man, he shouts as he swings by, *you should give this a try*.

Kitty and the twins stand behind a light standard. *Careful*, they call out to Chip. *You don't have a helmet.*

High-end watches? Eugene joins me on the bench. *Jesus, Birdman. What kind of pathetic asshole pays that kind of money for a watch?*

Mimi has joined the tour group and is doing her Ginger Rogers impersonation.

Chip tries a grind on the iron railing and crashes into a trash can.

Eugene shakes his head and starts to laugh. *You really want to be Two-Cent Jim?*

When they blew up the Stalin monument, says Kitty, *was anyone killed in the blast?*

Didi and Desi help Chip to his feet. He has scrapes on his elbow, and his pants are torn at the knees.

I ignore the demons and concentrate on the clouds hanging over the city. One of them looks like a bear, while another looks like a swarm of bees.

It's an allegory, says Eugene. *The greed of the wealthy and powerful. The impotence of the hoi polloi.*

"I know that," I tell Eugene.

All the Bees have is a stinger, and each time a Bee stings a Bear, the Bee dies.

Who dies? says Kitty.

There's only one way that the Bees win. Only one way they can hold the Bears at bay. Eugene rocks off the bench. *When you see your breakfast buddy, tell him he's full of shit.*

Anaphylactic shock, says Kitty. *It's terrible.*

Tell him the Bears will always win, says Eugene. *As long as Bees make honey, the Bears will come for it.*

I leave Eugene on the bench and wander over to the wall. Mimi has left the tour and is heading towards me.

"Good view," she says when she reaches my side.

A sharp wind rolls through the park and turns the air chilly.

"But I'm cold."

Mimi doesn't wait for me to offer. She snuggles up against me and jams her hands into my armpits. Her fingers are freezing, but I don't object or pull away.

"How was the tour?"

"The world looks peaceful from here," says Mimi.

"Most things look good from a distance."

"Are you sorry you didn't get that T-shirt?"

"A little."

Mimi gives me a squeeze. "What about the watch?"

"Didn't see one I liked."

Mimi stays where she is. "Watches and refugees," she says. "How is that possible?"

I hold Mimi and rub her back.

"And yet this is the world we've created."

We stand there, the two of us. The evening shadows have softened the land and turned the river silver. Soon, it will be dark, and all we'll be able to see are the lights of the city.

VIII

In the middle of the night, I go to the bathroom in the dark and feel my way to the front of the toilet. I've just begun my business when I'm startled by a moan.

Mimi is slumped next to the tub, clutching a towel.

"You okay?"

Another moan.

I feel her forehead. "You have a fever."

If either of us was going to get sick on the trip, I would have expected it would be me.

"The toilet," she says. "I think I'm going to throw up."

There are a number of things that men do better than women. Peeing is not one of them. For some reason, we're trained to do it standing up. Women sit, and there's nothing to say that men couldn't sit too.

"Don't throw up just yet."

I grab a washcloth and clean up the area around the toilet where being startled has left a bit of a mess. Which, technically, was not my fault.

"I'll get you some water."

I flush the toilet, rinse out the cloth, and let the tap run cold.

"Here," I tell Mimi, "you should drink some water."

Some people, when they get sick, are good patients, and some are not. But you can't tell by looking at a person. To look at Mimi, you would guess that she would be an agreeable patient, someone who would value the effort others make, someone who would appreciate a kindness.

"I don't want water."

"How about a cold compress?" I say, before I remember that the only washcloth is now unavailable.

Mimi lurches to a sitting position and crawls to the toilet. I step back into the bedroom, so she doesn't feel crowded while she retches.

I check the travel clock. Four thirty. Three hours before the breakfast room opens and I can get Mimi something to help settle her stomach.

I cast back over the evening meal. We had eaten at a restaurant where we sat at long tables with other people and shared plates of sausages and boiled cabbage. I want to blame the boiled cabbage, which came in large bowls and smelled like the boys' locker room at a high school, but we had eaten the same thing and I'm not sick.

"Little help in here."

I go as far as the doorway. "What do you need?"

"A pillow would be nice."

More retching.

When I was a kid, whenever I got sick, my mother would give me a glass of ginger ale and dry toast. I can't imagine that either had any medicinal properties.

Mimi is lying next to the toilet. I try not to look in the bowl.

"You can't sleep on the floor."

"Just get me a pillow."

I get a pillow and a blanket, make Mimi as comfortable as possible.

"Go back to bed," she tells me. "You can't do anything."

"I can be sympathetic."

Mimi turns on her side and buries her face in the pillow. "Why does the floor smell like urine?"

I lie on the bed, drift off every so often, but I don't go to sleep. I hear Mimi throw up a couple more times. I'm tempted to get out the guidebook to see if it lists the hospitals in the area.

But I don't.

Kitty paces the room. *You do not want to take her to a hospital in Prague.*

Eugene sits in the chair with his legs stretched out and his hat pulled down over his eyes.

They make a mistake, says Kitty, *and she could wind up in a coma.*

Atta boy, says Eugene, *just sit there and do nothing.*

I go to the suitcases and sort through the medical supplies that Mimi always brings along on a trip.

"We have Imodium," I call out.

I can hear Mimi change position on the bathroom floor. "That's for diarrhea."

"Acetaminophen?"

"For headaches."

I find a box with long, blue tubes. "Vagifem 10?"

"Gravol," says Mimi, her voice enhanced by the acoustics of the toilet bowl. "Find the Gravol."

Around seven, Mimi stops throwing up and the fever breaks. I help her back into bed.

"I'm feeling better," she says, but she doesn't mean it.

"I'm going to have to eat," I tell her. "How about I bring you back something?"

"Not hungry."

"Sure," I say. "Not now. But you will be."

"Before you go," says Mimi, "could you move the toilet closer to the bed?"

I'm early for breakfast. The room is closed, and there is no sign of activity. I'm debating waiting around or taking a quick constitutional on the Charles Bridge when Oz comes in the front door with a newspaper under his arm.

"There you are," he says with great delight.

"Here I am."

"And without your wife again."

"She's sick."

"Sick?"

"Stomach flu or something," I tell him. "She's getting better."

Oz nods. "Whenever I travel, I get sick. In Los Angeles I get sick. Also in Cape Town. And always in Mumbai."

"But not in Prague."

"Yes, of course in Prague, but not today." Oz gives me a wink. "It is the airplane. The bad air. You must travel by train."

"Or ship?"

"Yes," he says. "Or horse. Indians and horses. You are friends. This is true?"

I have a flash of Yellowstone and the two-hour ride from hell.

"May I join you for breakfast?"

I start to tell him that the room is not open yet, when I turn and discover that it is.

"And I have news," says Oz. "Not good. Not bad. There is a saying in English: 'No news is good news.' Is this a recommendation for ignorance?"

The breakfast room is empty. We're the first ones in, so we have our pick of tables. Oz chooses the one in the back corner.

"The best table." Oz sets the newspaper on the table. It's the

English edition of *The New York Times*. "From here you can see the world as it comes in."

The headline is about the US president and the conviction of another of his top aides.

"For lying to Congress." Oz smiles as he taps the paper. "As though this is a crime in politics."

I look over at the buffet and try to imagine what a sick person would like to eat.

"So, the news," says Oz. "I spoke with a friend who works at the National Museum. And yes, Wild West shows did come to Prague. There is a story, he says, of an Indian man who falls off a horse and is injured. My friend says that this Indian stays in Prague to recover from his injuries."

I feel a small surge of excitement. "Leroy Bull Shield?"

"Why not."

"But your friend doesn't know. Was there any mention of a medicine bundle?"

"This can be added to the story," says Oz.

"So, the man wasn't Leroy Bull Shield."

"Who can say," says Oz. "This is how it is with stories. What we wish to be true can be made to be true."

The items on the menu have changed, and I don't know what to order for my hot entree.

"Imagine," says Oz. "Uncle Leroy comes to Prague. And during the show, he is injured while attacking a wagon train."

"Injured?"

"A fall," says Oz. "He is placed in a hospital, where he recovers. Perhaps he is treated by a nurse, a beautiful Czech woman. They fall in love, marry, and move to Karlovy Vary, where is her family."

"Karlovy Vary?"

"This is to the west. Karlovy Vary is famous for its hot springs. There, in Karlovy Vary, our Indian is a celebrity."

The server comes by, and I let Oz order for the both of us. "They have three, no, four children and live happily ever after."

"Which is why he never comes home."

"Yes," says Oz. "That part is sad, but unavoidable."

"And the medicine bundle?"

"Ah," says Oz. "It is still with the family. The children have it, and each time it is opened, they remember their father."

"Grandfather."

"Yes, of course. Grandfather."

"Good story," I say.

"This is how realities begin," says Oz. "But first, we must tell a story again and again, until it can walk on its own."

"Even if it's not true."

"Adam and Eve," says Oz. "Supply-side economics. Weapons of mass destruction. Stories don't have to be true in order to prosper. A great lie can be a great success."

I get up and go to the buffet. Oz stays at the table and reads his paper. Making up a new medicine bundle to replace the old one is one thing. Making up a story about Uncle Leroy and his life after he left Canada is another.

The story Oz is suggesting is certainly plausible. Maybe Europe in the early 1900s wasn't as racist as the Canadian frontier. Maybe Leroy had come to understand that working in a Wild West show was better than living under the tyranny of church and state. Maybe never seeing his family again or the land he was born to was the price of freedom.

It would have been a high price.

Oz is waiting for me when I return. "Of course, there are other stories we could tell," he says. "Stories not so pleasant. Your uncle Leroy is a drunk. He gets into trouble with the law, and because he is a coward, he steals the medicine bundle and joins a Wild West show. In Europe, he is forced to sell the bundle for cash to support his drinking. In the end, he dies face down in a gutter in Pilsen."

"Pilsen?"

"It's on the way to Nuremberg." Oz wipes his fork on the napkin. "Which of these stories should we tell?"

"Maybe we don't need to make up a story."

"Ah," says Oz. "A mystery."

"Maybe there's nothing wrong with not knowing."

"The imagination always wants to know." Oz leans back and smiles. "This is why we have stories."

"And what's your story?"

"My story?"

"For instance," I say, "do you live here at the hotel?"

"No one lives at a hotel. One only rents a room."

"Okay," I say, pressing ahead, "then who are you?"

"Which story would you like?"

"How about the Bees and the Bears?"

"Ah," says Oz. "The Bees and the Bears. The Bees make the honey. The Bears destroy the hives of the Bees in order to take the honey. The Bees try to drive the Bears away to save their homes and food. What can be done?"

"The Bees have to organize."

"A union of Bees."

"The Bears are vulnerable," I point out. "Their noses are exposed. So are their eyes and ears."

"And each Bee who stings a Bear dies."

"Yes."

"And there is your answer," says Oz. "In order to bother the Bears, the Bees must be committed beyond expectations."

"This doesn't sound like much of a game."

Oz stands and buttons his jacket. "Please," he says, handing me the newspaper, "give this to your wife with my compliments. In it is a story about the refugees that she will enjoy."

« »

Oz is hardly out the door before Eugene helps himself to the vacant chair. I concentrate on my breakfast and try to ignore him.

He's right, Birdman, says Eugene. *If you're a Bee, you better be committed.*

The pastry is particularly good today. Cinnamon and apple.

But you're not committed, are you?

I may take one back for Mimi. If she can't eat it, I will.

You just talk a good fight. Eugene spreads out in the chair, his fingers interlocked behind his head.

I check the clock on the wall. Mimi hasn't come down, so I suppose that she's still in bed. I gather up the banana and the pastry and head to the room. Eugene stays behind.

Buzz, buzz, buzz, he shouts after me. *Writing-on-Stone? Lois Paul? How about we talk about Lois Paul?*

As I expected, Mimi is still in bed.

Kitty is sitting in the chair by the window, her face swollen from crying. *She's dying*.

I put the banana and the pastry on the table by the bed.

Kitty stares at the food. *Are you trying to kill her?*

I lean over and pat the lump that I guess is Mimi's butt. "You feeling any better?"

"Did you bring me anything to eat?"

"A banana."

Mimi rolls over and pokes her head out of the covers. "No pastry?"

"Don't know that you want to eat something like that."

Mimi sits up. "That looks like a pastry."

"You should probably start with the banana."

"Then you'll eat the pastry."

"No, I won't."

Mimi uses the sheet to wipe her nose. "Do you love me?"

Kitty turns to the wall. *He left you to die.*

"Yes," I say. "Very much."

"Then give me the pastry."

Mimi eats the pastry, and then she eats the banana. "Is that it?"

"I could get a pizza."

"Smart ass," says Mimi, and I can see that she is much better. "What's that?"

"What?"

"Under your arm."

I had forgotten about the newspaper.

"Is that a newspaper?"

"*New York Times.*"

"English?"

In addition to reading menus and historical markers, any kind of signage, Mimi loves reading newspapers. And not just the stories.

"Read it to me."

"It's a big paper."

Mimi scoots back under the covers. "I'm sick."

I catch Kitty's eye and hold it. "But you're not dying."

"Of course I'm not dying," says Mimi. "Start with the headlines."

Mimi commandeers all the pillows and blankets and makes herself a nest. I sit on the edge of the bed and read the paper.

Presidential adviser convicted of lying to Congress. Bank profits at all-time highs. Multinationals, the new face of organized crime. The iPhone everyone has to have.

Another school shooting in Florida.

"You're not skipping any stories, are you?"

"No."

"What about the real-estate ads?"

"You want me to read real-estate ads?"

Mimi snuggles down into the pillows. I'm hoping that she might offer me one, but she doesn't.

I read a story about the refugees from Syria, which shows the routes they take as they make their way to Germany, and another about a scientist in Japan who claims to have created an enzyme that will extend the shelf life of fish.

"I'll skip the sports?"

"Why?"

"You don't like sports."

"That's not true," says Mimi. "The scandals are pretty interesting."

The fashion section almost puts me to sleep.

"Let's do the obituaries," says Mimi. "Over-under."

Whenever Mimi gets her hands on a newspaper, she inevitably winds up at the obituaries, where she compares the ages of the people who have died with ours.

Over-under.

I work my way down the column. "Under, under, under, under . . ."

"That's four in a row, Bird."

"Here's another."

"Are we that old?"

"Here's an over."

Mimi sits up. "Are you okay?"

"Sure."

"Still thinking that you're going to die?"

Kitty pulls her feet up on the chair and raises her hand, as though she knows the answer to this question.

"You think about it." Mimi snuggles down under the covers. "I'm going to take a nap, and when I wake up, I'll expect an answer."

So we're in Prague, and it's late afternoon. Mimi wakes up from her nap, and now she is feeling better.

"I'm going to take a bath," she says. "A soak in the tub is always a good idea."

"Sure."

"You want to join me?"

"In the tub?"

"You know what happens when I have a slight fever."

"You get horny."

"Women get sensual," says Mimi. "Horny is what men get."

There's no profit in trying to argue this point.

"Are you horny?"

I fill the tub with hot water and sit on the toilet, while Mimi has a long soak.

"Why do you put a washcloth on your breasts?"

"So the girls don't get cold."

At intervals, Mimi works the faucet with her toes, so the water in the tub stays hot. I go back to reading the newspaper.

"There's a story about a new sock technology that is supposed to help circulation. The company claims that if you wear their socks, it will help with energy levels."

"Socks?"

"They're recommended for diabetics."

"Maybe you should try them, Bird."

"I don't need socks."

"The ones you have cut into your calves." Mimi rearranges the washcloth. "Every time you take off your socks, it looks as though someone has tried to strangle your legs. What else are the socks supposed to do?"

"Says they help with depression."

"Maybe the socks would save you from your demons."

At the top of the article is a small box that says "Paid Advertisement."

"It's not real," I say. "The company who makes the socks paid for the article."

"Ah," says Mimi, "the line between reality and fiction."

"There's a line?"

"Find the classifieds," says Mimi. "The classifieds are always fun, especially the personals."

I flip through the sections of the paper. Then I do it again. "Nope, no classifieds."

"What?"

"It looks as though *The New York Times* no longer has a classified section. Maybe it's only online."

"Well, that's disappointing." Mimi soaks the washcloth and puts it back on her breasts. "Then we'll just have to make up our own."

I fold the paper and set it down beside the toilet.

"Ravishing Blackfoot woman seeks virile Indigenous man," Mimi calls out from the tub. "Must have newer pickup and his own teeth. Steady employment a plus. Likes travel and adventure, pizza and hot dogs. Smoking and drinking are turnoffs."

Mimi paddles the water. Little ripples form and break against the sides of the tub. "Okay, your turn."

"I don't want a turn."

There's no food left from this morning, so I'll probably have to go out and find something to eat.

"What would yours sound like?"

"What?"

"Your personal ad," says Mimi. "If you put a personal ad in the paper, what would it say?"

"I wouldn't put a personal ad in the paper."

"None of us would," says Mimi, "but if you did . . ."

"I still wouldn't do it."

"Broken-down Cherokee photojournalist wishes to share his life with beautiful Blackfoot woman," says Mimi. "Or beat-to-shit Greek photojournalist wishes to share his life with beautiful Blackfoot woman. Which one do you like?"

"Broken down? Beat-to-shit? Really?"

"Okay. 'Senior.'"

"What's your point?"

"Here we are," says Mimi. "You on the toilet, me in a warm tub. This is life, Bird. This is our life. This is our life right now."

When Mimi gets out of the tub, she is all brown and wrinkly. It is not an attractive look, and while I enjoy her naked, I don't object when she gets into her clothes.

"Don't throw the paper out," she tells me.

"We've already read it."

"Nothing wrong with reading a newspaper twice," says Mimi. "You always miss something the first time through."

It's evening now, and I can feel my blood sugars beginning to drop. "I need to eat."

"What about me?" says Mimi. "I didn't have breakfast."

"You had a banana and that pastry."

"And I didn't have lunch, either."

The light has softened. In another hour or so, it will be dusk. If we go out now, I won't need my sunglasses.

"How are you feeling?"

"We're in Prague, Bird," says Mimi. "We didn't come all the way to Prague to stay in a hotel room."

"Oz thinks we should make up a story about Uncle Leroy."

"Make up a story?"

"Sure," I say. "We could tell your mother that we found out that Uncle Leroy was injured in an accident in Prague, that he met a woman, got married, had a bunch of children, and died a happy man."

Mimi looks skeptical. "Okay," she says. "So what happened?"

"What do you mean?"

"In this story. How was he injured?"

"He fell off a horse."

"What was his wife's name?"

"We'd have to make one up."

"Maybe you should ask this Oz," says Mimi. "Since it's his idea."

"I'm just telling you what he said."

"And why would we do this?"

Truth be told, we make up stories for all sorts of reasons. To protect ourselves. To feel superior. To deflect blame. To turn disaster into advantage. For no better reason than that we can.

"I'm not saying we should," I tell Mimi. "But it's an option."

"Lie to my mother?"

"You lie to her all the time. Remember the time when you—"

"I don't lie," says Mimi. "Sometimes I leave details out."

"Like the time you . . ."

Mimi sits up on the edge of the bed. I can see that she's thinking about getting up, but her face has an unhealthy tint to it, and her eyes don't sparkle.

"You okay?"

"Evidently not," she says and lies back down. "Maybe I'll just stay here."

"I can go out and get more food."

Mimi pulls the blankets over her body and curls up into a fetal position. "You know what I really want?"

"To go home?"

"Canned peaches," says Mimi. "I'd like some canned peaches."

"We could get canned peaches in Guelph."

"Did you think about what I asked?" Mimi peers at me from under the covers. "About dying?"

I stand and stretch.

"You're not dying, you know."

I stretch some more.

"And when you get back," says Mimi, "you can read the newspaper to me again."

IX

So we're in Prague.

The sky is dark, the city is aglow, the streets are busy with happy tourists. I wander around trying to think of what I can bring back to the hotel. Bananas should be easy enough to find. I'm not sure about the peaches, but I can always pick up a box of crackers.

White rice.

I don't know why I didn't think of this sooner. Invalids and white rice. Upset stomachs and white rice. Bland, bland, bland. And available at any Chinese restaurant in the world. If Uncle Leroy and the Crow bundle had been a Chinese restaurant, we would have found them years ago.

And I find one on a side street just before Old Town Square. It's a small place, brightly lit, with pictures of the available dishes on a sandwich board. In terms of quality, this is never a good sign, but there is little one can do to ruin white rice.

I'm reaching for the door when it flies open, hits me in the chest, and knocks me to the ground. I don't even know that I've fallen until I look up and see a woman standing over me.

"Oh my god!"

My head hurts, and my eyes don't want to focus. I've hit my head.

That much is clear. And my right hip aches. I move my hands. Then I move my legs. I don't think anything is broken.

"Are you all right?"

The woman is young. Not yet thirty. Dark hair. Brown eyes. Not White. Not Black. Sturdy. A handsome woman. Not pretty, though I doubt I would feel any better if I had been run over by a lingerie model.

A man comes out of the restaurant and closes in on the woman. "Jesus, Kal, what the hell did you do?"

"It was an accident," she tells him.

"Is he hurt?"

"It was an accident."

"Hey, old-timer." The young man bends down and squints at me. "You okay?"

I don't like him already.

"How many fingers?"

The woman helps me to my feet and starts brushing me off. "I am so sorry."

"It's okay," I tell her.

"See," says the young man. The accent is American. East Coast. "He's okay. No harm, no foul. Am I right?"

"I'm Kalea," says the woman. "Are you sure you're okay?"

"He's okay," says the man. "Come on back inside."

"Jesus, Bryce, show a little respect."

"Our food is going to get cold."

"I'm fine," I say. "Don't let your food get cold."

Kalea stands there with her hands on her hips, and for just a moment, she reminds me of Mimi.

"Please join us," she says.

"What? Come on, Kal!"

"I insist," says Kalea. "It's the least I can do. Please." And she holds out a hand.

« »

Kalea Tomaguchi and Bryce Osbourne. Kalea is Hawaiian and Japanese. Bryce is white-collar Boston. He's the third Bryce Osbourne, but doesn't use "Bryce Osbourne the Third," because it sounds stuffy and old-fashioned.

"My grandfather's era," he tells me.

"Blackbird Mavrias." I shake their hands in turn.

"Italian?" says Bryce.

"Mavrias is Greek," says Kalea. "Isn't it?"

"Greek and Cherokee," I say.

"See, Bryce," says Kalea, "all the best people are mixed bloods."

Bryce smiles and throws up his hands. "What?" he says. "Now it's a crime to be White?"

Kalea and Bryce have a table for four, so it's no problem to squeeze me in. All the staff have to do is bring a plate and utensils.

"I hope you like General Tsao chicken," says Kalea.

"Every time we do Chinese," says Bryce, "Kal orders that."

"And you always order the chow mein."

"We're predictable," says Bryce. "But we're also compatible."

"Maybe," says Kalea.

"Come on, Kal," says Bryce. "How many times do I have to say I'm sorry?"

Whatever the offence, it's easy to see that Kalea is not ready to forgive or forget. It's not a comfortable situation, but having been attacked, I discover that I'm hungry.

"We can order more if we need to," Kalea says.

"We still have dumplings coming," says Bryce. "And Sizzling Beef in Black Bean Sauce."

Kalea takes some of the General Tsao chicken. "Are you married, Mr. Mavrias?"

"Come on, Kal."

"I'm with someone."

"How long?"

I smile. "Longer than you've been alive, I'm afraid."

Kalea turns to Bryce. "You hear that, Bryce. That's the kind of relationship I want."

Bryce turns petulant. It happens quickly, as though there's a switch that he can throw at will. "Yeah," he says in a lilting sneer, "and just where is his wife?"

"At the hotel," I say. "I'm afraid she's sick."

"And you're getting medicine for her?"

"Kinda hard to do that when he's sitting eating with us," says Bryce.

"I figured I'd find her some white rice. Maybe a banana."

"That's sweet," says Kalea, and she reaches out and touches my hand.

NAOMI GALLANT.

Tally was five years old when Mimi and I broke up. No particular reason. Just a series of annoyances and frustrations, angry words and callous actions. We were young, full of ourselves, with no real sense of what it meant to live a life together. We were apart for about six months before we decided to try again, before we began working on our relationship with a firm purpose of amendment.

"A firm purpose of amendment." That was the crap phrase the Christian Brothers had taught me in parochial school. But it wasn't religion that kept us from drifting away.

It was our daughter.

At first we asked the question, what would she do without us? And when we had gotten that bit of egotism out of our system, we asked the more important question: what would we do without her?

But in that time, in those months out of sight, out of mind, I had had an affair.

Naomi Gallant.

WHEN KALEA TOUCHES my hand, she reminds me of Naomi Gallant. It is an unexpected memory. It is also pleasant, and I don't pull my hand away.

Bryce taps the table with his chopsticks. "Then I guess you better get going."

"Yes," I say, "I should."

"Not yet," says Kalea, and she squeezes my hand. "Maybe you can help us."

"Come on, Kalea," says Bryce, "we don't need the advice of some stranger."

"In all that time," says Kalea, "you must have learned a thing or two about love."

"You should ask Mimi about that."

"But I'm asking you."

Now I'm not so hungry. "Just take care of each other."

"You mean respect each other."

"Sure," I say. "That's always a good start."

Kalea turns to Bryce and waits.

"I respect you," he says, but he's too slow off the mark, and it sounds as though he has had to think about it.

"Doesn't feel that way much of the time."

"Who wanted to come to Prague? Did I say no?"

Kalea turns back to me. "Your wife is sick, and you go out to find her something to eat. That's love."

I shrug.

"And have you ever had an affair?"

Bryce's face turns red. "I told you I was sorry. Jesus, you don't need to tell the world."

Kalea keeps her eyes on me. "Have you?"

"No."

"When I asked Bryce," says Kalea, "he said the same thing."

"We agreed to put that behind us." Bryce slumps in the chair and crosses his arms on his chest. "It's not going to work if you keep bringing it up."

The server comes by, and I order white rice to go. I ask for some soy sauce as well in case Mimi is feeling much better and wants something to brighten an otherwise bland meal.

"And did your wife forgive you?"

"Yes," I say, "she did."

I MET NAOMI GALLANT when I was researching a fluff story on the resurgence of typewriters. A café on Toronto's east side had organized a "Type-In." Turned out the event was just a display of about thirty antique and vintage typewriters that you could look at and try.

If you were so inclined.

I didn't see the allure.

Sure, the machines from the mid-twentieth century were interesting to look at, but I couldn't imagine any of them competing with the ease and convenience of a computer keyboard. I had sat down in front of a light-green machine that looked a little like a sea turtle and was playing with the keys when she walked over.

"Naomi Gallant." And she held out a hand. "You have good taste," she said. "That's a Hermes 3000. 1963. Swiss-made. Iconic shape. Excellent typing action. You a collector?"

"No. Afraid not."

"You have a typewriter?"

"Had one."

"But you work on a computer now."

As soon as I told her I was doing a story on typewriters, she insisted on taking me around to each machine.

"This is an Olympia SM3. Beautiful machine. Great lines. Little heavy on the typing action because of the carriage shift. Olympia didn't switch to a basket shift until the SM9."

I tried taking notes, but Naomi didn't wait for me to catch up.

"Here's a Smith Corona Silent Super. It's one of the better machines they made. Hard to find one in mint condition."

"And this one's in mint condition?"

"And here's the one everyone wants."

The typewriter was a little on the squat side, as though it had been flattened by a press, and the keyboard stuck out like a mouthful of bad teeth. But it was the bright red colour that got your attention.

"The Olivetti Valentine. Designed by Ettore Sottsass and Perry King. Launched in 1969. It was a commercial flop. Iconic design, but technically mediocre. Terrible typing action. It came in white, green, and blue, but everyone wants the lipstick red."

Naomi took me to every machine in the café. Remington, Royal, Underwood, Voss, Oliver, Adler.

"L. Frank Baum, the guy who wrote *The Wonderful Wizard of Oz*, used a Smith Premier. Hemingway's favourite was a Royal Quiet Deluxe. Orson Welles used an Underwood."

Naomi was from Barbados, a small community called Pie Corner. The family had moved to Toronto when she was eight.

"Tom Hanks has a fine collection of typewriters," Naomi told me. "Started with a Hermes 2000."

Naomi rolled a sheet of paper into a yellow Olivetti Lettera 10 and typed a couple of lines. The sound of the keys striking the paper was surprisingly satisfying.

"I have a degree in business. Worked retail clothing for a while, but that didn't stick. Tried banking, and that was worse."

"So now you sell typewriters?"

"Buy them, fix them, sell them, collect them. I do it all. My business, my hours. The only downside is that I have to put up with a grumpy Black woman."

"I thought you worked alone."

Naomi had a great smile. "I do," she said.

Naomi invited me back to her workshop. I took notes, photographed the space, watched her remove the platen on a Halda.

And then she invited me to her apartment.

BRYCE ISN'T A patient man.

"I'm going back to the hotel," he says. "You can find me there."

I suspect that he's hoping that Kalea will follow him. But she doesn't. She sits at the table and waits, doesn't even look up.

"Is he gone?"

I nod. "He is."

"That must have been unpleasant for you."

"No problem."

"Bryce can be an ass without even trying," says Kalea. "He thinks because I love him that I'll put up with his crap."

My rice order arrives. The server has insulated the container with newspaper and put everything into a plastic bag.

Kalea pours the tea. "So, what's the difference between an affair and a one-night stand?"

I hold the cup in my hands, enjoying the warmth.

"I mean, is an affair something that goes on for months? And a one-night stand is just that? One night? One time?"

Mimi and I have had numerous discussions about sexual activity and contemporary mores. Is sex an "affair" if neither party is married or in a relationship at the time? If one of the parties is married, is the single person simply having sex, while the married person is having an affair? If you engage in a series of one-night stands, is this sexual freedom or promiscuity? Do such terms mean anything? Is it simply a matter of being committed or not, of being trustworthy or not, of being loyal or not? Where does polyamory fit into the conversation? Is sexual activity black and white or a decidedly foggy landscape?

Keeping in mind that in all cases, the same body parts are involved in much the same activity.

"So, Bryce had an affair?"

"He said it didn't mean anything." Kalea's eyes are dry. "If that's true, you have to wonder how the other woman felt. And if it didn't mean anything, why'd he do it? Men and women have to pee, but they don't necessarily have to have sex. You see what I mean?"

I touch the bag with the rice. It's still warm.

"So, he had an affair with one of my friends. I haven't talked to her, so I don't know the details. Were they in love? Was it just sport fucking? Are they still screwing around? Is there someone else I don't know about?"

"I really should be going."

"Your wife, right?"

"Don't want the rice to get cold."

"See. That's the difference between you and Bryce."

Kalea pays the bill. I walk with her to the street.

"Can I ask a favour?"

"Sure."

"Can you walk me back to my hotel? It's not far from here."

I can't say no, so I don't.

"Prague's a safe city. It's just that it's dark, and I'd feel safer if I had someone to walk with."

"Absolutely."

"You could give Bryce lessons."

It's none of my business, but I ask anyway. "Why do you stay with him?"

"He loves me. In his own way," says Kalea. "Besides, I think I'm pregnant."

"Ah."

"He doesn't know it yet. I was going to pick a romantic moment to tell him."

"As in dinner tonight?"

"Yes." Kalea starts laughing. "As in dinner tonight. That didn't go so well, did it?"

"Are you going to tell him when you get back?"

There's a trio of street musicians playing Leonard Cohen's "Hallelujah." Kalea stops to listen.

"I love that song. Did you ever see *West Side Story*?"

"That's Leonard Bernstein. Cohen's Canadian."

"Really? You're sure?"

"Positive."

"Well, it doesn't matter." Kalea takes my arm. "I still like the song."

We walk along a well-lit street that's alive with tourists. I wonder what the people who pass us think of this young woman and this old man. I try to straighten up as much as possible.

"Your back hurting you?" Kalea asks.

"No, I'm fine."

"I'm really sorry for knocking you down."

"Then we wouldn't have met."

Kalea slows down and stops. "This is my hotel. Thank you."

"Good luck with Bryce."

Kalea reaches into her jacket pocket. "Here," she says, "give this to your wife."

A purple tube with silver filigree.

"Perfume," says Kalea. "Bloomingdale's was giving away free samples."

"Bloomingdale's?"

"Manhattan. Bryce took me there to look at china and place settings. Do you guys have china and place settings?"

"No."

"It's been a wonderful evening." Kalea kisses me on the cheek. "Your wife is a lucky woman."

I find a small grocery and buy two bananas and a box of crackers that are supposed to be organic. I get a can of ginger ale as well. I look for canned peaches, but there's none to be found.

Eugene and the Other Demons are waiting for me when I come out of the store.

Pathetic, says Eugene. *Death and the Maiden. You look in the mirror lately?*

What if that Bryce had had a gun? says Kitty.

So, is this what old feels like? says Didi.

I don't think I like it, says Desi.

If that guy had made a move, says Chip, *they'd have been picking up pieces for the next week.*

You were thinking about it, weren't you? Eugene smiles and makes an obscene gesture.

This is why you should always carry a condom, says Kitty.

NAOMI AND I WERE together for the better part of a month. We'd meet at the St. Lawrence Market, wander yard sales and thrift stores looking for typewriters. Then we'd go back to her place.

"You and your wife going to get back together?" Naomi asked me one afternoon.

"Don't know."

"You think she still loves you?"

"Don't know."

"Then I suggest you ask her." Naomi had gotten out of bed and made coffee. "'Cause there isn't any 'us.'"

"Okay."

"You might try for a sentence of more than two words."

"You like your own space."

"Of course I like my own space. Everyone likes their own space."

That evening, Naomi walked me to the train station. When we got there, she handed me a black case.

"Something to remember me by," she said. "Talk to your wife. Give your little girl a hug."

I waited until I was on the train and it had pulled out of the station before I opened the case. An Olympia SM9 in mint condition. There was a note in the carriage. "Write Something Amazing," it said.

When I get to the room, Mimi is sitting up in bed, watching television.

"I can't understand a word they're saying, but you can tell from the action what's happening."

I take the rice out of the bag and open the ginger ale.

"It's the Syrian refugees." Mimi gestures at the screen. "They've left the train station in Budapest, and now they're trying to walk to Germany."

I find a small towel and use it as a plate for the crackers and the banana.

"Banana." Mimi gives me a smile. "Yum."

"I had a mishap."

Mimi hits the mute on the remote.

"No big deal. A woman knocked me down. By accident."

"Am I supposed to drag the story out of you, or are you just going to tell me?"

"It's a pretty good story," I say. "You can't tell a good story all at once."

"I'm sick," says Mimi. "I could die. I may not have time for the seven-day, winter-tipi version."

So, Mimi eats the rice and the banana. I help her with the crackers and the ginger ale.

"Aren't you the knight errant," Mimi says when I've finished the telling.

"Kalea reminded me a little of you."

"Which makes you Bryce?"

I hadn't thought of that, but now that Mimi says it out loud, I realize that Bryce and I have more in common than I'd like to admit. I try to remember what I was like at his age, and I don't like what I find.

"So, you met a young woman in a shaky relationship with a guy who's full of himself, and she's pregnant?"

"Maybe she's pregnant."

"Still, it doesn't sound good."

"We got through it."

"By then, we had already had a child," says Mimi. "That probably helped."

"What would you have told her?"

Mimi motions for me to lie down on the bed. I move the towel with the food and put my head on her lap.

"Too heavy?"

"No," she says. "So, what's really on your mind?"

I close my eyes. It's comfortable here. All things considered, I might just stay.

"Are you wondering how we got from there to here? From this Calley to me?"

"Kalea."

Mimi smiles and strokes my head. "And from this Bryce to you?"

Sometimes jokes cut deeper than the truth.

"Is this about that woman in Toronto? The one with the typewriters?"

MIMI AND I DIDN'T get back together all at once. It took the better part of a year to sort everything out and put the past behind us. She had spent the "lost time," as we called it, with family and friends. So far as I knew, she had not taken up with anyone, no affairs, no one-night stands, whatever the difference might be.

If there was a difference.

The typewriter I had in those early days had been an old Remington portable that I had dragged around the country with me. And then I had switched to a word processor, a computer with a keyboard that beat the typewriter hands down for efficiency but had all the charm of a sock.

Mimi had complimented me on my flexibility, had supported the technological move. She had even made a joke about the change. A dinosaur, she would begin, walks into the twentieth century.

But now that we were back together, here was another typewriter, a nicer typewriter than the Remington. A strange and unexpected typewriter. A typewriter that had appeared out of nowhere.

Mimi didn't take it head-on. She'd come into my office, ask me how the writing was going. She'd run a hand over the machine and wait for me to offer up an explanation. At first, I kept my mouth shut, pretended that the typewriter had been there all along.

I'm not sure why I thought the matter would end there. One day, she caught me over espresso.

That's not your old typewriter, is it?

No, I told her, it isn't.

So, you bought a new one?

To this point, I hadn't been lying. I was careful not to fall into that trap. But each time I sidestepped the question, it felt as though I was.

It was a gift, I told her. That was the truth. Not the whole truth. And she knew it.

A friend?

Yes.

Do I know him?

Shit.

And that had been that. That was as far as I could carry the story without the weight of it crushing me.

A woman, I told Mimi. Naomi Gallant. She fixes typewriters.

MIMI AND I LIE on the bed together. The spiders are gone. I figure that they're just out foraging and that they'll be back.

Mimi shifts her weight. "You want to do anything?"

"For instance?"

"A walk," she says. "I'm feeling better. The rice helped. So did the banana."

"You want to go for a walk? Now?"

"I've been in the room all day. Fresh air might be good for me."

"Or we could stay here."

Mimi plays with my ear. "You like it here, don't you."

I make the same sound that I make when Mimi bakes an apple pie and cuts me a large piece while it's still warm.

"Unfortunately," she says, "my bladder is full, and you're pressing on it."

I sit up and run a hand through my hair.

"Oh, Bird, your left eye is starting to swell again." Mimi touches my face. "Come on," she says, "let's get a cold compress on that."

The eye has not only swollen up, but now the white of the eye is red, as though I've suffered a hemorrhage when I wasn't looking. I stand in front of the mirror and pull the lid to one side.

Red everywhere.

"It's not eye cancer," says Mimi. "So don't go there."

I work on the eye with a cold towel. I'd prefer that the towel was warm, but Mimi insists that anything hot could encourage the swelling.

"Have you ever thought what your life would be like if you had made different choices?"

"Like what?"

"Everybody wonders about that. What if I had gone into law instead of fine art? What if I had stayed on the reserve? What if I had married Martin?"

"Martin?"

"Or Guido?"

"Guido?"

"They're just examples, Bird," says Mimi. "They're not real people. And I would have shot myself before I became a lawyer. But what if I had? How would my life be different?"

"Okay."

"What if your father hadn't deserted the family? What if he had stayed and moved everyone back to the reserve in Oklahoma?"

"In the States, it's reservations, and the Cherokee don't have one."

"Or if your grandfather had moved your grandmother and your mother back to that little village in Greece. Where would you be today?"

"In Greece, I guess."

"Come on, Bird, don't tell me you've never thought about the possibilities."

"I guess."

"That woman tonight. Kalea. When you were with her, did you wonder what might have happened if you were single?"

"I wasn't *with* her."

"Did she really remind you of me?" Mimi gets a piece of toilet paper and dabs the corner of my eye. "Or did she remind you of the typewriter woman in Toronto?"

There's no good answer to such questions, so I continue to look at my eye and feel sorry for myself.

"You never asked me what I did when we were apart."

"Nope."

"But you must have been curious."

I check my other eye in case the hemorrhage has spread.

"Or are you afraid to ask?"

"We're in Prague," I say. "We're in Prague, and we're together."

"Is that your final answer?"

"It is."

"You don't want to call a friend?"

Mimi gets her light jacket. It's not cold, but after the day she's had, it's probably smart to stay warm.

"I'm missing a day," she says. "I want it back."

"Hard to do."

"How about a partial replay. How about we start with the Chinese restaurant?"

"Where I got the rice?"

"Where you met Kalea."

"I didn't meet her," I say. "She knocked me down."

"And then we can walk over to the hotel where she's staying," says Mimi. "Who knows, maybe we'll run into her. We might even run into her guy."

"Bryce?"

"You think I'm weird?"

"A little."

"I'm curious to see how much this Bryce reminds me of you," says Mimi. "That's all. I'm just curious."

From time to time, Naomi would send me a typewritten letter, the kind of letter you might send to an acquaintance you hadn't talked to in a while. She would tell me about the machines she had found. Or she would allude to the growing number of young people who were becoming disenchanted with modern electronics.

Twice, she sent me invitations to a typewriter show she had organized. She never mentioned the time we had spent together.

What she said in her letters was always said from a distance.

I never wrote back. I don't think she expected that I would. Still, I liked getting the letters, liked running my fingers over the paper and feeling the impressions each key had made.

I found the Chinese restaurant, and I showed Mimi where I had been knocked down. I'm sorry I hadn't been cut. Finding dried blood on the pavement would have been dramatic.

And somewhat heroic.

I made one wrong turn, but I found the hotel.

"This is where she's staying?"

"This is it."

"Let's go in."

"Why?"

"I'd like to meet this woman."

"Are you upset with me?"

"Curious, curious, curious," Mimi says. "What's wrong with being curious? What was her last name? Tomaguchi. Right?"

There is no one registered under Kalea Tomaguchi.

"She's registered under Bryce's name," says Mimi. "That's disappointing."

"Yes, there's a Bryce Osbourne staying at the hotel," the desk clerk tells us. "Would you like me to ring the room?"

"What do you think?" Mimi turns to me. "Maybe she'd like to meet me."

I say, sure, why not, we have nothing better to do. Here we are in Prague looking for a dead Indian and a lost bundle, without a hope in the world of finding either. Bothering a young couple in the middle of a crisis is certainly more interesting than touring another church.

Mimi doesn't appreciate the sarcasm. "I think it would be nice to meet her. Then we'd have a story to tell, and so would they."

The desk clerk tries the room.

"I'm sorry," he says, "but there is no answer. Do you wish to leave a message?"

We wander around for a while. The evening is pleasant. The cloud cover has moved on, and the stars have come out to glisten in the night sky. Every time we pass a couple in the street or we see a man and a woman in a café, Mimi asks if it's Kalea and Bryce. I make the effort, but the truth is their faces have already faded away, and all I see, as we make our way back to the hotel, is a city of strangers.

When I wake up in the middle of the night to go to the bathroom, Eugene and the Other Demons are waiting for me. I stand by the toilet and ignore them.

And then the first cramp hits, and we all start screaming.

THE YEAR I GRADUATED from high school, I hitchhiked to Oklahoma to try to find my father. I didn't tell my mother, wasn't sure how she would feel about my chasing after a man who had left her hanging like laundry on a line. I didn't think she would be angry, but I was pretty sure she'd be hurt. So I told her that I had a job roofing A-frame chalets at South Shore, Lake Tahoe.

It wasn't a lie. I did have a job roofing chalets. It lasted two weeks, and by then I had enough money to get me to Oklahoma and back.

I had hitchhiked before. It was no big deal. Those days, everyone was on the move. Hobos, hippies, the unemployed, kids looking for an adventure. The on-ramps to the major highways looked like commuter bus stops.

My first ride was from Truckee to Reno. The guy who picked me up was on his way to a poker tournament in the Biggest Little City in the World.

You going to Oklahoma?

I am.

What the hell for?

It took me two days to get to Denver. Another day to Tulsa. Better part of a morning to Tahlequah.

I didn't know much about my father. My mother hadn't spent any time on the subject. Name, rank, serial number. He had been a soldier in the war. At one point, he had been stationed at Fort Sill, and with me in her arms and my brother in her belly, my mother had taken the train across the country to visit her husband. That was the one and only time he ever saw me, and I suppose it would have been the only time I ever saw him.

All that I knew about my father had come from my mother, and she had barely known the man.

"Where was he born?"

"Tahlequah," my mother told me, "but he was raised in a town called Clinton."

Tahlequah was a small town in the foothills of the Ozark Mountains. Clinton was one of the many dots along Highway 40.

"Did he have any brothers or sisters?"

"Couple of half-sisters. Why do you want to know?"

"No reason."

I figured that Tahlequah was going to be a bust, but I wanted to see where his life had begun.

And to make sure that he hadn't returned.

I started my search in a small café just off the main street with a copy of the *Stilwell Democrat Journal*. I read it cover to cover over coffee, a bowl of chicken vegetable soup, and a piece of butternut-squash pie.

The top news story was Lake Tenkiller and the determination by the US Army Corps engineers that fishing there had improved.

There was no mention of any Blackbirds in the paper. I was hoping that I might stumble upon relations left behind when his parents had moved out of the hills and onto the flats, aunts or uncles or cousins, extended family who might have been able to tell me if he was still alive and where he might be found.

I asked the guy at the register.

Blackbird?

Melvin Blackbird. Cherokee.

This here's the capital of the Cherokee Nation, the man said with a smile. Toss a rock.

Do you have a phone book?

Public phone in front of the drug store. How was the pie?

I found the booth and the book hanging from a chain. There was a handful of Blackbirds scattered around Tahlequah. I got a bunch of dimes and began calling the numbers.

I ran out of people before I ran out of dimes.

THE SCREAMING WAKES MIMI, and she rushes into the bathroom.

"Bird, it's two in the morning."

The inside of my right thigh feels as though someone is trying to tear tin off a roof.

"You're going to have to try to be a little quieter."

"I'm trying!"

"What if I rub your leg?"

"No!"

"If you keep screaming," says Mimi, "someone is going to call the police."

"Don't care!"

"Then we better get you into your underpants."

I'm bent over the sink, holding on to the edges, my knuckles white from the exertion, and Mimi starts singing "Ten Little Ducks," the song we sang to Nathan whenever he was upset.

Eugene and the Other Demons join in on the chorus.

When she gets down to three ducks, she stops. "Any better?"

The cramps are still coming in waves, but they're not as fierce now. "A little."

"Try singing," she says.

"I don't want to sing."

"Not even if it helps?"

I'm awash in sweat from the pain. Mimi gets a towel and drapes it over my back.

"Come on," she says, "*Three little ducks . . .*"

I STAYED IN TAHLEQUAH overnight, checked out some of the bars, with the same results. The next afternoon, I caught a ride to Oklahoma City, where I got stuck at an on-ramp for the rest of the day, until a guy in a station wagon picked me up.

A salesman. Floyd something. Auto parts.

"Where you headed?"

Clinton.

"Clinton?"

Clinton.

"Hell, son, nobody goes to Clinton 'cept peckerheads and salesmen. You got business there?"

Maybe.

"Hour thirty. More if I have to stop. Prostate. You wouldn't know about that."

Guess not.

"Atlanta to Las Vegas," Floyd told me. "If it's auto parts, my name's on it."

Floyd had a bottle of Old Fitzgerald in the glovebox, a carton of Camels on the back seat.

"Help yourself," he told me. "You work for a living or you just on the wander?"

Visiting family.

"Used to live down south in Ardmore. Second wife. Got kin all over the state. Turn over a stone, and there's a cousin."

We pulled off the interstate at El Reno. "Too bad we're not close to a Furr's. Salisbury steak, fried okra, lemon meringue pie. Damn."

Floyd drove into town and parked across the street from a small white stucco building with red awnings.

"Robert's Grill," he said. "You ever had an onion burger?"

The grill was stuck on a main corner. No interior to speak of. Counter seating only. We found a couple of stools where we could see the burgers being cooked.

I asked Floyd if he had ever run across a Melvin Blackbird.

"Your daddy? How'd you get Blackbird for a first name?"

The onion burger was pretty good. Floyd had a burger and a Coney dog with chili and slaw.

"Man's got to keep up his strength. You want to tag along and watch me work? Car parts ain't a bad career."

We got to Clinton after lunch.

"None of my business, but I'm not sure you chasing after your old man is all that smart."

Don't disagree.

"Lot of people do things for no good reason, but once they're done, well, that's it."

No good reason.

"Your old man could have come back. Women are always willing to make allowances. But he didn't."

No, he didn't.

"And what if you find him? What you going to do then? Man's going to be a stranger. And he could be a whole lot worse."

I thanked Floyd for the ride and for lunch.

"Long as you're in Clinton, you should see the big plastic Indian in front of Howe Motors. Can't miss it. Number one tourist attraction hereabouts."

So we're in Prague.

The cramps finally relent. I lie on the floor, exhausted, my leg jammed between the toilet and the wall to keep pressure on the muscle.

And I have no plans to move.

Mimi brings a blanket and a pillow. "I'm going back to sleep," she says. "Try not to wake me."

Kitty sits by the door, her arms wrapped around her knees. *Muscle cramps can be an indicator of debilitating diseases such as ALS and muscular dystrophy.*

How come we always wind up with the shit? says Chip.

What are you going to do when Mimi leaves you? says Kitty. *She's not going to want to live with a cripple.*

Eugene tries to look sympathetic. *Can't say you don't deserve it.*

The twins lie down beside me and take most of the blanket.

I don't get much sleep. The floor of the bathroom is hard. Each time I have to get up to pee, my leg threatens to seize up. I give up on sleep around seven. Mimi is on the bed in the aftermath of a crocodile death roll, the covers wrapped around her so tightly, it would take a chainsaw to cut her free.

"You awake?"

"No."

"It's time for breakfast."

"You go," she says. "I had a late night."

"You should meet Oz."

"I should sleep."

I find the lump in the covers that appears to be Mimi's head and kiss it. "They stop serving at nine thirty."

"Stay away from the pastries," she tells me. "You know what they do to your blood sugars."

FLOYD DROPPED ME OFF on South Fourth Street.

"What'd I tell you." Floyd tapped out a quick rhythm on the steering wheel. "Big sucker, ain't he?"

The Indian standing in the car lot was enormous.

"Back in the day, if you guys had looked like that," said Floyd, "things might have gone a lot different."

On the big Indian's belt was "Howe Motors." I didn't get the joke right away. And then I did. Indian. Howe. Howe. Indian. Not terribly funny, not terribly stupid. Something out of a high school yearbook.

Floyd pulled the car into gear. "Not much to the town," he said. "Follow this street, take a left at West Gary, and you'll wind up back at the highway."

I stood next to the big Indian and took in the town. My father had been six or so when the family had moved here from the green hill country of northeastern Oklahoma. Looking at the streets and the buildings, the cars and the people, I couldn't help but wonder what offence the Blackbirds had committed to have been banished to such a place. Maybe Clinton was where Adam and Eve had landed when they were thrown out of the garden.

Under the bright sun and fierce heat, the town felt as though it had been pulled hot from a forge and beaten flat on an anvil, the kind of place where people lived their lives in front of open refrigerators, and dogs melted on the sidewalks.

I didn't have anywhere to go, and I wasn't eager to brave the sunshine, so I waited in the shade of the big Indian until a woman in a lime-green Suburban shirt and dark brown slacks came out of the sales office.

"You look like you might could use a car."

The woman wasn't heavy-set, but neither was she small.

"Every one of these beauties has air conditioning. If they ain't got air, we don't sell 'em."

The heat had raised a heavy sweat and turned parts of her shirt transparent.

"And I can make you a sweet deal right now." The woman smiled and wiped her face with a handkerchief. "How about we talk inside? You like a soda?"

WHEN I GET to the breakfast room, Oz is sitting by himself, a globe of the world on the table in front of him.

"You are late." He holds out both wrists. "I thought perhaps you had gone back to Budapest."

"Why would I do that?"

"The refugees are the news," says Oz. "They are now exciting and possibly a tourist attraction."

I stare at the globe.

"For my granddaughter," says Oz. "She wants to know about the world. This is the safe way to do that."

"It's a nice globe."

"But erroneous," says Oz, "as is much of our knowledge of the world."

I sit down and gently turn the globe. I don't find the Czech Republic immediately.

"Mercator," says Oz, "Gall-Peters, Robinson, Winkel tripel, AuthaGraph. Do you have a favourite?"

I turn the globe some more and find Canada.

"This globe is a Mercator," says Oz. "1569. The Flemish cartographer Gerardus Mercator. Very popular. Unfortunately, it inaccurately increases the relative size of land masses the farther away you get from the equator."

The server comes by with coffee. Oz orders the egg special. I order the ham and cheese.

"This is why Greenland looks to be the same size as Africa, when in fact Africa is more than thirteen times larger." Oz rubs his hands together. "And Scandinavia. All of those countries are shown to be larger than India even though India is actually three times their size."

The globe has a small imperfection in the middle of Texas, and I wonder if it has been dropped or bumped.

"The most accurate map of the world is the AuthaGraph, invented by the Japanese architect Hajime Narukawa in 1999, which divides the planet into ninety-six triangles. This allows the land masses to be shown in their correct relationship to one another."

It could also be a used globe that Oz has picked up in a second-hand store.

"The Mercator method tends to accentuate the size of 'White' countries." Oz places a finger on Africa. "You can put all of the United States and China and India right here, along with Spain, France, Germany, and Italy with room to spare."

We don't have a globe at home, but I can imagine having one would be handy.

"So, you see, even a globe can be concerned with politics and race."

Oz gets to his feet and shuffles to the buffet. I follow him. We move along the line, helping ourselves.

"Your wife? She is feeling better?"

"I think so."

"But she is still asleep?"

I help myself to the sliced tomatoes and cucumbers.

"So, you will look again today for the uncle Leroy and the bundle?"

"How's your friend's game going?"

"The Bears are still winning," says Oz. "But the Bees are organizing."

THE WOMAN'S NAME was Bobbie Sherman Darnell.

"Bet you're surprised to find a woman selling cars."

I admitted that I was.

"Daddy owns the dealership," Bobbie told me. "My husband's normally here, but he's off playing golf with the boys, so I got the keys to the kingdom."

There were pictures on the wall of a large man in a football uniform, down in a three-point stance.

"That's my husband, Buddy. Played ball for the University of Oklahoma Sooners. He was on the team that beat Maryland twenty to six for the national championship in 1955." Bobbie grabbed two bottles from a small refrigerator in the corner. "Buddy never started. He played centre behind Jerry Tubbs. But coach let him in for a couple of plays towards the end of that game so it would be official."

It was cool in the sales office, the air conditioner going, the radio tuned to a local station that was playing Bill Haley's "Rock Around the Clock."

"Buddy don't care much for rock and roll. Hope you don't mind."

Clinton had a high school. It was on West Gary.

"I went there. Went to OU too. That's where Buddy and I met."

Over a cold RC, I told Bobbie I was looking for my father.

"Knew a Blackbird when Buddy and I were in Norman." Bobbie flipped through the phone book but didn't find any Blackbirds. "Doesn't mean your folks weren't here. People in Clinton come and go all the time."

The clock on the wall said four thirty. It was probably too late to stop in at the high school and look at the yearbooks. Next to the clock was a photograph of a young woman leaning over the hood of a car.

"That was me. I was going to pack my bags. Jump on the interstate. Drive off into a Saturday-matinee future. But then Buddy showed up and the girls came along and that was that."

I figured I'd eat before I left town. With any luck, I'd catch a ride before it got too dark and make Albuquerque by morning.

Bobbie tapped her empty bottle on the desk. "So you're Cherokee and Greek," she said. "How's that working out for you?"

OZ PILES HIS FOOD around the globe. "All over the world," he says, cutting into his omelette, "people are starving."

The part of the globe that is facing me shows Europe and Africa. Greece is in the centre. I can't see Evia, but I know it's there. I'm sure that Syria is in the same neighbourhood, but I can't find it.

"The Kingdom Trio," says Oz. "Do you know these singers? They sing about riots in Africa and starving in Spain."

"Kingston Trio."

"Yes," says Oz. "The world festering with angry souls."

"Unhappy souls."

"Did you find Syria?" Oz spins the globe back a little. "Here," he says. "Below Turkey."

Seeing Syria on the globe doesn't help. "So, they come through Turkey?"

"Yes," says Oz. "Sometimes they stay. But most take boats to Greece."

"Boats?"

"Bodrum to Kos. Very dangerous. Not enough boats, always the problem of sinking."

"Greece isn't very close to Hungary."

"Then they must walk or perhaps a bus, if they can afford it. Germany is the number-one place. Also, Sweden."

Between Greece and Hungary are a number of small countries I know nothing about. Macedonia, Bulgaria, Albania, Kosovo, Montenegro, Serbia, Croatia, Romania.

"Who knows how they get to Budapest." Oz shrugs. "Many don't. And now Hungary has shut the doors."

"The trains still aren't running?"

I have no eye for distances, but Syria to Greece must be over a thousand kilometres. From Athens to Budapest looks to be even farther. Walking to Germany seems improbable. Sweden impossible.

"We have seen the refugees," says Oz, raising his glass of orange juice in a toast, "and they are not us."

I HAD DINNER in Clinton at a small café that was attached to a service station. The waitress was an older woman with hair that reminded me of a mouthful of hay and a limp that threw her from side to side. The badge on her uniform said "Gladys."

I ordered the burger and a milkshake. "You know any Blackbirds here in town?"

"Indian?"

"Cherokee."

"Little far west for that. You tend to find them folks around Tahlequah and Muskogee. You headed east?"

"West."

"Come through Oklahoma City?"

"I did."

Gladys filled my cup. "Don't go to the City anymore," she said. "Too many coloureds for comfort sake."

The milkshake was thick. The burger was overcooked, and the fries tasted as though they had been boiled in crankcase oil. I was tempted to suggest that Gladys might try rubbing a french fry on her bad hip.

"And when you get to Texas, make sure you keep going. Friend of mine had a car break down in Amarillo, and she's still there."

I had a piece of apple pie for dessert. Scoop of vanilla ice cream. It wasn't any better than the fries. I drank more coffee, watched the cars go by on West Gary, read a local advertiser that offered everything from end-of-the-year discounts on trailers to water-well drilling. Howe Motors had a big ad on page three.

Gladys was waiting at the register.

"If you get to Gallup," she said as she rang up the bill, "be sure to stop in at Earl's. North side of the road by the tracks. Not much to look at, and it's run by a bunch of Navajos. But the food's jake."

It was getting on evening when I stepped out of the café and started walking to the interstate. The air had cooled. It wasn't comfortable, but it gave you hope that the world wasn't going to go up in flames anytime soon.

I had gotten a couple of blocks when a white Cadillac sedan pulled over to the curb. And I hadn't even put my thumb out.

"Hey, there."

Bobbie Sherman Darnell.

I squatted down next to the open window.

"How was the food?"

"Don't order the fries or the pie."

Bobbie laughed. "I should have warned you. But they got good milkshakes."

"Nice car."

"Perks of the job," she said. "I can drive anything I can stick a key in."

"So, you're done for the day?"

"Off to get Buddy," said Bobbie. "He's out at the club."

"Golfing, right?"

"More like bullshitting and drinking. Probably reliving the high school state championship again."

The light was dropping. I liked talking to Bobbie, but I needed to get to an on-ramp with enough light left for people to be able to see me.

"Buddy don't realize it yet," she said, "but for him, high school is as good as it's ever going to get."

"You know how far it is to Gallup?"

"I'd give you a ride, but there's not much point." Bobbie smiled and turned the radio up. "Runaway" by Del Shannon. "You're going somewhere, and I'm not."

IT'S AFTER NINE, and Mimi has yet to make an appearance.

"Today, in *The New York Times*," says Oz, "there is an article on Prague."

I'm still working the globe, trying to see how the refugees might get from Syria to Sweden.

"'Behind Dilapidated Doors Lies a Secret Prague,'" says Oz. "This is the title of the article. Very provocative."

"Secret Prague?"

"Old buildings," says Oz. "The artists of Prague are taking over abandoned factories, electrical substations, military barracks. Quite exciting."

"If you're a Prague artist."

"Exactly," says Oz. "But not so exciting if you're a tourist. Tourists like to go to the places other tourists go. The Eiffel Tower. Piccadilly Circus. The Great Wall of China. Disney World. Then when tourists talk to each other, they have much in common."

Oz closes his eyes and leans back in the chair.

"Of course, many tourists do not want to be tourists. They wish to slip away and find the hidden gems." Oz closes his eyes. "But this is not practical. I have a friend who went to Bottovo. With whom can he share this experience?"

"So, these places in Prague are . . . dangerous?"

"Paris is dangerous. Berlin is dangerous. Naples is very dangerous. Artists are always dangerous."

"Metaphorically speaking."

"This is why we kill artists before we kill lawyers."

"So we should stay on the Charles Bridge?"

"Only if you are tourists." Oz takes out his cellphone and taps the screen. "Your last story was to be in three parts. About the social-service system in Canada and how it took Indian children away from their parents."

I turn the globe so I can see Japan.

"But only the first part was published."

I'm surprised just how long and thin the country is.

"And now you are hiding in Prague."

"I'm on vacation."

"But your home is Canada. At some point, you will have to go home."

"Probably."

"And then what will you do?"

This is the question Mimi has asked me any number of times.

"If you don't write, what will you do?"

I could feel myself being backed into a corner. "What about you?"

Oz put a hand to his chest. "Me?"

"Sure," I say, coming off the ropes. "Who are you? What are you doing in Prague? And this game. Bears and Bees. If the Bears always win, what's the point of playing?"

Oz stops fiddling with the globe. "Is this an interview? Am I to be a story?"

Sitting in the breakfast room, arguing with Oz, is not what I should be doing.

"How exciting."

I should be gathering food and taking it to Mimi.

"You will ask questions, and I will answer them, yes or no. Later, you can take my picture."

"This isn't an interview."

"Sometimes, when we ask questions about others," says Oz, "we reveal something about ourselves."

"And I'm not doing a story."

"Of course, the problem with questions," Oz says with a smile, "is that we often ask the wrong ones."

I DIDN'T CATCH a ride out of Clinton until late, and I wound up spending most of that night at a gas station in Groom, Texas. Early morning, a guy in a minivan took me as far as Bernalillo. From there, I got to Farmington, on to Salt Lake, and then dead west across Nevada and the mountains.

Four days out to Oklahoma. Five days back. And in all that time, I hadn't learned a thing about my father.

I didn't tell my mother where I had been, what I had done.

Roofing pay well? she had asked.

Well enough.

You going to do more roofing?

Probably not.

Any thoughts on what you might want to do with your life?

A few.

Don't wait too long.

I won't.

That fall, I enrolled at a junior college, in their journalism program. And I never looked for my father again.

OZ CUPS A HAND around his mouth. "I will give you hints," he whispers. "Ready?"

It's Mimi's fault. If she wasn't in bed, I wouldn't be sitting at a table playing twenty questions with a man with different-coloured eyes and a watch on each wrist.

"Heterochromia." Oz blinks his eyes a couple of times to get my attention. "This is why I have one blue eye and one gold eye. It is genetic. You might think that this curiosity has a geographical centre, but it does not. This will save you a question."

I didn't come all the way to Prague to play games.

"Neither are the two watches cultural." Oz holds his wrists out. "They are not worn for social or religious reasons. This will save you another question."

Of course, we're not going to do anything or go anywhere until Mimi gets out of bed.

"You could ask me if Czech is my first language."

"Is Czech like German?"

"No. And Czech is not my first language. See. I've given you two answers for one question."

I check the doorway for Mimi.

Oz glances at his watches. "But it's late. I have an appointment." Oz picks up the globe. "Tomorrow," he says. "We must continue tomorrow."

"Tomorrow?"

"Of course," says Oz. "How else will we get the answers if we don't ask the questions?"

XI

As I let myself into our hotel room, I wonder, not for the first time, why I spend my time chasing after men who are missing or dead.

My father.

My grandfather.

Leroy Bull Shield.

My mother died just after Nathan was born, but Mimi's mother is still alive. We don't visit her much. We talk to her on the phone, but only when the guilt becomes uncomfortable.

And we have a daughter and a son who deserve our attention, even if they don't want it.

I know that Eugene has an opinion on such matters, but I'm able to unlock the door, slip through, and leave him in the hall by himself to talk to the walls.

"Honey," I call out, "I'm home."

I expect to find Mimi still in bed, wrapped up in the sheets and the blankets like a giant burrito, but instead, she's sitting in the chair with her sketch pad.

I know better than to disturb her when she's working, so I sit on the edge of the bed and wait. She doesn't like me looking over her shoulder, but I look anyway. Outside, on the bridge, the day is bright and cheery. The sky is blue with wispy clouds. Even the river looks pleased with itself.

But on Mimi's pad, the day has become night, black and oppressive. Instead of the crush of tourists, Mimi has drawn a solitary figure slumped against a stone wall, shoulders hunched, face turned away from the light.

Mimi normally paints water, so this image is somewhat disturbing.

"Is that me?"

Mimi doesn't look up from the drawing. "Do you want it to be?"

"I like it."

"Maybe it's Eugene."

"Eugene?"

Mimi uses a charcoal stick to turn the background a black velvet. "I'm feeling better."

"Good." I take the perfume tube out of my pocket and hold it out. "You might like this."

Mimi turns the tube over in her hand. "Perfume?"

"From Bloomingdale's in New York."

Mimi waits.

"The woman who knocked me down, she gave it to me to give to you. I think it was her way of thanking me for walking her back to her hotel."

"My hero," says Mimi. "And now my hero can feed me."

"You're hungry?"

"I'm hungry."

"The breakfast room is closed."

"I know." Mimi puts the pad to one side.

I gesture to the pad. "What about Eugene?"

Mimi slips into her shoes. "He's not going anywhere."

« »

Mimi is down the stairs and out the door, and I have to hurry to keep pace with her. She strides up the street, takes a left and then a right, trots through a small square without even looking at the crazy statue made up of parts of a horse, a table, and a granite column. On top of the column is the bust of someone most likely famous, but Mimi picks up speed at this point, and I don't have time to read the plaque.

Nor do I have the inclination.

A few more turns before she comes to a stop.

"Let's eat here," she says.

"Is this a guidebook recommendation?"

Mimi pushes her way through the doors and strides up to a woman holding menus. "A large table by the window. We may have friends joining us."

The woman guides us through a large, open room.

"Friends?"

Mimi takes a seat with her back to the wall. "I like to have space when I eat."

"You know that this is a hotel restaurant," I say. "And that the menu has photographs of the food?"

The restaurant is nice enough. Dark wood and stone, an ambience that splits the difference between a Gothic church and a medieval dungeon.

"Did someone tell you that the food here is good?"

The breakfast selections are proudly North American. Cholesterol rich and deep-fried yummy.

Two eggs any style, potatoes, bacon, and toast pledging allegiance. Pancakes with maple syrup and sausage humming an anthem. Eggs Benedict with ham waving a flag.

This is the kind of restaurant we try to avoid, the kind of restaurant that gives travel a bad name.

"Are you feeling okay?"

"Why don't you get the eggs Benny?"

"I hate eggs Benny."

"That way, I can have some of your food."

The place gets crowded fast. Men in shorts and polos. Women in sundresses and sandals. Children in branded T-shirts and running shoes.

"Tourists," I whisper to Mimi. "We're in a tourist petting zoo."

"We're tourists."

Mimi orders a side of toast and a fruit cup.

"I thought you were hungry."

Mimi watches a young couple as they weave their way through the restaurant, looking for a table.

"Is that her?"

"What?"

"The woman who knocked you down."

"What?"

"Last night. At the Chinese restaurant. The one you walked back to her hotel."

It takes a moment for me to catch up to Mimi.

"That's this hotel?"

"What was her name?"

"Can you spell 'stalking'?"

Mimi slow-eats her toast and picks at her fruit cup. "Don't eat too fast," she tells me. "We're on vacation. There's no need to rush."

I can't believe that Mimi has dragged me here on the off chance that we might bump into Kalea and Bryce.

"You know what the odds are?"

"What about those two?"

I'm nursing a piece of apple pie that Mimi has ordered for me when Kalea Tomaguchi and Bryce Osbourne appear.

"That's them," Mimi says with no hesitation, "isn't it."

According to one of the postcards, Captain Trueblood's Wild West Emporium had made a swing through the Netherlands, Sweden, and Norway. The card that Uncle Leroy sent home from Amsterdam showed a windmill and several low-slung barges tied up to a dock.

Weather cold, it said. How are you?

We went to Amsterdam the year after we went to Paris. Mimi had found an article that mentioned a pipe museum on Prinsengracht that had an American Indian pipe in its collection.

"Don Duco," Mimi told me. "He found a bunch of antique pipes while he was doing renovation work, and the hobby just got out of hand."

"Eight euros to see a bunch of pipes?"

"They have an American Indian pipe," Mimi told me with authority, "so maybe they have the Crow bundle as well."

The museum wasn't all that large, but then pipes don't take up much room. And the collection was pretty impressive.

"I wonder why there's no information on the pipes." Mimi wandered the display cases looking for some sort of signage. "Be handy to know the history."

There was a display of elaborate pipes that looked as though they had been created by Hieronymus Bosch, and a series of French pipes with people's faces carved into the bowls.

"That's a Maori pipe from New Zealand." Mimi pointed to one of the cases. "And over there are opium pipes from China. You find the American Indian pipe yet?"

As it turned out, the museum had more than one pipe from the Americas. There was an argillite pipe from Haida Gwaii and a pipestone calumet from the Great Lakes.

We wandered through the rest of the museum, and then we went downstairs to the pipe and tobacco store.

"How about I buy you a pipe, Bird? You wouldn't have to smoke it.

You could just stick it in your mouth and look distinguished."

I tried to imagine myself packing the bowl of a pipe with tobacco, tried to imagine the clouds of choking smoke, tried to imagine the stink on my clothes and the bad taste it would leave in my mouth.

Then again, looking distinguished wasn't to be underestimated.

"Well," said Mimi as we climbed the stairs to street level, "no luck with the bundle, but we know more about pipes than we did before."

MIMI DOESN'T WAIT for an answer. She's out of her seat and waving at Kalea as though they're old friends. Kalea waves back tentatively. And then she sees me.

I close my eyes and wait.

"Mr. Mavrias."

I open my eyes.

"I can't believe it," Kalea says. "What are the odds?"

"Yeah," says Bryce, "what are the odds."

"Join us, please."

All the tables are taken. Bryce looks anyway. He has my sympathies. I wouldn't want to share a table with a couple of strangers.

"I'm Mimi Bull Shield." Mimi helps herself to my pie. "And you already know my partner, Blackbird Mavrias."

"Bull Shield and Mavrias?" says Kalea. "See, Bryce. Lots of women keep their own names."

Mimi turns towards Bryce like a shark who has just caught the scent of blood in the water.

"Kalea Tomaguchi," says Kalea. "And this is Bryce Osbourne."

"Bird has told me so much about you."

Kalea blushes. "I suppose he told you how I knocked him down."

Mimi smiles. "He was embarrassed."

Kalea sits next to Mimi. Bryce stays standing, hoping that a table will come free.

"We were at this restaurant."

"Chinese."

"Yeah, Chinese. Bryce and I were having an argument."

Bryce sits down quickly. "Pretty dull stuff. I don't think they want to hear it."

"We don't mind," says Mimi, "do we, Bird?"

I keep my head down and try to protect my pie with an elbow.

"We're getting married in the fall, and there are so many things to decide. Bryce wants a destination wedding in Costa Rica, and I'd rather save the money and have a simple ceremony in my parents' backyard."

"That's not a wedding, honey," says Bryce. "That's a barbecue."

"And he wants me to take his last name."

"Kalea Osbourne," says Bryce. "It's a great name."

"But then all our children would be named Osbourne."

That pretty much kills the conversation. There's no way I'm going to be the first to say anything.

"Do you have children?" Kalea asks.

"Two," says Mimi.

"How did you handle the last names?"

"Bull Shield," says Mimi with no apology in her voice. "I did all the work."

Bryce grunts. "Is that like an Indian tradition?"

"I like it," says Kalea.

"So, you argued," says Mimi, not one to be deterred by a grunt.

"We did," says Kalea. "And then I got angry and left the restaurant in a rush, and that's when I hit your husband with the door."

"Don't worry," says Mimi. "He didn't mind."

"He was very kind to walk me back to the hotel."

Mimi glares at Bryce. I'm used to her glares. Still, I feel my body tense.

"But after I got back, he apologized." Kalea smiles across the table at Bryce. "And we made up."

"Did we ever."

"Bryce!"

"I'm going to the bathroom," says Mimi. "You want to come?"

"Sure," says Kalea.

Bryce and I sit at the table and try not to look at each other. "You know why women do that?"

"Go to the bathroom together?"

"Yeah."

"Besides the obvious."

"Is it so they can talk about us?"

"Probably."

"You don't mind your kids having her last name?"

This is not the first time I've been asked this question. "Bull Shield. It's a good name. It has a long history among the Blackfoot."

"But you're Mathias."

"Mavrias," I say. "It's my mother's name."

"Not your father's?"

"Nope. My father's name was Blackbird."

"That's your first name."

"It is."

"So, you have your mother's last name, and your kids have their mother's last name?" Bryce shakes his head. "My parents are never going to go for something like that. You got any advice?"

"On how to change Kalea's mind?"

"Yeah," says Bryce. "I really want to go to Costa Rica."

Besides pipes, a couple of major art museums, the hotel where Chet Baker died, and the remarkable maze of canals, Amsterdam is known for its public brothels. De Wallen is the most famous of the red-light districts in the city, and after dinner at an Asian restaurant, Mimi decided that we needed to walk around the area.

"There's a bronze sculpture that shows a hand fondling a breast." Mimi pointed to the top of an ornate spire in the distance. "It's near the Old Church."

"A hand fondling a breast?"

"And there's a statue celebrating sex workers of the world in the same area."

"Near a church?"

"Sure," said Mimi. "Sex and religion? A match made in heaven."

We had to hunt to find the sculpture. It was set in the ground, small and somewhat creepy, as though there was a woman buried under the cobblestones with only one breast showing, while a hand reached out from the grave to fondle the nipple.

"My mother," said Mimi, "is going to be sorry she missed this."

The statue was equally problematic. A full-length female figure standing on steps, looking back through an arch.

"She's supposed to be standing in a doorway."

"Is that what that is?"

"Belle," Mimi told me. "Her name is Belle."

The statue was roughly rendered, as though the artist had finished off the piece with hot metal lumps thrown against the woman and hammered into place. Large breasts, heavy hips. Belle was wearing pants and a tight top of some sort. She had her hair twisted up into a tight bun and was staring off into the distance.

If it weren't for the guidebook, I might have thought that Belle was standing on a gallows, waiting for a rope.

Instead of a prostitute waiting for a customer.

"Sex worker," Mimi corrected me. "They prefer the term 'sex workers.'"

Mimi had me take a picture of her standing in solidarity with Belle, and then Mimi took a picture of me with Belle.

"Try to look happy, Bird."

"I am happy."

"There's supposed to be a place around here where the women talk about the profession. Sort of a lecture. We should go. Might be something you can use for the book."

"Pass."

"Have you ever thought about it?"

"The book?"

"No," said Mimi. "Having sex with a prostitute."

"Didn't you want to find Trumpeter Alley?"

"Don't change the subject."

"The narrowest alley in Amsterdam? Only a metre wide? I'd like to see that."

Mimi stood next to Belle with her hands on her hips. "So, have you ever been with a sex worker?"

"Mimi . . ."

"Do you know the percentage of men who have been with sex workers?"

"Mimi . . ."

"Let's go see the brothels." Mimi tucked the guidebook into her pack and took my hand. "Don't worry," she said. "I'll keep you safe."

THE WOMEN DON'T RETURN right away, and when a table opens up at the far side of the restaurant, Bryce is quick to grab it.

"Where's Bryce?" says Mimi.

"Table," I say. "Over there."

"I should probably go," says Kalea.

"He does look lost," says Mimi.

Kalea smiles. "And I'm hungry."

"Don't forget what I said."

« »

Mimi watches Kalea cross the restaurant. I tap my fork against my glass to get her attention.

"Okay, what was that all about?"

"What?"

"You know."

"Have some more coffee, Bird."

"I don't want any more coffee. Why did we come here? And what did you say to her?"

"You really want to know?"

Of course I don't want to know. I'm not even sure why I asked, but it's too late now.

"When we saw the refugees in Budapest, did you want to help them?"

"Sure."

"But we couldn't, could we? We don't speak the language. We had no idea what we could do, what could be done. We were helpless."

"Okay."

"Did that feel good? Were you proud of yourself?"

"Mimi . . ."

"But with Kalea, I can do something. I can help."

"Mimi . . ."

"Or I can mind my own business. Is that what you're about to tell me?"

"You don't know her."

"I know she has a boyfriend that she's about to marry. I know she's not sure that she loves him. Last night, you told me that she thought she was pregnant. Do you know what that's like for a woman?"

"No."

"No is the correct answer." Mimi takes a forkful of my pie. "So, she's not pregnant. After they had sex last night, her period started."

"That's good, right?"

"Yes, that's good. It means she has a chance to reconsider her decision."

"To marry Bryce."

"Would you want to be married to Bryce?"

Across the restaurant, Kalea and Bryce are locked in conversation. Kalea is sitting upright in her chair. Bryce is slumped over his food. Neither of them is looking happy, but I'm too far away to be sure.

"You told her to dump Bryce?"

"Not exactly."

The groan escapes before I can stop it. "You didn't tell her the story about fishing?"

"Maybe."

"The one your mother tells. Just because you catch a fish doesn't mean you have to keep it? That story?"

Mimi shrugs.

"I'm going to get another piece of pie."

"You've already had one."

"You ate most of it."

"If she were your daughter," says Mimi, "what story would you have told her?

So WE STROLLED UP and down several streets in Amsterdam with names neither of us could pronounce. The evening light played off the canals, while women in bikinis swayed back and forth in windowfronts.

"You think Uncle Leroy would have visited a sex worker?"

A group of young men came down the street, drunk, laughing, egging each other on. They stopped in front of various windows and stared at the women, and the women stared back. One of the men took a photo with his cellphone, and as he turned away to show it to his buddies, the woman flew out of her room, grabbed the cellphone, and threw it in the canal.

Mimi whacked my shoulder. "Did you see that?"

At first, the man stood there, stunned. The woman went back into her room, shut the door, and pulled the curtain.

"Way to go!" Mimi whispered, loud enough for the men to hear.

Not that they were listening. The man who had lost his phone started shouting in a language other than English, but it wasn't hard to figure out what he was saying. He went to the door and began pounding on it, until he was dragged away by his friends.

Mimi snuggled up against me. "So which woman would you want to have sex with?"

"You."

"Sweet, but you have to pick one."

"No, I don't."

"I don't mean for real," said Mimi. "Think of it as though you're looking at a painting. Some people like realism. Some like abstract. How about I go first."

"How about we go back to the hotel."

"See the dark-haired woman in the white bikini?"

"Mimi . . ."

"She's cute."

"Mimi . . ."

"And I really like the bikini."

Mimi dragged me up and down several more streets, stopping every so often in front of the lighted windows.

"Okay," I said at last. "The blonde."

"The one in the panties and the halter top?"

"Yes."

"Really, Bird?" said Mimi. "A blonde?"

IT'S ALMOST ONE by the time Mimi and I step out of the hotel restaurant and into the sunshine of a beautiful Prague day.

Mimi pulls out her guidebook. "So now," she says, "we have our choice of the Prague Zoo or Stromovka Park."

My stomach is somewhat upset, and my body is beginning to ache, as though there's a fever in my immediate future.

"I thought we had decided against zoos."

I don't think it's anything serious, but I wonder if I might be getting what Mimi had.

Kitty takes a step backwards. *Is it contagious?* she asks.

"Prague is supposed to have one of the best zoos in the world," says Mimi.

"That's not a recommendation."

"Then let's go to Stromovka. It's the largest park in the city. We just have to find tram 91."

"You know, we have parks in Guelph."

"When was the last time we went to Riverside Park?"

"And we could walk the river from Victoria past the Boathouse and all the way to the Hanlon."

"Stromovka has a duck pond."

"The Speed is lousy with geese," I say. "And every spring, we get to see the goslings."

"We're not in Guelph." Mimi's voice is low and sad. "We're in Prague."

Normally, Mimi is able to manage my depressions and bad moods. But every so often, I wear her down.

"Would it be easier for you if we weren't together?"

I shake my head, but Eugene is already on the job.

Way to go, champ, he whispers.

"Is that what this is about?"

I tell Mimi I'm sorry, that I'm not feeling all that well, that I'm tired, that I'm not comfortable in foreign places, that I don't do well when I'm not at home. These are excuses that I've used so many times, they feel like amiable ruts in a hard road.

"Are you unhappy with me?" says Mimi. "With our lives?"

Tell her the truth, says Eugene. *Tell her you hate yourself and what you've become.*

"Because I'm not unhappy with our lives." Mimi is crying now. Softly, so you wouldn't notice unless you looked. "I just wish you weren't so miserable."

Tell her you've become a Bear.

"What do you believe in, Bird? Is there anything left that you believe in?"

ALL THE WAY BACK from Amsterdam's red-light district, I went over my choice of sex worker. I told myself I should have picked the brunette in the green leotards, or the woman with the short black hair and the tattoo of a rose on her shoulder.

As though there were a right choice in the first place, and I was annoyed with Mimi for making me choose.

Mimi didn't say anything until we got to Dam Square. "That was disappointing."

"What?"

"The brothels. I thought the women had their own apartments. I thought they were in control of their space and their bodies."

I didn't know what to say, so I said nothing.

"I thought they lived normal lives. Normal women. Doing normal things. Watching television. Ironing. Washing dishes. Sitting in their living rooms with the blinds open. With a dog or a cat. And every so often, when they felt like it, they had sex for money."

There was a young man at the far side of the square with a didgeridoo. He was playing a rhythmic piece that had nothing in common with American show tunes.

"But those places were cages. A room with a door. A hole in the wall. A zoo for men."

I thought about the lectures on the sex trade that we could have attended. Perhaps, if we had gone to one, Mimi would have been able to ask questions, and maybe if she had heard the women talking about how they lived their lives, she'd have felt better.

Maybe they did have pets.

WE FIND TRAM 91 and take it to the park. When we get there, we start walking.

"Are there sights we're supposed to see?"

"There are," says Mimi, but she doesn't stop, and she doesn't look at the guidebook. "There are always sights to see."

We walk past something that looks a bit like a church but turns out to be a planetarium. I'm not feeling much better, but I'm optimistic that the fresh air will help.

Prague is currently under a smog advisory. Kitty holds up her cellphone. *Respiratory disease and heart problems.*

"You want to go in the planetarium?"

Mimi doesn't break stride. "Not really."

She picks up speed through a large meadow with an old-time trolley off to one side, parked in the grass. I'm thinking that she's trying to leave Eugene and the Other Demons in the dust, but even though he's not as young as he used to be, Eugene manages to keep up.

This could also be her version of a death march.

When we come to a lake, Mimi slows down. There's a small dock that extends into the water. On either end is a large duck's head carved out of wood.

I take out my camera. "How about I get a photograph of you and the duck dock?"

I think that "duck dock" is mildly funny, but I don't even get a smile.

"How about we sit on the bench and talk?"

Eugene puts his hands in his pockets and takes four steps back. Kitty herds the twins to the edge of the lake to search for bugs. Chip goes for a jog.

"Sure."

"Do you want to talk?"

"Talking's fine."

Mimi settles herself on the bench, and we sit there for what feels like hours, but isn't.

A mother comes by with her three children. The older girl skips along the path, playing an imaginary game. The younger boy shuffles behind, kicking at the gravel, making little puffs of dust with his feet. The woman pushes a stroller, her shoulders hunched, her eyes set on something in the distance that isn't there.

"You remember those years?"

I nod. "Hard to forget."

"And we only had two."

"After one," I say, "I don't think it matters."

"But you're not the expert."

The girl is suddenly twirling around, her arms flung away from her sides, her head thrown back to the sky.

"She's having a good time." Mimi pats my hand. "Do you think our kids had a good time?"

"The time Nathan chased that goose?"

"And then the goose chased him."

"And you came to the rescue with your umbrella."

The woman comes to the front of the stroller and lifts a baby out. The child looks to be about a year old, and she's determined to walk. She stands upright, measuring her new-found balance, then staggers forward for a few steps and sits down on the path with a thump. The mother turns to say something to her son, and the baby picks up pieces of gravel and begins putting them in her mouth.

"Remember when Tally found that piece of cat shit in the sandbox?"

"That's what you remember from your children's childhood?" Mimi hits me on the shoulder. "Angry geese and cat shit?"

"We still managed to raise two pretty good kids, didn't we?"

"And yet here we sit on a bench in a park in Prague, feeling sorry for ourselves. Why is that?"

The woman turns to find her baby with a mouthful of dirt and a face drawn up into the beginnings of a good scream. The older girl hurries to her sister's side and begins using a finger to scrape the gravel out. It's clear that this isn't the first time the two have played this game.

"We have a good life," Mimi begins. "You write. I paint."

"I've stopped writing. You still paint."

"I do," says Mimi. "Course, I paint the same thing over and over."

"Nothing wrong with water."

Mimi settles against me. "I'm not going to change the world."

The woman hikes the baby on her hip and leads the girl and her brother onto the duck dock. She takes out sandwiches and bottles from the stroller, along with a blanket. I feel my stomach rumble.

"My paintings aren't going to prevent wars. They're not going to stop climate change. They're not going to end poverty or restrain greed."

Eugene wanders back in our direction. I don't want him anywhere near this discussion, but here he comes.

"Does that mean we're failures? The both of us?"

I watch the woman on the dock with her three children. I wonder if there's a father in the picture or if he has already run off. Or been killed. Maybe this is Mimi's mother, when she was a young woman.

Or mine.

"Is that it?" says Mimi. "Is that what happened?"

Eugene sits down on the end of the bench and makes himself at home.

"Is there anything you still believe in?" says Mimi.

Go ahead, says Eugene. *Tell her the truth*.

I turn my back to Eugene. "You mean like militaristic religions, unprincipled governments, rapacious economies?"

Eugene leans on my shoulder. *Tell her about justice*, he whispers.

"What about me?" says Mimi. "Do you still have faith in me?"

The sandwiches the woman has brought have had the crusts removed. There are sliced bananas and apples in a plastic container. She and her daughter make a game out of putting pieces of grape in the baby's mouth.

"Or yourself," says Mimi. "Have you lost faith in yourself?"

Eugene stands up and starts walking away. I don't know where he's going, and I don't care.

Mimi and I sit on the bench and watch the picnic on the duck dock. The woman has the baby tucked in against her breast, while the older girl runs from one duck head to the other, her brother hard on her heels.

"Remember when Nathan wouldn't go to sleep unless he was lying next to me?"

"And every time you moved, he'd wake up."

"And how he'd only nurse for a couple of minutes at a time?"

"And then we'd have to sing him back to sleep."

"'Ten Little Ducks.'"

"I should hate that song," says Mimi, "but I don't."

"Please don't start."

"There's no one around to hear us."

"Yeah, but there could be."

"And you'd be embarrassed? Singing in a park?"

The little boy has torn part of his sandwich into pieces and throws the bits into the water. The ducks on the far side of the pond see the motion and rush over to the dock.

"Perfect timing," says Mimi, and she counts the ducks that cluster around the dock and the family. "*Sixteen little ducks went out one day.*"

I shake my head.

"Come on, Bird," says Mimi. "If we don't believe in ourselves, let's try believing in ducks."

XII

The family doesn't stay on the dock for long. The boy and the girl begin fighting. The mother ignores them. She packs up the food, tucks the sleeping baby into the stroller, and they all head out, the boy running ahead, shouting insults back at his sister.

"Any idea what he's saying?"

"What all brothers say to their sisters." Mimi stands and stretches. "Remember when Nathan called Tally a poopy-heady?"

I start to stand, and this is when things begin to go sideways. A wave of nausea comes out of nowhere, and my legs buckle.

"Bird!"

And down I go in a heap. My first emotion is embarrassment. Blackbird Mavrias, famous photojournalist now retired, collapsing in a park in Prague.

And then I throw up.

Mimi is immediately at my side, but I don't really hear what she's saying. And then more nausea and then the cramps. My face is buried in the grass. I can smell the dirt and my own vomit, and I don't really care. All I want is to find a position for my body that doesn't hurt.

Mimi rubs my back. I continue retching, but now nothing is coming up, so that's an improvement. Mimi continues to talk, and that's when I realize that she's not talking to me.

"No, he's not drunk."

"He is sick?"

"Yes, he is sick."

I try to raise my head so that I can join the conversation, but that just brings on another wave of nausea.

"He has eaten something?"

"I don't think so. But he's diabetic."

"The blood sugars," says a male voice. "My father is diabetic also."

I can feel Mimi rummaging in my pack. And then I feel a sharp pain in my finger. More nausea, but not as strong as before.

"His blood sugars are okay," I hear Mimi say.

"You are sure he is not drunk."

I open my eyes, and what I see are two sets of scruffy runners and the cuffs of two pairs of dark pants.

"He's not drunk." Mimi's voice has hardened a bit.

"There is a fine," says one of the men.

"For being sick?"

"A public park. Fifty American dollars."

I angle my head. The runners and the pants are joined by light-blue shirts.

"That's ridiculous."

Two men. One tall with blond hair. The other shorter and wider, with dark hair cut tight to his head. Early twenties.

"It is law."

"And we must check your money," says the tall man.

"There is much counterfeiting going on in our country," says the shorter man. "This is being done by foreign tourists."

I get myself to a sitting position. I'm feeling better. Not good, but better.

"And you're the police?" says Mimi.

"Yes, of course," says the tall man. "Undercover."

"And you want me to pay a fine *and* you want me to give you our money so you can check it?"

"It is police business." The shorter man takes a badge out of his pocket and flashes it. "Or we must take you to the jail."

I lean back against the bench and breathe slowly.

"Take us to jail? Because my husband is sick?"

"Yes," says the taller man. "Unless you pay the fine immediately."

"And let us check your money for counterfeits."

"Because you're the police?"

"Of course."

"Czech police with ridiculous accents?"

I straighten my glasses. Now that I can see clearly, both men look younger than I would have expected. And worried. The tall one looks at the shorter one, who tries to impress Mimi with a scowl.

I could tell him that that's not going to work. But I don't.

"If you persist, we will have to take you to jail and charge you with many things."

Mimi puts her hands on her hips. "You know what I think," she says, her voice sharp enough to cut bone. "I think this is a scam. I don't believe you're the police at all."

"We are the—"

"And I'm going to start screaming as loud as I can, and we'll see what happens when the real police arrive."

"Look," says the tall man, his Czech accent all but gone. "Just give us the money."

I'm feeling better, and now I'm also angry. I push myself to my feet and try to flex the muscles in my chest. Hercules and the Nemean lion. Samson in the temple. Atlas hoisting the world over his head.

"Fire!" yells Mimi.

Both men jump.

"Fire!"

"Okay, okay," says the shorter man, and he pushes his hands down in an attempt to get Mimi to lower the volume. "Give it a rest, yeah?"

"Fire!"

Flexing for battle isn't a good idea. I can feel my stomach lurch forward. I put my hands on my knees and wait for the nausea to find me again.

"Now you've upset Bird."

I'm in the middle of a dry retch and don't see what happens next, but I hear one of the men scream.

"My eyes!"

"It's just perfume," says Mimi.

"I'm blind!"

"Here. Wash your eyes with this."

I hope Mimi isn't giving away our water. The nausea passes, and I'm able to stand up straight. The shorter man is on the ground. The taller man is pouring water into his partner's eyes. It's our water, all right, and he's using most of it.

Mimi is standing firm, the purple perfume atomizer at the ready. "No way you two are police."

"You're in a lot of trouble," says the taller man, but his voice has lost all its conviction.

Mimi cocks her arm, the atomizer at the ready. "Let me see that badge," she says. "Now."

"All right, all right," says the taller man, "so we're not the police."

Mimi turns the badge over in her hand. "Shit," she says, "you drew a badge on a piece of cardboard?"

"It's not a bad job. Nigel's got a gift for art, yeah?"

"Christ, Trevor," says the short man, "don't use our names."

"You've actually robbed other people with this?"

"No," says Trevor.

"Maybe," says Nigel. The skin around his eyes is red, but he seems to have recovered. "Couple euros here and there. What's wrong with your husband?"

"You should get that checked out," says Trevor. "My old man got a bad stomach. Six months later, he's dead."

"Your man probably ate something," says Nigel. "No proper food in the whole city."

"Look," says Trevor, "we're sorry about this, but we're broke. We blew our money and don't have enough to get home."

Nigel rubs his eyes. "Trevor's mum will send us the money for a ticket, but he don't want to stand for the lecture."

"So, you rob people."

"Just the tourists," says Trevor. "They don't really care, you know. Gives them a story to tell."

"Yeah," says Nigel. "Some ways, we're doing them a favour."

"And if the real police catch you?"

"Yeah," says Trevor, "that wouldn't be good."

Mimi pulls a five-euro bill out of her pocket and hands it to Trevor. "When we get back to the hotel, I'm going to report the two of you to the police. If I were you, I'd call Trevor's mum immediately and get out of Prague."

"Christ," says Nigel, "you Americans are as mad as a bag of ferrets."

"Canadian," I manage to say before Mimi can leap in.

"I thought Canadians were polite," says Trevor.

Nigel is on his feet. He seems none the worse for wear for having been perfumed. "What about my badge?"

"I'm keeping it," says Mimi, and she points the atomizer at Nigel. "The five euros is for the badge."

"Fair enough," says Trevor as he and Nigel back away. "Hope your man feels better."

I sit down on the bench. The nausea has passed, but it has left me exhausted.

"Is there any water left?"

"How you feeling?"

"Lousy." The first sip of water is wonderful. The second is even better.

"Don't drink too much," says Mimi. "It could upset your stomach."

I sit back and let the afternoon sun warm my face. All things considered, it feels good sitting here, doing nothing.

"Why'd you give them money?"

Mimi shrugs. "I felt sorry for them."

"They were crooks."

"They were kids."

"This part of your 'save the world' tour?"

"The skinny one reminded me a little of Nathan." Mimi puts her arm around my shoulders. "What about Eugene and the Other Demons? I'll bet Kitty has something to say about your little episode."

"Nope," I tell Mimi. "As soon as I started to puke, they took off."

Mimi takes out the guidebook. "As I see it, we have two choices. One, we can go back to the hotel."

I close my eyes and imagine we're back in Guelph having a sandwich at Miijidaa or the Boathouse. "What's number two?"

"As it turns out," says Mimi, "it's close by."

"What's close by?"

Mimi smiles and pats my cheek. "The Prague Zoo."

THE YEAR I TURNED eighteen, I stole a car. Well, technically, I didn't steal it. It was more an unauthorized borrowing. My mother was friends with a woman whose husband was a doctor. I didn't know Dr. Philips all that well, but what I did know was that he had a car.

A 1960 red Plymouth Fury convertible.

Mom didn't have a car, couldn't afford one. I don't think she even had a licence. I didn't have a licence either, but I knew how to drive.

One of my best friends in high school was Doug Crook. Doug's father owned a service station on Washington, and Doug and I would drive cars around his father's lot. We'd park them, move them in and out of the service bays, take them around the block when no one was looking.

I could drive anything. Standard. Automatic. It didn't matter. If it had wheels and a motor, I could drive it.

Anyway, whenever Dr. Philips and his wife went to Hawaii, they'd get my mother to collect the mail and check on the house to make sure everything was working, and they'd hire me to cut their grass and water the yard.

And they'd leave their car in the garage, where the battery might go dead and the carbon could build up on the cylinders. So, if you looked at it from the standpoint of automotive maintenance, I was doing them a favour.

Mimi was just kidding about the zoo.

She can see that I'm not up for much, so she finds a tram that takes us near Old Town Square, and we walk back from there. The room is still hot, but I don't care. I fall onto the bed and melt into the mattress. I can hear Mimi marching about the room.

"What are you doing?"

"I'm thinking."

"Thinking about what?"

"The other things I could have said." Mimi flops down on the bed beside me. "To Trevor and Nigel."

"Our young felons?"

"Clever stuff. Cut-them-off-at-the-knees remarks. God, I wish I could do it over again."

"We could have gotten hurt."

"True enough," says Mimi. "You were in no condition to fight them off if they had gotten physical."

"But they would have had to go through you to get to me."

"That's sweet." Mimi giggles. "And you know what? I'm horny."

"Again?"

"It was the excitement. I think it was the excitement."

"I thought you said women get sensual."

"Are you horny?"

"Not really."

"Maybe a little?"

"I just spent the afternoon throwing up."

Mimi slides her leg over my groin and runs her hand under my shirt. "How about now?"

I WAITED UNTIL MONDAY to take the car. My mother worked from eight until six. I figured I'd go over to Dr. Philips's house just after she left and grab the keys, drive around for three or four hours, and then put the car back in the garage, with no one the wiser.

The keys for the car were on a hook behind the front door. Next to the key hook was a notepad with a pen attached. There were three items on the pad. The first said "Insurance review." The second simply said "Gauge." The third said "Call Howard."

I told myself that when I was rich, I was going to have hooks for my keys and a notepad to remind me of things that needed to be done.

So I had the key, but I couldn't just take the car and drive it around town. I wasn't sure how many 1960 red Plymouth Fury convertibles there were in Roseville, but lots of people knew my mother, which meant they knew me. And if they saw me in the car, they'd know that the two of us didn't belong together.

Instead, I headed up Highway 80 towards Auburn and the mountains, a full tank of gas, the top down, the wind in my hair, the sun shining. I remember promising myself that this was the way my life was going to be.

Roseville to Truckee was about eighty-five miles. A little over two hours non-stop. I made it there in under that. Dr. Philips had great taste in cars. The Plymouth flew up the highway like a rocket bound for the moon.

So we're in Prague, lying on the bed, and it turns out I'm a little interested after all. Mimi senses this and presses her advantage.

"You don't have to do anything," she tells me. "You lie back, and I'll do all the work."

This is not as easy as it sounds. I'm still not feeling great, and not sure I can hold up my end. But Mimi takes her time, and before I know it, we're off to the races, a couple of sweaty horses hitting the finish line together.

More or less.

"Imagine that," she says, as she rolls off me. "You should be sick more often."

"You did all the work."

"Still, you were impressive."

Mimi sits up and holds out the cardboard badge she took from Nigel. "Fornication in Prague hotel room is against the law," she says in a terrible accent that sounds like a Russian who has spent too much time in Newfoundland. "You will have to pay fine."

"It wasn't fornication. You assaulted me."

"Fifty American dollars or more sex."

I do my best impression of being dead. "The fifty dollars."

Mimi bends down and kisses my stomach. "You don't have fifty dollars."

I WAS HUNGRY by the time I got to Truckee. I had about three dollars on me. Maybe some change. A burger joint next to a Standard gas station was advertising an "American Meal"—burger, fries, and a soft drink—for $1.50.

"Seems a little high," I told the girl at the window.

"Olympics," she said. "Now we're a tourist trap."

I ate the burger sitting at a picnic table and took in the forest and the mountains all around me. I could hear the Truckee River, but I couldn't see it. At that moment, I thought about getting into the car and driving into the rising sun. Nevada, Utah, Colorado. At that moment, the last place I wanted to be was home.

The last person I wanted to be was me.

I took my time with the french fries. I knew I wouldn't have another chance to enjoy life like this for a long time. Thomas Blackbird Mavrias and his Plymouth Fury on their way to the stars.

I hit the restroom at the back of the café, washed my hands so that I wouldn't get any french-fry grease on the car, and slid back under the steering wheel. I wasn't in any hurry. I thought I'd head down to Lake Tahoe, drive around the Nevada side, maybe stop at one of the casinos, see if I could get in.

There was plenty of time to tour the lake and still get home before my mother got off work. Plenty of time before Dr. Philips and his wife returned from Hawaii.

I turned the key in the ignition, punched the drive button, backed the car out of the parking space, and swung around just as the engine lurched several times and died.

MIMI WAS RIGHT. Sex was the better option. Fifty American dollars had just been a ploy.

"You know what," says Mimi, who is more awake than she should be. "I'm hungry."

"Sleep first," I say. "Then we eat."

"I'm hungry now."

"I think I'm still sick."

As Mimi sits up, the sheet falls away from her breasts. Even in my diminished condition, they are lovely to look at.

"Are you listening to me or looking at my boobs?"

"Both."

"So, you're not that sick."

"I'm definitely weak."

Mimi bounces out of bed. "Maybe I'll go out and get you some white rice. Maybe I'll be knocked down by some handsome stranger, and he'll have to help me back to the hotel."

"Maybe he'll have a badge."

"Like this one," says Mimi, and she holds up Nigel's little masterpiece.

"What are you going to do with it?"

"The bundle," says Mimi. "Maybe this will be the contribution from Prague."

I TRIED STARTING the car again. The battery was charged. The starter motor was turning over. But the engine wouldn't catch. And that's when I saw it. The gas gauge. It was still set on full.

And then I remembered. The note on the pad next to the keys. "Gauge."

Shit.

The attendant at the gas station was a young kid about my age. I tried to be nonchalant.

"Sometimes the gauge doesn't work," I told him. "I think I'm out of gas."

"Nice car."

"It's a beauty, all right."

"You want me to help you push it?"

I couldn't think of anything else to do, so I said sure, and we started pushing the car the hundred feet or so from the café to the pumps. The Fury drove like a dream, but pushing it was like trying to shove a boulder up a down escalator.

"Fill it up?"

"How many gallons will a dollar buy me?"

"A dollar?" The kid gave me a cockeyed smile. "Gas is forty-one cents a gallon, so you'd get about two gallons."

"It's thirty-one cents in the valley."

"We're not in the valley."

I started to do the math in my head. "You know how many miles to the gallon this car gets?"

"You don't know?"

"It's my father's car. He lets me use it."

"Cool," said the kid. "Pop the hood, and we'll take a look."

Which was more easily said than done. I had never opened the hood of a 1960 Plymouth Fury. So I hung back and let the kid take the lead.

"Your dad's got good taste."

"That's Dad."

"This is the 361 Sonoramic. Two Carter four barrels, 310 horses, 435 cubic inches of torque."

"Lot of power."

"At the top end," says the kid, "but it's a little slow off the mark."

"What do you think it gets to the gallon?"

The kid made a low whistling sound. "The four barrels will suck a tank dry pretty quick. At this altitude, you'd be lucky to get ten, maybe twelve."

"Ten miles to the gallon?"

"Lucky."

No matter how I did the math, the dollar plus change wasn't going to get me home.

"You broke?"

"Naw," I said, "but I left my wallet at home."

"Guess you'll have to call your dad."

"Gone." I shook my head. "He and Mom went to Hawaii."

"Damn," said the kid. "I've always wanted to go to Hawaii."

I stood there and tried to look pathetic.

"If this was Nevada," said the kid, "you could put your dollar in one of those slots and take your chances. But I wouldn't recommend it. Those places don't make money by giving it away."

Stuck in Truckee. It was almost biblical. Steal a car. Get stuck in Truckee. Divine retribution. Mom was going to find out I had taken the car. Dr. Philips was going to know that Katheryn Mavrias's oldest boy was a thief.

Standing there at the service station in Truckee, I wondered if it was possible to push the car to the top of a hill, throw it in neutral, and coast all the way down to the valley and back to town.

"Course there might be a way I can help you out."

"Okay."

"Let's pop the trunk and see what we got."

Mimi takes a bath. I lie in bed and watch the spiders on the ceiling. They've become part of the family now, along with the air conditioner that doesn't work.

Eugene sits on the edge of the bed. Kitty has found her favourite corner. Chip is on the floor doing push-ups, while the twins count out each rep.

Busy day, says Eugene. *Smart move, pretending to be sick.*

An upset stomach, says Kitty, *is one of the first signs of pancreatic cancer.*

Twenty-eight, say Desi and Didi, *twenty-nine, thirty, thirty-one . . .*

I hear Mimi splashing in the tub. "For a sick guy," she shouts out, "you were pretty good."

Some lover, says Eugene. *Lie on your back and think of mother England.*

"Matter of fact," says Mimi, "you were great."

Or bowel cancer, says Kitty. *It's probably one of the two.*

"And I was proud of you. The way you were prepared to protect me."

"Maybe we should try to get robbed more often."

Let's not do that, says Desi. *Confrontation makes Didi anxious.*

Chip is up to fifty-three and is sweating pretty hard. *Why does this shit always happen to me?*

"When you get out of the tub," I call out to Mimi, "you want to grab Chinese?"

THE KID'S NAME WAS Randy. His uncle owned the service station, and he was teaching his nephew how to be a mechanic.

"I finished high school, so it's not like I can fool around. My dad's a plumber, but I like cars."

"You got a car?"

"Not yet," said Randy. "But I got my eye on a '56 Bel Air."

I opened the trunk. The spare tire was off to the left. Dr. Philips had arranged the rest of the trunk in boxes. Tire chains. Jumper cables. Two cans of 30 weight motor oil.

"Your dad takes good care of his car."

"I help," I say.

Randy took a step back and leaned on one foot as though he was thinking. "Okay," he said, "here's what I can do."

MIMI COMES OUT of the bathroom all warm and smelling of soap, and climbs into bed with me.

"We don't have to go out," she says.

I quickly roll on my stomach.

Mimi runs her fingers down my back. "We can just stay here and cuddle."

I slide out of bed quickly and put my underpants on. "Thought you were hungry."

Mimi thinks about this for a moment. "You're right," she says at last. "I am hungry. We can sleep when we get back to Guelph."

I already have my pants and shirt on. But I can't find my socks.

"We're not going to be here much longer. Prague is the end of the line. No more postcards."

I throw the covers back and check the sheets, and sure enough, there they are.

"We won't have an excuse to travel."

I put my socks on. "You'll think of something."

"Maybe, when we get home, we should try starting over." Mimi has put on her green silk dress with the red flowers. This is the dress she brings for special occasions. "I could work some social relevance into my paintings."

"And I could write a book?"

"You were a hell of a journalist."

I sit back down on the edge of the bed. "My writing isn't going to save the world. My articles aren't going to prevent wars. They're not going to stop climate change. They're not going to end poverty or restrain greed."

Mimi sits down beside me. "Maybe they don't have to. Maybe that's the mistake we make, why we're so easily defeated."

Outside, somewhere in Kampa Park, a band begins to play big-band tunes. First up is Cole Porter's "Begin the Beguine."

"But in the meantime, how about we go dancing?"

"Dancing?"

"Why yes," says Mimi, "I'd love to."

I COULD HAVE GONE over to Tahoe and circled the lake. Now that I had a full tank of gas, I could go almost anywhere. Instead, I got back on the 80 and headed home.

Randy had been as helpful as he could have been.

Under the circumstances.

A full tank of gas came to just under $7.50. The spare was worth about $40. Randy figured he could sell it for around $20, which meant that with the trade, he'd come out about $12.50 ahead, especially as the spare tire was on a rim.

"Most people never even touch their spares," Randy told me. "Lot of my customers trade their cars in every two years. Most of them don't even know they have an extra tire. Your dad like that?"

"Sort of."

"Probably won't even miss it."

"Right."

"Just don't get a flat."

I drove the speed limit down through Emigrant Gap, past Gold Run and Colfax. I thought about stopping in Auburn, but I didn't have any money to speak of, and I didn't want to take the chance that the car might break down.

On the drive up to Truckee, I had been a high roller out to see the world. Coming down, I was a fugitive in a stolen vehicle with no licence, trying to make it home without being arrested.

And I did.

I was sure that everyone was watching me as I drove along Main Street and pulled into Dr. Philips's driveway. I backed the car into the garage and left it as I had found it. I hung the key back on the hook and locked the door to the house.

Then I went home and waited for my mother to return from work. And for the sky to fall.

KAMPA PARK IS FULL. There are food vendors everywhere. I get a sausage plate with brown bread, sauerkraut, and hot mustard. Along with a glass of beer. Mimi gets a cheese sandwich. She drinks most of my beer.

"Let's get one of those *trdelnik* thingies," she says. "We can split it."

Along with the food vendors, there are craftspeople selling all sorts of stuff. Mimi buys a small bottle of beer shampoo. I buy a box of something called "spa wafers." The food and the wandering have settled me, and I'm feeling better.

At the far end of the park, we find the band. Several couples are dancing on the grass.

"'Sentimental Journey,'" I tell Mimi. "1940s."

"Can we dance to it?"

"If we knew how to dance."

"We're in Prague," says Mimi. "Who's going to care."

"Sentimental Journey" ends, and the quintet slides into "Embraceable You."

Mimi drags me onto the grass and puts her arms around me.

"I could stand on your feet, and you could lead."

"Or we could just stand here and hum along with the music."

Mimi snuggles in against my shoulder. The night is warm. You can't see the stars, but there are lights in the trees and on the bridge. All around, the city glitters, as we sway back and forth.

THE PHILIPSES RETURNED two weeks later, tanned and happy, with photographs of blue water and white sand beaches. Mrs. Philips brought my mother a red patterned muumuu and a set of four drinking glasses that said "Blue Hawaii."

Each morning, I would watch Dr. Philips drive his car out of the garage, expecting that any moment, he would stop, open the trunk, and discover the theft. But he didn't.

Then in late August, he left for work in the Plymouth and came home with a brand-new Ford Galaxie 500. Springtime Yellow.

And that was that.

IT'S LATE WHEN WE leave the park. The band is playing "At Last," and Mimi and I slow dance our way past the food stands and under the bridge to the small square in front of the hotel. A soft, high fog has settled on the city, but tonight, we won't get lost.

"The door's open," says Mimi. "That's a good sign."

"Unless we want to spend the night on the Charles Bridge."

"But then we couldn't have sex."

"We've had sex. Twice."

"Are you tired?"

"Exhausted."

"But not too exhausted."

"Completely exhausted."

"Tell you what," says Mimi. "You pretend to be a tourist, and I'll show you my badge."

We stand outside the hotel and listen to the music in the distance. Mimi leaves me, walks over to the small canal that runs along the side of the bridge, and looks down into the water.

"We never did find out what happened to Uncle Leroy or the Crow bundle."

"Nope."

"But that's no reason why we should give up." Mimi leans against me. "Maybe we should take one of those dinner cruises."

"On thc Vltava?" I shake my head. "Expensive, and the food will be horrible."

"We might see the world from a different point of view," says Mimi. "Sometimes that makes all the difference."

I'm still a little weak from the episode in the park, but as I stand there with Mimi, I realize that for the first time in a while, Eugene and the Other Demons are nowhere in sight.

XIII

Oz is already in the breakfast room by the time I get there.

"Good morning," he says. "I was hoping you would arrive."

"Here I am."

"Yes, here you are." Oz folds his newspaper. "Today, I leave Prague, so there is much to discuss."

"You're leaving?"

"Yes, of course. Prague is beautiful, but one cannot walk back and forth on the Charles Bridge and call it life."

Oz takes an envelope out of his jacket and places it on the table next to his coffee cup. "So, tell me what you did yesterday. The Infant Jesus of Prague? The Lennon Wall? The Farmers' Market? Mala Strana?"

"We went to Stromovka."

"The park? But you have parks in Canada?"

I tell Oz that we do.

"And they are different than Stromovka?"

"No."

"That is the sadness of travel. Everything is much the same."

"We were almost robbed."

Oz's face fills up with concern. "A robbery?"

"Almost."

I tell Oz how I got sick in the park. How two young men pretended to be police. How Mimi had saved the day.

"Wonderful," says Oz when I've finished. "A thrilling story. You will tell this story when you go back to Canada?"

"Probably."

"Of course, probably. And these young men had a badge?"

"The one guy had drawn it on a piece of cardboard. It was pretty good."

Oz leans in. "In many places, criminals buy police uniforms on the Internet for this exact purpose. In other places, the police themselves rob you."

"They were just kids."

"In the United States," says Oz, "the police are the new army of the powerful. This has always been true in Russia and China, but now is also true in Germany and France. Spain as well. South Africa. Did you go to the zoo? It is very near Stromovka. There you will find honest animals."

"I'm not crazy about zoos."

Oz smiles sadly. "And yet we live in one."

I look at the buffet. I should be hungry, but I'm not. "Where will you go?" I ask. "When you leave Prague?"

"Ah," says Oz, "that is the question. There are few safe places left in the world. Copenhagen. Stockholm. Perhaps Amsterdam."

I remember Mimi's concerns about New York.

"At one time, New Zealand was a possibility," says Oz, "but now it is not."

"Don't go to the US."

"Of course not." Oz frowns. "Yet you were born in California. And now you are Canadian. How did this happen? Do you find that Canada is safe?"

"You should talk to Mimi," I tell Oz. "She likes to tell that story."

Oz taps the envelope. "This is for you," he says. "And for your Mimi."

The envelope is thick and heavy, the kind of envelope that you see in movies when blackmail or bribery is involved.

"Here is the story of Uncle Leroy. I have typed it, so you do not have to argue with my handwriting."

"The story you made up? The one about Uncle Leroy and his Czech family in the town with the hot springs?"

"Karlovy Vary," says Oz. "Yes. I've added a few extra possibilities that you can keep or take out."

I leave the envelope in the middle of the table.

"Your uncle Leroy. Dead, but now brought back to life through postcards and travel. Such a resurrection."

I'm not sure I want to encourage Oz in his inventions and philosophizing, so I turn my mind to remembering the names of the seven dwarfs.

"Story and memory. Memory and story." Oz rubs one eye. "Together they are history."

I get six of the names right away but can't think of the last one.

"There is the story of a young man during the time of the Russians coming to Prague."

Oz pauses for a moment, as though he's trying to recall the details. "This young man was angry that his country had been invaded, so he picked up a piece of charcoal and found a wall. Here was his opportunity to write something that might stop the slaughter, something that might push back the tanks and change what was to happen."

Doc, Sneezy, Bashful, Grumpy, Dopey, Sleepy . . .

"But because his task seemed so monumental, so impossible, he wrote nothing."

Grumpy, Sneezy, Dopey, Doc, Sleepy, Bashful . . .

"But your uncle Leroy," says Oz. "Look what he is able to do with a bucket of shit and a brush."

Happy. I always forget Happy.

"When you look for him," says Oz, "do you ever find yourself?"

I can see where Oz could be annoying.

"What about the game?"

"Game?"

"The Bees and the Bears."

"Ah," says Oz, and he taps the side of his head. "No, the game is dead. The trials, they were disappointing. Such a shame."

I wasn't sure that it was much of a game in the first place, but I don't tell Oz this.

"A good idea," says Oz. "But there is a fatal flaw."

"Too complicated?"

"No. It is a simple game." Oz shrugs and makes a sad gesture with his mouth. "But it seems no one wants to be a Bee. Everyone wants to be the Bear."

I glance at the clock. I can see that Mimi is going to be late again.

"I will miss you, my friend." Oz reaches over and pats my hand. "Such wonderful conversations. Cowboys and Indians. Robbers in the park. Lost relatives and injured enthusiasms. Did you know that many tourists who come to Prague attempt suicide?"

"Really?"

"Yes, a great many jump off the Charles Bridge."

"Doesn't look high enough."

"Perhaps that is the point. Sometimes a failure is a success." Oz extends his arms and holds his wrists out. "Which one?"

Somehow the conversation has taken a left turn when I wasn't looking.

"Watch," says Oz. "I wish to give you one of these watches."

"I don't want your watch."

"You pick. A gift."

"I still can't take it."

"Ah," says Oz, "you are worried that you will pick the expensive one."

"I don't need a watch."

"No one needs a watch." Oz slips the watch with the emerald-green face off his wrist. "What we need is time."

Oz sets the watch on top of the envelope. "So, we will not see each other tomorrow."

"What will you do in Amsterdam?"

"What does anyone do in Amsterdam?" Oz pushes the chair back and stands up. "But what about you?"

"Me?"

"Will you finish that article? The one with the three parts?" Oz straightens his jacket. "Or have you run out of hope and happy endings?"

Lois Paul had been a single mother in Saskatchewan, working a minimum-wage job, when her six children were taken from her and put up for adoption.

I interviewed Elsie Tolmar, one of Paul's children, for a three-part story on social services.

The Adopt Indians and Métis Program.

Tolmar had been adopted by a Norwegian couple who didn't tell her she had been adopted until she forced the question.

"I was probably in my late twenties when I figured it out," Tolmar told me. "I mean, look at me. You going to mistake me for a Norwegian?"

I WANDER TO THE buffet and put food on my plate. I'm still not hungry, but I know that I need to eat. I figure that Mimi will come rushing into the breakfast room at the last minute.

But she doesn't.

I sit at the table until the buffet has been cleared away and the staff begins looking at me sideways. This is not the first meal that Mimi has missed, and as I climb the stairs, I find that I'm somewhat irritated.

After all, we paid for these meals.

Mimi is sitting in the chair in her bra and underpants, her feet propped up on the window ledge. She has her sketch pad out and is working on another drawing.

"I wasn't hungry," she says without looking up, "so I thought I'd do some work."

"You missed breakfast, again."

"We'll have an early lunch."

"And you missed Oz."

"Your imaginary breakfast buddy."

"He's not imaginary. He's going to Amsterdam."

"We went to Amsterdam," says Mimi. "You remember?"

The sketch is similar to the other one Mimi had drawn. A solitary figure walking on the Charles Bridge. She's laid in a dark background that is cut with the lights from the ornate standards set on the stone walls. It appears that the figure is carrying something.

"Uncle Leroy?"

"Maybe," says Mimi. "I haven't decided."

"It's moody."

"It could be you."

"Is that supposed to be a bundle?"

Mimi darkens a shadow next to one of the statues. "I could put Eugene and the Other Demons in right about here."

"Or a bucket and a brush."

"Then it wouldn't be you."

I lie on the bed, my hands on my chest. I could probably stay here all day. My eyes feel normal. My legs aren't threatening to cramp. My stomach is still a little tender from the day before but seems mostly settled.

"Don't get too comfortable," says Mimi. "As soon as I finish this, I'll want to find food."

I TOOK A PHOTOGRAPH of Tolmar, and then I took a photograph of Tolmar and her three children.

"Mom and Dad are dead now, so it doesn't matter."

Tolmar had all the information on the adoption and a copy of her mother's file.

"You know why they took us away from her?"

I said that I would have to guess it had something to do with alcohol or drugs. Tolmar showed me a copy of the social-services form, pointed to the bottom of the page.

In a section marked "Reason for Apprehension," someone had scrawled a short note in a clumsy cursive that simply said *Single Indian mother, unable to care for children*.

MIMI AND I COME out of the hotel and get as far as the steps up to the Charles Bridge.

"I think we should split up."

"Split up?"

"For the day." Mimi adjusts her backpack. "I want to wander around and do some sketching."

"Okay."

"But I'd like to wander on my own."

I don't have to look. I know Eugene and Kitty are standing right behind me.

"You haven't had breakfast."

"I'll find a place. Is that a problem?"

"No. It's fine."

"You'll be okay?"

"Sure."

"You could find a café and work on the book."

"Sure."

"I better get going, or I'll lose the light."

There's a shout from the bridge. A young man has climbed one of the statues and is leaning out over the water. He holds on to the saint's crown with one hand and flails his free arm around over his head, as though he's just come out of a chute on a bull.

Mimi steps inside my arms and gives me a hug. I watch the young man on the bridge. He's taken off his shirt and is waving it in circles. In the distance, two policemen are working their way through the tourists.

"So, you're going to be gone the entire day."

"Don't read anything into it."

"Maybe I'll go to the Sex Machines Museum."

Mimi gives me a quick kiss. "That's the spirit."

I watch Mimi head off across the bridge and disappear into the crush of tourists. Splitting up isn't anything unusual. Mimi and I have done this many times before. Both of us going off on our own.

But it doesn't feel the same in Prague, and now I'm faced with the prospect of spending the day with Eugene and the Other Demons.

Which I have no intention of doing.

So I start walking. I figure that I'll walk the day away, stop for coffee every so often, see some of the lesser-known sights on the fly, grab a quick meal, and keep walking.

If nothing else, the exercise will do me good.

So, says Eugene as he trots by my side, *what's the plan*?

Stay in the hotel room, says Kitty. *Where it's safe.*

We should stand in the sunshine, says Didi.

Sunshine makes us happy, says Desi.

Sports bar, says Chip. *I vote for a sports bar.*

Maybe you want to hang off a statue, says Eugene, *and howl at the sky.*

Someone who didn't know any better might think that Eugene and I were close, that he was a good friend.

But if you're going to try to kill yourself, says Eugene as we cross the Charles Bridge on our way to Old Town, *we get to watch.*

The Sex Machines Museum is very near the astronomical clock. I stop in the square for a moment to see if they've got the clock working yet. There's a large crowd of tourists with their cellphones and iPads at the ready, and a feeling of high enthusiasm in the air.

I check the time. The watch Oz gave me says that it is a couple of minutes to the hour, so I decide to wait to see what might happen. When I look at the watch, I can't help but wonder if this is the expensive watch or the cheap one. It doesn't matter, but I am curious.

You think he's going to give you an expensive watch? says Eugene.

It's probably stolen, says Kitty. *And you know what happens then.*

The hour comes and goes. The clock doesn't move, and neither does the crowd. It's as though the people are fixed in place. The clock is a major tourist attraction, one of the reasons to come to Prague, so it stands to reason that it has to work.

Even if it doesn't.

The enthusiasm turns to annoyance and disappointment.

"What a rip-off."

"I could have watched the video at home."

"So, this is the famous clock?"

A woman carrying a purse the size of a steamer trunk swings around and cuts a game trail through the crowd.

"If it was in Trenton," she says as she tramps past me, dragging two teenagers along behind her, single file, "the thing would sure as hell work."

The Sex Machines Museum is just down a narrow street. I stand at the entrance and look at the lipstick-red banners. I don't mean to, but I begin to keep track of the people who go in.

All couples.

I probably stand at the entrance for a good twenty minutes, and the only people who go into the Sex Machines Museum are couples.

Go ahead, says Eugene. *Single guy in a sex museum? What's the worst they can think?*

What happens if they raid the place? says Kitty.

That you're pathetic? Eugene tips his hat back. *No secret there.*

I vote we go in, says Chip.

I'll stay outside with the twins, says Kitty.

I take a step towards the entrance, money in hand, when an older couple comes out. The woman is checking her camera. The man is leaning over her shoulder, watching the screen.

"Are you sure," he says, "you deleted the one of me and the giant wood dildo?"

I make a graceful turn and walk away.

Chip is slow to leave the doorway to the museum. *How come we never do what I want to do?*

Tolmar had a photocopy of an old social-services poster. A dark-haired child posed against a white backdrop.

"That's me," she said. "I was two. When they put us up for adoption, they made up posters with our pictures. You know, the kind of thing people do for lost animals."

How did you justify that kind of racism? Tolmar had wanted to know. How did you explain that kind of hate?

I was tempted to tell Tolmar that at the time, social services made up the same kind of posters for White kids as well.

"I'm a single mother," Tolmar told me. "I'm Native. My husband died of cancer last year. So now are they going to take my kids?"

THE WALK TURNS into an aimless stroll with stops in front of store windows filled with glassware and clothing, puppets and pastries. I wander up and down streets and narrow lanes, through small squares with statuary and water features, into the shadow of old churches and the golden arches of McDonald's.

Wenceslas Square, says Kitty as we break out onto a broad boulevard with a wide centre median. *At the far end is where Jan Palach burned himself alive.*

Protest against the Soviet invasion, says Eugene. *Now there's someone who lived his principles.*

For all the good it did him, says Chip.

Why are there so many people? ask the twins. *Big crowds make us nervous.*

The twins are right. There are more people in Wenceslas Square than I would have expected. The closer I get to the top of the boulevard, the denser the crowd becomes.

Maybe it's a celebration, says Didi. *We like celebrations.*

Like a circus, says Desi. *We like circuses.*

Celebrations and circuses make us happy, says Didi.

A group of men are putting up a wooden structure of some sort. I don't recognize it right away.

And then I do.

Is that a gallows? says Kitty. *Are they going to execute someone?*

Hey, Birdman. Eugene makes a hanging gesture with his hand. *Maybe they heard you were in town.*

I back up against the side of a Burger King and let a squad of grim-faced men and women push their way through. They wear helmets and carry placards. One of the men has a bullhorn. Several have brought Czech Republic flags that they wave over their heads.

Kitty squeezes up against me. *Everyone stay together and watch for white panel trucks.*

I've never seen this many people in one spot. In Barcelona, we stumbled upon a Catalan independence march that filled one of the wide avenues of that city, but this crowd looks to be even larger.

Up ahead, a shout goes up and the crowd erupts. Someone steps on my foot. I try to push away, when something flashes across my face and the world explodes. I don't remember what happens next, until I find myself on the ground.

"Blackbird Mavrias," says a familiar voice. "Such a surprise."

I'm dizzy, and my nose hurts like hell.

I feel hands assist me to my feet, and I imagine that it's Eugene and the Other Demons trying to help for a change.

But it's not.

It takes a moment for me to focus. "Oz?"

"Your nose is bleeding," says Oz. "But it is not serious."

"What happened?"

"Some pushing," says Oz. "Some shoving. A large man and his elbow. Such a crowd is not gentle."

I can feel something warm run down the side of my face.

"You will have to soak the shirt in cold water." Oz hands me a handkerchief. "Come," he says, "we will sit down so you can recover."

Oz helps me through the crowd and into a building We go up an escalator and into a second-floor coffee shop.

"Oliver's," says Oz. "Good coffee. A pastry. And we can watch from a safe distance."

We get a table at a large window that looks out over the square.

"Here," says Oz. "Pinch the sides of your nose with your fingers. It will stop the bleeding."

The mass of people on the street below moves back and forth like waves on water.

"So good to see you again."

"I thought you were going to Amsterdam."

"I am." Oz gestures to the rally. "But I am delayed. Did you bring your camera? Are you writing a story about Czech intolerance? Did you come to help, or do you just want to watch?"

My head hurts as much as my nose. I take my fingers away and hope that the bleeding has stopped. Oz orders coffee for the both of us, along with a slice of chocolate cake.

"We will share the cake," he says. "Too much sugar can be unpleasant."

I nod. My nose seems to be holding its own.

Oz looks out the window. "Here you can see the whole of history. Pro and con. Left and right. Conservative and liberal. Love and hate. Do you see the dividing line? The partition between the two camps?"

"The median?"

"On one side of the square are those who do not want immigrants to come into the Czech Republic." Oz takes a breath. "On the other side are those who wish to welcome people less fortunate than themselves. On one side, apprehension and anxiety. On the other, hospitality and welcome."

The coffee is hot, but I can't really taste it.

"Sadly, it is never this simple."

Same with the cake.

"Over there are flags of the Czech Republic and signs that say the Czech Republic is for Czechs only. But there are also signs concerned with employment and health care. Others with cruelty to animals."

Standing on a concrete flower box is a man with a sign that says "Fuck Hope, Take Action." For a moment, I think that it's Eugene.

"What about the people dressed in yellow?"

"Ah," says Oz. "The ones carrying the flags with an image of the sun."

"Are they for the refugees or against?"

"Against," says Oz. "They are dressing up like . . . *slunickar.* This is difficult to translate into English. Gullible. Naive. The people dressed in yellow are saying that anyone who supports the refugees is naive."

At the top of the square, several men in masks are climbing onto a tiered monument. On the highest tier is a knight mounted on a horse, holding a lance.

"It is a bit of humour, all this yellow. Still, it is also serious."

As I watch, two of the men reach the knight and take out a large piece of red cloth.

"But most of the people are here because it is a sunny day, and with such gatherings, a party is always a possibility."

At first, I think it's a flag of some sort. But then I see that it's an enormous pair of red underpants.

"Are those underpants?"

"Yes, of course," says Oz. "This is a protest against the president of the country."

"Red underpants?"

"This is to indicate that he is in bed with the Chinese, that he is a man who is ashamed of nothing."

At the top of the boulevard, just past the knight on the horse, a group of men stand in a tight bunch, surrounded by a wall of police.

"When the president supported the Russians in their harassment of the Ukraine, Czech activists pelted him with eggs."

Several of the men walk around in circles, their cellphones to their ears.

"Eggs. Giant underpants. The people of the Czech Republic enjoy the drama of democracy. Everything is possible at a protest."

"Who are those guys?"

Oz looks down on the square. "The men in suits with their noses pointed at the sky?"

"The ones behind the police perimeter."

"Politicians," says Oz. "Local and federal. They are sniffing the air, trying to catch the scent of popular opinion." Oz raises his head and makes quiet snorting noises. "See how they stay away from windows."

"Windows?"

"In Prague," says Oz, "standing by a window can be dangerous. How is the cake?"

TOLMAR MADE A POT of coffee, and we sat in her backyard in the late afternoon sun.

"Why are you doing this?"

The question had caught me by surprise.

"Why talk to me?"

I explained that the interview was part of a larger three-part story about the role of social services in the bureaucratic "scoops" that had taken Native children from their families.

"It's not going to give me back my mother."

I agreed that it wouldn't.

"And it's not going to give my mother back her six children." Tolmar had sat in the chair and waited for me to say something.

"I don't want another apology," she said. "You can tell those bastards to keep their apologies in their pants."

I turned off my tape recorder and slipped it into my pocket.

"Why waste your time writing about something that can't be changed? Where is the good in that? What do you expect will happen when you publish this story?"

That evening, I dropped the rental off at the airport and caught the red-eye back to Toronto.

SUDDENLY, ON THE STREET below, singing breaks out, first on one side of the median and then on the other.

Oz points his fork at the far side of the square. "The Czech national anthem."

Some of the politicians begin smiling and waving at the crowd.

"And here," says Oz. "On this side, 'Close the Gate, Little Brother.' Do you know the song?"

"No."

"'*The wolf hungers for the lamb, brother, have you closed the door?*'" Oz sings the words softly, under his breath. "Karel Kryl."

More songs break out, and the square is filled with a cacophony of sound, with no form other than volume and enthusiasm.

"Wonderful," says Oz. "Such singing is good."

My nose starts to bleed again, and I have to pinch it shut.

"It is hard to kill each other when we sing together." Oz sits up suddenly, as though he's been hit. "But where is your Mimi?"

"We split up. Just for the day," I add quickly. "She wanted to go off by herself and sketch."

"Sketch? She is an artist?"

"She is."

"And you are just . . . wandering?"

"I am."

"Ah," says Oz. "Just a Bear looking for honey."

« »

The rally breaks up slowly, like winter ice on a pond. The singing stops, the banners and the flags are put away, and the people begin drifting back into the city.

"You see," says Oz, "like all protests. Great emotions. High spirits. Firm resolve."

"It was pretty impressive," I say.

"And in the end, little changes."

Oz stares out the window. There are still a great many people in the square, but all of the passion is gone.

I scrape up the last of the chocolate cake. "I went by the Sex Machines Museum this morning."

Oz turns back to me and smiles. "But did you go inside?"

"No," I say. "I was tempted, but I came here instead."

"Such a shame," says Oz. "You missed the giant wood dildo."

XIV

When I come out of the building, the square is still busy, but the demonstration is over. The boulevard is littered with flyers and pamphlets, with coffee cups and plastic water bottles. Fast-food containers.

Eugene picks up a sign with a picture of a middle-aged man. There's a red circle around his head and a red slash across his face. Eugene rattles it in my face. *Friend of yours?*

The twins pick up little flags on sticks and wave them around as they skip along behind me.

Kitty keeps both eyes open for trouble.

Chip kicks at the trash in the street.

Oz's handkerchief is brown and crusty, and each time I press it against my nose, it hurts. I don't mind the blood on my shirt. It's a badge of the moment. And as I make my way through the dregs of the protest, people step aside out of respect for the hero, bloodied but unbowed.

Hero, my ass, says Eugene. *You just forgot to duck.*

White panel trucks, says Kitty. *Keep watching for white panel trucks.*

We walk down the street single file, me in the lead, Eugene right behind, Chip and the twins with their flags, Kitty bringing up the rear. I don't spend much time window shopping. It's late afternoon now, and I want to get back to the hotel.

How about the Sex Machines Museum? Eugene shouts at me. *Still time to see the big dildo.*

We breeze through Old Town Square. There's a crowd in front of the clock, and for all I know, it could be the same crowd as earlier in the day or from the day before, waiting patiently for the Apostles to make an appearance.

Or for the rooster to get off its ass.

I don't slow down to see whether or not the clock has been fixed. Frankly, I don't care.

Mimi is waiting for me when I get back to the room. She's sitting in the chair, her feet on the windowsill. Her sketch pad is open on the bed, which is her way of telling me that I am to look at the images.

"Good day?" I ask.

"See for yourself," she says without changing position.

The sketches are all of water patterns around the abutments of the Charles Bridge. One is a close-up detail of a plastic water bottle floating in the current.

"These are great."

Mimi pulls her feet off the sill and comes out of the chair.

"My god, Bird," she says as soon as she sees me, "what happened to you?"

I try to look as injured as I can.

"Are you all right?"

There are people who don't like to be coddled. Luckily for Mimi, I'm not one of them.

"What?"

"Your nose. Is that blood on your shirt?"

"Oh, that."

"Did you get into a fight?"

"Not exactly." I want to tell her about the protest and about meeting Oz, but I don't see where there is any rush.

"Come here, you silly puppy," says Mimi in her soft, motherly voice that I like so much. "Let's get you cleaned up."

"It hurts quite a bit."

"Good news." Mimi rubs my head. "It's not as bad as Venice."

UNCLE LEROY HAD SENT a postcard from Venice. On the back, he had written, "Pretty, but the place smells." Mimi had always wanted to go to Venice, so tracking down a lost relative and a missing bundle had been the perfect excuse.

"We'll go in the winter, when the prices are better and there aren't as many tourists."

"It'll be cold."

"Not as cold as Guelph."

We took the train from Nice to Venice. It wasn't much of a trip. Nice to Genoa, Genoa to Milan, Milan to Venice. The Rocky Mountaineer Escape Circle from Vancouver through the Canadian Rockies would have been more fun and with better scenery.

I mentioned this to Mimi as a point of reference. "Does the Mountaineer run in the winter?"

"No."

"Whereas the train to Venice does."

When we arrived at the Santa Lucia station, the island was shrouded in fog.

"Now what?"

"The *vaporetto* stop is right over there." Mimi dragged her bag down the walkway to the Grand Canal. "We want number 1 or 82."

"Okay."

"Number 1 makes all the stops on the Grand Canal," Mimi told me. "Number 82 is an express."

"Let's take 82."

"If we take the express, we might miss something."

"We can't see much in the fog."

"It isn't that thick."

Mimi was right. The fog wasn't that thick, but what there was gave the place a faint, hazy appearance, as though the city didn't really exist.

Mimi held the guidebook up so I could see the map of Venice.

"It's not a big place," she said. "Not sure where they would have put a Wild West show."

"Maybe the show didn't come here," I told her. "Maybe the show was close by, in Padua or Marghera, and Leroy took a day off to see Venice and send a postcard home."

"Doesn't matter," said Mimi. "We're here now."

The number 1 *vaporetto* wasn't as large as I had imagined, and it did stop everywhere.

"Tell me this isn't great."

"It's great."

"Look at that, Bird. Gondolas. You don't see gondolas in Guelph."

"We have kayaks and canoes on the Speed."

"Venice is over fifteen hundred years old. Guelph hasn't cracked the two-hundred-year mark yet."

"That means Guelph is in better shape."

I had my camera out, ready to take a picture of a crazy sculpture, a large, white hand coming out of the water and grabbing one of the buildings, when the *vaporetto* was hit by a wave from an enormous cruise ship that was lumbering its way out of the lagoon.

So we're in Prague, and letting Mimi clean my nose is not as pleasant as I had imagined.

"We have to get the crust off."

"No, we don't."

"Hold still."

"Don't disturb the scab."

Mimi soaks the shirt in the sink in cold water.

"You were at a protest for the Syrian refugees, and someone hit you?"

"It wasn't just about the refugees. It was for a whole bunch of other stuff," I tell her. "It was a multitasking protest."

"I'm sorry I wasn't there to protect you."

"Oz bought me coffee."

"Oz? Your breakfast buddy?"

"We ran into each other. He was supposed to go to Amsterdam," I say, "but he stayed for the demonstration."

"He hit you?"

I explain what happened. The protest. The guy who caught me with his elbow by mistake. The second-floor coffee shop. The chocolate cake.

"Prague is beginning to become problematic." Mimi touches the side of my nose. "You get knocked down, and now you get knocked down again."

"And we both get sick."

"Don't forget our two felons in the park," says Mimi. "You see the dilemma."

I don't see the dilemma, and I don't tell Mimi that I don't.

"I mean we were right there with the refugees in Bupapest, and what did we do?"

I don't think I need to tell Mimi what we didn't do. So I don't do that either.

"Nothing," says Mimi. "We did nothing. Oh, we were sympathetic and we were outraged, but we didn't do anything."

"We thought about it."

"And yet when we almost get robbed by a couple of juvenile delinquents, what's our response?"

Mimi waits. No problem. I can wait as well.

"We give them money." Mimi shakes her head. "Does that make any sense?"

I look out the window. There are clouds piled up on the horizon behind the bridge. Some of them are dark, and it appears as though a storm may be on its way.

"So, you sketched all day?" I say.

"Most of it," says Mimi. "I had lunch in Old Town. Did you know the Sex Machines Museum is right around the corner from the clock?"

I go back to the bathroom to look at my nose.

"I have to say the museum was interesting," she says. "You'll never guess what I saw there."

IN VENICE, MIMI HAD booked us a room at a small hotel tucked in behind Piazza San Marco. The Locanda Orseolo. Our room overlooked a narrow canal, and we could sit in chairs and watch small boats slide past our window, loaded with supplies that they dropped off at the hotels along the waterway.

The room was red brocade and gold trim with two high-back chairs that the owners might have borrowed from a museum.

"Well, one thing is for sure," said Mimi as she wandered the sitting room and the bedroom. "It beats the Holiday Inn."

"It's really nice," I agreed. "And we get a homemade breakfast."

"You hit that metal support pretty hard." Mimi checked the cut on my forehead. "It's split pretty good. Who knew riding in a *vaporetto* could be dangerous."

"Do I need stitches?"

"The bleeding is almost stopped," she said, "so I think you'll live."

"It hurts."

"Of course it hurts. 'Blackbird Mavrias versus the *Vaporetto*. A limited engagement.'"

"It wasn't my fault."

"No," said Mimi, "it wasn't."

"Am I going to have a scar?"

"And a really nasty black eye."

So WE'RE IN PRAGUE, and Mimi takes me to a restaurant she has found. Terasa U Zlate studne. Up by the castle.

"This is fancy."

We get a table by the window and look down on the city laid out in evening light.

Mimi turns sideways in her chair. "Look at that view."

"Just how expensive is this place?"

"Tomorrow we fly home." Mimi looks sad. "This is our last night in Prague."

"That expensive?" I stretch my arms out and take her hands in mine. It's romantic moments like this that strengthen relationships.

"You bought a watch?"

"What?"

I had forgotten about the watch. But there it is. On my wrist. All emerald green and sparkling gold.

"No," I say. "Oz gave it to me."

Mimi squeezes my hands. "You know, if you decided to buy a watch, you can just tell me."

"I told him I didn't want it. But he insisted."

Mimi opens her menu. "Don't order the black caviar."

"Five thousand, one hundred Czech crowns?"

"About three hundred dollars Canadian."

"For fish eggs?"

"The steak is only eighty-five."

Mimi gets a pumpkin soup, which we share, and orders a beetroot risotto carnaroli for her main course.

"Look, Bird," she says, "they have Canadian lobster."

I order the pork chop on mint lentils, with carrot purée and apple glaze.

"When we get home, remind me to call my mother."

I take the envelope out of my jacket. "You could give her this."

Mimi looks at the envelope and then she looks at me.

"It's the story that Oz made up about Uncle Leroy and the Crow bundle."

"The one where he stays in the Czech Republic? Gets married? Has a family and a bunch of kids? So forth and so on?"

"I'm sorry you never met him."

Mimi leaves the envelope where it is. "Did you think about what I asked you?"

"Sure."

"About believing in something?"

"Good food." I tap the menu. "I believe in good food."

"What about that three-part article you started and didn't finish," says Mimi. "Lois Paul. Maybe you could start there."

I shake my head. "I'll never finish that story."

Mimi cocks her head at me. "The problem with human beings," she says, "is that we can describe what we do. We just can't explain why."

The soup is excellent, and the pork chop is not overcooked. Mimi offers me some of her risotto to taste, but I'm not a fan of beets.

"Think of it as pieces of red potato, Bird."

For dessert, we share a pecan cake with bourbon, caramel cream, pineapple chutney, and sour-cream ice cream. I would have preferred plum cake or a fruit pie of some sort, but neither is on the menu.

The bill comes to 2,320 Czech crowns, which, with tip, is around $150.

"It wasn't all that expensive," says Mimi as we walk down the hill to our hotel.

"We only had one appetizer," I say. "And no wine."

Mimi takes my arm. "Maybe, in the end," she says, "there are no happy endings."

VENICE, THAT FIRST DAY, reminded me of Tofino and the coast of British Columbia.

"This is your kind of weather, Bird," Mimi told me. "Grey, damp, miserable."

"It is."

"I couldn't live in this."

"Maybe you could try."

"We've already had this conversation."

We didn't stay in the room. I hadn't even begun to unpack before Mimi had her guidebook out and at the ready.

"I thought you said we were supposed to get lost in Venice."

"There's lost," said Mimi, unfolding her map, "and then there's lost."

That first day in Venice, we wandered. Venice is not a large city and it was surprisingly busy. Evidently, even in winter, tourists came to slosh their way through Piazza San Marco and weave their way through the hawkers selling selfie sticks, corn for the pigeons, roses.

Disposable plastic-wrap boots.

"Where do you want to start?"

"Coffee."

"I said start, not stop."

"I've been injured," I said. "Coffee will energize me."

Mimi consulted her book. "We could go to Caffè Florian."

"Does it have good coffee?"

"It's a neo-baroque coffee house that dates back to the early eighteenth century."

"And the coffee."

"Very expensive," said Mimi. "An espresso is over six euros."

We walked by Caffè Florian, and it did look elegant. The walls were covered with murals. All the furnishings looked old, as though the tables and chairs might be original and generally uncomfortable.

"A little circle of quiche lorraine is sixteen euros."

We stood outside and looked in the windows of the café at the people sitting at the tables in the soft light.

"It's nice," said Mimi, "but everyone in there looks like us."

So WE'RE IN PRAGUE, and when we come out of the restaurant, the moon is waiting for us. Full and bright. In the distance, we can see the bridge and the river. I can't breathe out of one nostril. My left leg feels as though it's about to cramp up. Halfway down the hill, I remember that I left my diabetes kit in the room.

"Muffy will be happy to see you," says Mimi. "And I think you'll be happy to see her."

The night air is warm, and all things considered, it's a better-than-average evening. Even Eugene and the Other Demons would be hard-pressed to complain. Tomorrow, we'll be back in Guelph, in our own house, in our own bed. Muffy will be delighted to see me, and I'll be happy to see her.

But for now, we're in Prague.